Acclaim for Kathleen Fuller

"This compelling series continues with a serious story of forgiveness and redemption, as Fuller returns to Birch Creek to develop new relationships and revisit old friends. Lighthearted moments . . . provide charming comic relief."

—*RT Book Reviews*, 4½ stars, TOP PICK! on *The Promise of a Letter*

"Evoking a simpler time, when letters were handwritten and partially narrated in an epistolary style, Fuller's (*Written in Love*) first volume in a new series introduces two charismatic protagonists and an appealing, heartwarming story line. With elegantly clear prose and evocative settings, the author delivers another captivating read fans will relish."

—*Library Journal* on *The Promise of a Letter*

"Fuller's refreshing portrayal of the Amish as complex, flawed children of God adds deeper dimension to a plot already filled with lovable characters and an artfully crafted world that draws readers in and invites them to stay. Passion and joy for God and the written word are evident throughout the book, woven into a heartwarming invitation to share the love."

—*Publishers Weekly*, starred review on *Written in Love*

"The first book in the Amish Letters series features a poignant love story made even sweeter by the humorous penpal exchange between Phoebe and Jalon at the start. These are standout characters with complicated emotional histories. Readers of Fuller's Birch Creek series will be happy to return to this community and discover new characters and new romantic possibilities."

—*RT Book Reviews*, 4½ stars, TOP PICK! on *Written in Love*

"Fuller's inspirational tale portrays complex characters facing real-world problems and finding love where they least expected or wanted it to be."

—*Booklist*, starred review, on *A Reluctant Bride*

"Fuller has an amazing capacity for creating damaged characters and giving insights into their brokenness. One of the better voices in the Amish fiction genre."

—*CBA Retailers + Resources* on *A Reluctant Bride*

"This promising series debut from Fuller is edgier than most Amish novels, dealing with difficult and dark issues and featuring well-drawn characters who are tougher than the usual gentle souls found in this genre. Recommended for Amish fiction fans who might like a different flavor."

—*Library Journal* on *A Reluctant Bride*

"Sadie and Aden's love is both sweet and hard-won, and Aden's patience is touching as he wrestles not only with Sadie's dilemma, but his own abusive past. Birch Creek is weighed down by the Troyer family's dark secrets, and readers will be interested to see how secondary characters' lives unfold as the series continues."

—*RT Book Reviews*, 4 stars, on *A Reluctant Bride*

"Kathleen Fuller's *A Reluctant Bride* tells the story of two Amish families whose lives have collided through tragedy. Sadie Schrock's stoic resolve will touch and inspire Fuller's fans, as will the story's concluding triumph of redemption."

—Suzanne Woods Fisher, bestselling author of *Anna's Crossing*

"Kathleen Fuller's *A Reluctant Bride* is a beautiful story of faith, hope, and second chances. Her characters and descriptions are captivating, bringing the story to life with the turn of every page."

—Amy Clipston, bestselling author of *A Simple Prayer* and the Kauffman Amish Bakery series

"The latest offering in the Middlefield Family series is a sweet love story, with perfectly crafted characters. Fuller's Amish novels are written with the utmost respect for their way of living. Readers are given a glimpse of what it is like to live the simple life."

—*RT Book Reviews*, 4 stars, on *Letters to Katie*

"Fuller's second Amish series entry is a sweet romance with a strong sense of place that will attract readers of Wanda Brunstetter and Cindy Woodsmall."

—*Library Journal* on *Faithful to Laura*

"Well-drawn characters and a homespun feel will make this Amish romance a sure bet for fans of Beverly Lewis and Jerry S. Eicher."

—*Library Journal* on *Treasuring Emma*

"*Treasuring Emma* is a heartwarming story filled with real-life situations and well-developed characters. I rooted for Emma and Adam until the very last page. Fans of Amish fiction and those seeking an endearing romance will enjoy this love story. Highly recommended."

—Beth Wiseman, bestselling author of *Her Brother's Keeper* and the Daughters of the Promise series

"*Treasuring Emma* is a charming, emotionally layered story of the value of friendship in love and discovering the truth of the heart. A true treasure of a read!"

—Kelly Long, author of the Patch of Heaven series

Words from the Heart

Other Books by Kathleen Fuller

The Amish Letters Novels

Written in Love

The Promise of a Letter

The Amish of Birch Creek Novels

A Reluctant Bride

An Unbroken Heart

A Love Made New

The Middlefield Amish Novels

A Faith of Her Own

The Middlefield Family Novels

Treasuring Emma

Faithful to Laura

Letters to Katie

The Hearts of Middlefield Novels

A Man of His Word

An Honest Love

A Hand to Hold

Novellas included in

An Amish Christmas—A Miracle for Miriam

An Amish Gathering—A Place of His Own

An Amish Love—What the Heart Sees

An Amish Wedding—A Perfect Match

An Amish Garden—Flowers for Rachael

An Amish Second Christmas—A Gift for Anne Marie

An Amish Cradle—A Heart Full of Love

An Amish Market—A Bid for Love

An Amish Harvest—A Quiet Love

An Amish Home—Building Faith

Words from the Heart

Kathleen Fuller

Thomas Nelson
Since 1798

Words from the Heart

Published in Nashville, Tennessee, by Thomas Nelson. Thomas Nelson is a registered trademark of HarperCollins Christian Publishing, Inc.

Thomas Nelson titles may be purchased in bulk for educational, business, fund-raising, or sales promotional use. For information, please e-mail SpecialMarkets@ThomasNelson.com.

Library of Congress Cataloging-in-Publication Data

Names: Fuller, Kathleen, author.
Title: Words from the heart / Kathleen Fuller.
Description: Nashville, Tennessee : Thomas Nelson, [2018] | Series: An Amish letters novel ; 3
Identifiers: LCCN 2017041996 | ISBN 9780718082567 (paperback)
Subjects: | GSAFD: Christian fiction. | Love stories.
Classification: LCC PS3606.U553 W67 2018 | DDC 813/.6--dc23 LC record available at https://lccn.loc.gov/2017041996

Printed in the United States of America

18 19 20 21 22 / LSC / 5 4 3 2 1

To James. I love you.

Glossary

ab im kopp: crazy, crazy in the head

ach: oh

aenti: aunt

appeditlich: delicious

bann: temporary or permanent excommunication from the Amish church

bruder: brother

bu/buwe: boy/boys

daag/daags: day/days

daed: father

danki: thank you

dawdi haus: smaller home, attached to or near the main house

Dietsch: Amish language

dochder: daughter

dumm: dumb

dummkopf: idiot

Englisch: non-Amish

familye: family

frau: woman, Mrs.

geh: go

grossdaadi: grandfather

grossmammi: grandmother

gut: good

gute nacht: good night

haus: house

kaffee: coffee

kapp: white hat worn by Amish women

kinn/kinner: child/children

maed/maedel: girl/young woman

mamm: mom

mann: Amish man

mei: my

mudder/mutter: mother

nee: no

nix: nothing

onkel: uncle

Ordnung: the set of rules, written and unwritten, by which the Amish live

schee: pretty/handsome

schwesters: sisters

seltsam: weird

sohn: son

vatter: father

ya: yes

yer: your

yerself: yourself

September 3

Dear Ivy,

I know we just said good-bye a few minutes ago, but I'm missing you already. I wish you didn't have to leave Michigan. I wish you didn't have to go back to Birch Creek. I wish you were here next to me. I wish for a lot of things, and hopefully, soon some of them will come true.

I'll visit you as soon as I can. In the meantime, expect a lot of letters from me. I'm not much of a writer, but I'll do the best I can. You'll probably get tired of hearing from me. I can't wait to hear from you.

Write soon, Ivy. It won't be long until we're together again.

John

Chapter 1

December (one year later)

Ivy Yoder stood on tiptoes as she reached for the dark-green dress she'd chosen to wear today. She had a stepstool in her room, but most of the time she didn't bother to use it. At four feet eleven, she was used to having to reach for things. Once she was dressed, her hair tucked neatly into a stiff white *kapp* and warm stockings covering her legs and feet, she grabbed her purse and then went downstairs to help her mother with breakfast.

"*Gute morgen*," *Mamm* said, scrambling what Ivy knew had to be a dozen eggs in a large cast iron skillet. She adjusted the gas burner underneath.

"Morning." Ivy set her purse on the kitchen counter near the mudroom and then started setting the table. Her father and three brothers were feeding the animals and milking their two dairy cows, and as usual they would be hungry for a big meal when they finished. Her brothers were all strapping boys who burned a lot of calories working on the family farm. After several lean years, the farm was a success. They had plenty of food, not only for themselves, but to share with other families as well. None of them took for granted the bounty they were experiencing after so many years of struggle.

Ivy quickly finished with the table, and then she started cutting a fresh loaf of bread into thick slices.

"Everything okay?"

Ivy looked at her mother, not liking the expression on her face. Mary Yoder was usually a happy-go-lucky woman, optimistic even in the worst of times. But occasionally she made *that* face, her eyes looking at Ivy with a mix of worry and confusion.

"*Ya*," Ivy said, placing the bread slices on a plate and carrying it to the table. "Why?"

"Today's *yer* last day at the Millers'. I know you've enjoyed working for them."

Ivy nodded. She'd been working part-time at Miller's Bookbinding over the past couple of years. Her younger sister, Karen, had also worked there before she married a little over a year ago. Now David Miller had told Ivy he and his wife were closing their business and moving back to Holmes County, where they were from originally. "I'll miss them a lot, but they're happy to be moving closer to their extended *familye*."

"That seems to be a trend around here." *Mamm* slid the scrambled eggs onto a large platter and handed it to Ivy. "The older people here when Emmanuel Troyer started the settlement are moving away." She smiled. "Meanwhile, our community is filling up with *yung* folks."

Ivy returned her mother's smile with a halfhearted one of her own. Yes, there were plenty of younger residents in Birch Creek now. Unfortunately, most of them were children, teenagers, or men who came to marry women in the community. Over the past three years, since Emmanuel Troyer left under a scandalous cloud and her father became the new bishop, a lot of changes had been made. But one thing remained the same. Ivy Yoder, at nearly twenty-six, was still unmarried—and had zero prospects.

Well, there'd been one. She thought about the letter from John still in her nightstand. The one and only letter she'd received from him, even though he'd promised to write to her every day. She hadn't been foolish enough to hold him to that specific promise, but she had expected him to write. At the very least to respond to her letters. Instead, she hadn't heard from him in over a year.

"Ivy? Are you sure you're all right? You seem a little preoccupied."

"I'm okay." And she was, except when she thought about John. Or her single status. Two things she preferred not to dwell on.

Mamm opened her mouth, but then she closed it—another sign that her mother was concerned. *Mamm* rarely failed to speak her mind.

Ivy knew she should let the matter drop, but after a few seconds and against her better judgment, she said, "What?"

"It's just . . ." *Mamm* swirled soapy water around her spatula in the sink. "I wondered if maybe you were having some trouble adjusting to Karen not being here."

"Karen moved out months ago. Besides," she said, shoving one of the kitchen chairs farther under the table, "there's *nix* to adjust to."

"But we've never really talked about . . ." *Mamm* sighed, dried her hands, and walked over to her. "I just want to make sure you're okay. And if you want to talk about anything, I'm here for you."

Ivy nodded, touched that her mother, even in her uncertainty, wanted to be sure Ivy was all right. But a small part of her knew if she had a boyfriend or even the prospect of a husband and a future, her mother probably wouldn't be worrying so much. *Maybe not at all.* Still, she appreciated her offer. "*Danki*," she said. "That's *gut* to know."

Her father and brothers entered the kitchen, and after they took turns washing their hands, everyone sat down at the table. When they'd finished eating breakfast, Ivy cleared the table and started filling the sink with fresh water.

"I'll do the dishes," *Mamm* said, turning off the tap. "You *geh* on to work."

"Are you sure?"

"*Ya.*" She wiped her hands on her apron. "Are you still planning to *geh* to Phoebe's after work?"

Ivy nodded. Phoebe Chupp had invited her and Karen over to make Christmas cards. Many Birch Creek residents sent homemade cards this time of year. Ivy's best friend, Leanna, who was also Phoebe's sister-in-law, was coming as well. Ivy was looking forward to spending time with her friends, even if she sometimes felt like an outsider because they were all married. And, in Phoebe's case, had two children.

"Do you want to join us, *Mamm*?"

She shook her head. "I've got plenty to do here. You have fun."

"I will." She went to the mudroom and put her navy-blue scarf around her neck, noticing the small hole at one end. She kept putting off darning it. Sewing wasn't her favorite activity.

But she needed to tend to it before the hole grew bigger and ruined the whole scarf. She slipped on her coat and boots before making her way outside.

As she headed to the barn, she wrapped the scarf more tightly around her neck. It was a crisp morning, and she looked up at the rising sun as it peeked out from behind puffy white clouds. Tucking her chin deeper into her scarf, she entered the barn, nodded at her sixteen-year-old brother, Ira, who was cleaning out the stalls, and hitched up the buggy.

By the time she reached the Millers', the sun had fully risen and the clouds had disappeared. She parked the buggy, unhitched the horse, led him to the fenced-in pasture behind the barn, and then went inside the small, modest Amish home.

The Millers had been in the bookbinding business for almost thirty years, bringing it to Birch Creek when they moved here ten years ago. She found it hard to believe this was her last day working for the kind couple. She'd miss them, but not necessarily the work. She found it tedious, especially the book repair orders that occasionally came in. David worked on the most valuable and delicate repairs, but Ivy had learned how to replace and repair pages in books that had more sentimental value than monetary value.

In the Millers' mudroom, she removed her boots and hung up her scarf and coat before going to the back room where the Millers had set up their workshop. When she walked in, David was hunched over his desk, the scent of glue, old books, and fresh paper hanging in the air.

"*Gute morgen*," Magdalena Miller said from her usual position at a large table in the center of the room. She was packing spiral-bound cookbooks into a small box. She paused, her lips forming a slight smile, deepening the wrinkles at the corners of her mouth. "I have something for you."

"For me?" She watched in surprise as Magdalena turned, picked up a large hardcover book, and walked toward Ivy.

"For you." Magdalena handed the book to her.

Ivy's surprise grew as she ran her hand over the beautiful linen cover. "What is this?"

"Open it and see."

She did, and what she saw nearly brought tears to her eyes. She'd worked on a genealogy project for her father for the last three years—another tedious job, but one she found more interesting as she delved into the histories of her family and others in Birch Creek. She'd brought it in last week to be bound, but she'd been expecting a simple, plastic spiral binding with a soft cover. "It's beautiful," she said as she turned the high-quality pages.

"Our gift to you, for doing such wonderful work." David joined his wife at her side.

"I wasn't expecting anything so lovely." Ivy closed the book and hugged it to her chest. "*Danki. Daed* will really like this."

"You put a lot of hard work into that project. It deserved a special binding." Magdalena smiled. "We're going to miss you and all of Birch Creek. But the time has come for us to retire and move closer to *familye*."

David removed his glasses and wiped the lenses with a handkerchief. "The business isn't what it used to be, with so many people now using those fancy e-readers." He put his glasses back on and pushed them onto his high-bridged nose.

"But we've made a *gut* living doing what we love and for that we're blessed." Magdalena took a deep breath. "Now, let's get to work. We still have plenty to do today."

Ivy set the book aside and started packing up the last shipments of books from Miller's Bookbinding. She also spent a few hours helping Magdalena pack up the workshop. "Don't worry about the rest," she said when Ivy's usual quitting time had come. "We'll finish it ourselves."

"Are you sure you don't need any help?"

"*Nee*, our *sohn* and his *familye* are coming tomorrow to help us." Magdalena looked around the workshop. "We'll have everything ready to *geh* by Saturday."

Ivy hugged her now former employer. "*Danki* for the opportunity to work here."

Magdalena hugged her back, and after Ivy said good-bye to her and David, she headed to Phoebe's. Phoebe and Jalon Chupp didn't live too far from the Millers, but the drive still gave Ivy some time to think. She'd been trying to find a new job ever since she learned the Millers were closing their business and moving away, but she hadn't had much luck. Either the jobs were temporary or she couldn't work the hours they required. Tomorrow she would have to step up her efforts. She didn't want to be without a job for very long.

But this evening she was spending time with friends. She pulled into the Chupps' driveway and mused about how much had changed in such a short time.

A little over two years ago, this residence had been a small, not-so-successful farm where Jalon and Leanna lived alone after their parents moved back to their hometown in Mesopotamia. Now there was an addition on the house, and Phoebe's family, the Bontragers, had built a house on the property next door. The modest *dawdi haus* behind Jalon and Phoebe's home was now a large house, where Karen and her husband, Adam, lived. Since

Adam's legs had been paralyzed in an accident when he was twelve, the house was equipped to accommodate his wheelchair. Leanna and Roman now lived in a new house near his brother, Daniel, and his wife, Barbara.

Ivy parked the buggy and got out. A large Maine coon cat trotted toward her on the fresh snow. As he curled around her legs, she bent down and patted his head. "Hey, Blue. Where's *yer* shadow?"

"Right here." A seven-year-old boy with pale-blond hair and striking blue eyes scampered to them. "*Aenti* Leanna and Karen are already here helping *Mamm* with supper."

"I better hurry inside and give them a hand."

Malachi picked up Blue. "See you later," he said, waving as he walked away, the huge cat snuggled in his arms.

After caring for her horse, Ivy went to the back door and knocked, but instead of waiting for an answer, she walked inside and kicked off her boots in the mudroom. The scent of apples and cinnamon filled the air as she hung up her coat and scarf. When she poked her head through the kitchen doorway, Phoebe was pulling a pie out of the oven, Karen was brushing butter over freshly baked rolls, and Leanna was setting the table—the best task to give her. Despite being married for more than a year, she was still hopeless in the kitchen.

"What can I do to help?" Ivy asked.

Leanna set down the last fork. "*Nix.* I think everything is done." She smirked. "*Yer* timing is impeccable."

Ivy grinned and looked up at her best friend of many years. Leanna Raber was unusual in several ways, starting with her six-foot height and very slim body. She was also the only female Amish mechanic in Birch Creek—and anywhere, as far as Ivy knew. She was quirky and outgoing and confident, traits Ivy had always appreciated. Years ago they'd vowed to be friends forever, and as they grew older and their friends were consumed with interest in boys, they also vowed never to do something as silly and conventional as getting married.

Ivy's smile dimmed. *So much for keeping that last vow.*

"Where's Hannah?" Ivy asked Phoebe.

Phoebe slipped the potholders off her hands. "With *Mamm*. She wanted to take her for the night." Phoebe shook her head. "You would think twelve *kinner* in the *haus* would be enough for her, especially since Hannah's starting to walk now."

"Twelve *buwe*," Leanna pointed out. "*Yer mamm* needs a little female balance, don't you think?"

"And we all know how she dotes on her granddaughter," Karen said as she put the rolls on the table.

The back door opened, and Jalon walked in from the mudroom, Adam close behind in his wheelchair and Malachi bringing up the rear. "*Geh* wash up for supper," Jalon ordered, looking at his young son.

"I'll *geh* with you," Adam said. Then he swooped Malachi up and parked him on his lap. As he wheeled out of the kitchen, he looked up at Ivy. "Hi," he said. "We'll be right back."

Ivy turned to look at Karen, and from the softness in her sister's eyes, Ivy could tell she'd been watching her husband with Malachi. She wondered how long it would be before Karen and Adam had their own child. Ivy knew Karen wanted to be a mother, but although she and her sister were close, Karen hadn't shared anything that personal with Ivy since the wedding. Which was fine with Ivy. Married couples deserved privacy, and she wouldn't pry.

She took in the scene in the kitchen—Jalon washing his hands in the sink as he talked to Phoebe, Leanna pouring the last glass of cold tea as Karen set Malachi's cup of milk in front of his place setting—and not for the first time, she felt like a seventh wheel. That feeling only increased as they all sat down at the table. She was seated next to Malachi and across from Leanna. Roman was working late on a broken generator, but even though he wasn't there, Ivy felt his presence.

The tiny stab of envy paled against how she'd felt when she returned from Michigan and learned Leanna and Roman were dating. Ivy had spent a few weeks with her cousin while she was on bed rest, and she'd had no idea Leanna and Roman had fallen for each other while she was gone. She hadn't known Leanna was even interested in Roman. She was happy for her friend when she told her of their unexpected romance, but a part of her felt betrayed—which was ridiculous since Ivy had been considering breaking her own vow to remain single.

Thanks to John, she didn't have to consider it anymore.

They all prayed and then ate the delicious meal—corned beef and cabbage, buttery mashed potatoes, fluffy rolls, and apple pie for dessert. After supper, the men cleared out while the women quickly cleaned the kitchen and then brought out the supplies to make cards—folded card stock; a few rubber stamps with simple Christmas designs; red, green, and black ink pads; and envelopes. Ivy chose a holly berry design and started stamping.

"Today was *yer* last day at the Millers', *ya*?" Karen asked. At Ivy's nod, she added, "I'm going to miss them. I enjoyed working there."

"They're happy to be moving closer to *familye*." Ivy examined the stamped image. A little crooked, but hopefully no one would notice.

"Do you have another job lined up?"

She shook her head. "Tomorrow I'm going to start getting serious about *mei* search."

"Funny you should mention that." Leanna tapped one slender finger on the kitchen table. "Aden came into the shop this morning. He mentioned offhand to Roman that he'll need to hire someone to work in the store soon. He's taken over running it since Sadie is in a *familye* way. None of the Schrock women are working in the store anymore, so they need another employee besides Barbara."

"It's hard to believe that just a couple of years ago all three sisters were working there." Karen inserted her finished card in an envelope.

"Things have changed around here so quickly," Leanna said, nodding. She looked at Phoebe. "Mostly *gut* changes, though."

Ivy was only half listening. Leanna was right about the good changes in Birch Creek, but the community had also experienced its share of tragedy. Schrock Grocery and Tools was a successful store owned by the Schrock family. When Sadie's parents died in a buggy accident three years ago, she and her sisters, Abigail and Joanna, took over running the store. Now all three sisters were married and had children, so Ivy wasn't surprised they needed help in addition to Barbara, who'd been working at the store for over a year.

"You should talk to Aden about it," Leanna said, affixing a stamp to the upper right corner of an envelope.

Ivy nodded. She would enjoy working at the Schrocks'—and not just because she was friends with the family. She liked being around people, something she didn't get enough of while working at the Millers'. It would also be a new challenge since she'd never worked in retail before. She made a mental note to stop by there tomorrow. Relieved that she now had an option, she focused on finishing the cards and enjoying time with her friends, the self-pity she'd felt earlier disappearing. She might not be married or even dating, but she wasn't alone. She had her family, her friends, and most important, her relationship with God. What more could she ask for?

Later that night Ivy yawned as she drove home. It had been a long day, and she was looking forward to climbing into bed and snuggling under her handmade quilt. But when she pulled into the driveway, she saw a familiar buggy. What was Cevilla Schlabach doing here? It was easy to recognize the older woman's buggy. On it was the maximum amount of reflective tape the district would allow, and probably not only because of safety reasons. Ivy's father had relaxed the restrictions several months ago, as he had with a lot of the rules since he became bishop. He hadn't thrown the *Ordnung* out the window, and he was devout when it came to his faith. But Emmanuel Troyer had held the community under his tight fist, and Ivy's father determined that not all the rules needed to be so strict.

She put the horse up in the barn and then went inside the house, where she heard voices coming from the front room all the way to the mudroom. When she entered the living room, she was a little surprised to see Noah Schlabach sitting on the hickory rocker her parents had owned since before she was born.

Ivy's brow shot up. She hadn't seen or heard from Noah since Karen and Leanna's double wedding. He'd approached her right after the ceremony and told her his great-aunt Cevilla wanted them to go through her deceased stepmother's belongings. Glenda's English family had shipped a load of boxes to her, eager to finally clean out one of the family homes. "For some reason, we have to *geh* through them together," he'd said. That was the way his aunt wanted it, and Ivy knew Cevilla well enough that she didn't argue.

That was over a year ago, and this was the first time Noah had returned to Birch Creek. She wasn't exactly surprised about that. He wasn't from the area, or even Ohio. He lived in Arbor Grove, an Amish community in Iowa, and he traveled extensively for his job as an auctioneer and antique specialist. That was an atypical career for an Amish man, but Cevilla wasn't the only quirky member of the Schlabach family. Ivy had assumed he'd changed his mind about helping his aunt since he'd been gone so long. "Hi," she said, hesitating at the edge of the living room.

"Noah stopped by to see you." *Mamm* gave Ivy an inquisitive look, since men never came to the Yoder household to visit Ivy.

"I wasn't expecting you," Ivy said to Noah.

"But now that you're here," *Mamm* said, getting up from the couch, "we'll leave you two to talk." She tapped her husband's toe with her foot. "Right, Freemont?"

"Oh. *Ya*. Right." He rose as well and stretched. "Nice visiting with you, Noah."

"Likewise." Noah stood and shook Freemont's hand.

After her parents left, Ivy moved to stand by the couch. Noah held out his hand to her. "Hi, Ivy."

She looked up at him. Way up, so she could see his face. He was an average-looking man, nothing extraordinary about him, except for one thing. He was tall. Very tall. Well over six feet, probably six four if she had to guess. He was also lanky and gangly. The complete opposite of John physically.

Why was she thinking about John right now? It wasn't as if Noah was a viable candidate to end her singleness. As far as she knew, he had a girlfriend—or even a wife—back home in Iowa.

She shook his hand. "Sorry it's been so long since we talked," he said. "I've been pretty busy with traveling and all."

She nodded. "Found any *gut* antiques?"

"A few. How have you been?"

"I've been . . ." She paused. "I've been *gut*." She smiled. "*Sehr gut.*"

"Glad to hear it."

"I'm assuming you're here to talk about Cevilla." At his nod, she gestured for him to sit back down as she lowered herself onto the couch. "I've asked her a couple of times if she wanted me to at least unpack a box or two. Especially since you told me at the wedding that another shipment was coming too."

"It did, and let me guess," he said, sitting back down in the hickory rocker opposite her. "She refused."

"*Ya.*" She folded her hands in her lap.

He leaned back in the chair and put his straw hat on one knee, his long legs bent, the toe of one foot tapping against the floor. He was one tall, thin man. "I still don't know why she insists we both need to do this, but we can *geh* through the boxes together per *mei aenti*'s instructions. If you're free, that is. I'll be glad for your help."

"I'm free." And she was a bit enthusiastic. She'd been itching to unpack those boxes and find out what kinds of things Cevilla's English stepmother kept. Cevilla said her stepmother was a pack rat, so Ivy assumed there would be some interesting finds up in her attic. "When do you want to start?"

"Tomorrow morning, if that's okay. I figure the sooner the better. Cevilla is eager to get her stepmother's stuff sorted and out of her attic."

"Did she say that?"

"Not in those exact words, but trust me, I got the message." He grabbed his hat and immediately started tapping the floor again. When he saw her looking at his foot, he stilled. "Sorry. Bad habit." Then he added, "I was hoping to be here sooner, but *mei* schedule wouldn't permit it. I feel bad that she's waited this long."

She didn't know Noah very well, but she did admire his commitment to his aunt, something she'd seen before. About two years ago Cevilla had invited her to go to Holmes County for the day. It was her first invitation from Cevilla, and while she had thought it odd that the woman invited her and not someone closer to her eighty-plus years, Ivy agreed to go. She had suggested Leanna go with them, but Cevilla said she wanted it to be just the two of them.

On the ride there, she said they were going to an auction Noah was involved in. Ivy didn't mind. She liked auctions. She enjoyed seeing the interesting, and at times unique, items being auctioned off. She also liked eating fresh hot donuts while she observed the action, both on the auctioneer podium and in the crowd milling around. At this auction, Noah was one of the auctioneers. She had to admit, he was good. Very good. Not only was his auctioneer's cadence smooth and fast, but he could also get the crowd going with a joke or a good-natured plea for more bids.

"Isn't he wonderful?" Cevilla had said a few minutes into the auction.

"He's definitely *gut*." Ivy ate the last bite of her donut.

"When he's finished I'll introduce you."

When they met, she was surprised at his height, especially noticeable when she was standing next to him. After Cevilla made the introductions, he bent down slightly to look at her, a move she usually disliked because it made her feel a bit insignificant. In his defense, though, he pretty much had to because of their extreme height difference. "Nice to meet you. *mei aenti* has mentioned you once or twice." He straightened and winked at Cevilla.

"I only mention people worth mentioning." Cevilla touched the back of her *kapp*. "I thought since the auction is over, we can *geh* get supper."

"Sounds like fun, but I can't. The auction might be over," he said, gesturing to the people cleaning up around them, "but there's still lots of work to be done. Since I'm the head auctioneer, I have to stay behind and make sure it all gets finished and people get paid."

"Oh."

He picked up on her disappointment right away. "But don't worry. I'll come to see you soon." Then he did something that surprised Ivy—he grabbed his aunt in a big hug, right in front of everyone. "I love you," he said, his voice clear and resonant. "Be careful on the way back to Birch Creek." Then he let her go, and as he backed away he nodded at Ivy. "Nice to meet you."

Ivy wasn't particularly shy with her affection. She hugged her mother and her sister regularly, her father less frequently since he was more reserved, and sometimes Leanna. But she hugged only in a private setting, like all the Amish she knew.

She watched Noah clap an English man on his back, saying

"Good job" in his deep, friendly voice. From what she could tell, he seemed respected and well liked, and Cevilla clearly thought the world of him.

He'd been true to his word that day, visiting his aunt a week later. Ivy hadn't seen him that time, but Cevilla had made sure to tell her he'd been there. "He's such a *gut bu*," she said as she poured Ivy a cup of peppermint tea, Cevilla's staple when Ivy came to visit. "I wish he would slow down, though. He doesn't take time to smell the pansies."

"Ro—" Ivy caught herself. If Cevilla wanted to smell pansies, Ivy wouldn't correct her.

"So is tomorrow morning okay?" Noah asked.

Ivy blinked as Noah's question brought her back into the present. "Sure. Tomorrow is fine." She picked off a piece of fluff on the edge of her sweater sleeve. "What time should I be there?"

"Cevilla gets up before the chickens, so I'm sure you couldn't arrive too early." He grinned as he stood. "After breakfast will be fine."

Ivy thought that would be perfect. She'd spend a few hours at Cevilla's, and then stop by the Schrocks' to talk to Aden about a possible job.

Noah plopped his hat on his head, covering up a mop of wavy, black hair. "Can't wait to see what Glenda's got in store for us."

"Me too. I'm still surprised Glenda's *familye* sent all her stuff to Cevilla, but I guess after Glenda's sister died too, they were eager to find someone to take it."

Noah shrugged as she walked him to the door. "I guess. Cevilla doesn't talk too much about Glenda's *familye*. Which is surprising, since she talks about everything else. Sometimes too much." He flashed another grin as he said the words. "Then again, compared to me and *mei aenti*, the rest of our *familye* is pretty quiet. A staid bunch, as Cevilla says."

Ivy agreed as Noah slipped on his boots. She knew only a little about Cevilla's family—that Glenda, Cevilla's stepmother, had been English before she married Cevilla's father, and that her brother, Noah's grandfather, was sixteen years older than she was. Otherwise, she kept information about her family, and pretty much her past, close to her chest.

Ivy followed him out on the front porch. He waved as he climbed into Cevilla's overly reflective buggy. She waved back, and as soon as Noah drove away, she turned and walked into the house, promptly running into her brother Seth.

"Who was that?" Seth shoved a piece of bread into his mouth. He was always eating. He was also growing faster than a weed, even at age eighteen. He was taller than their father now.

"Noah Schlabach," she said, glancing up at him and then moving toward the staircase to go up to her room. She wasn't in the mood for Seth's questions. Of all her brothers, he was the one who liked to poke his nose in her business the most. Or maybe he just enjoyed getting her riled up.

"Noah, huh? I've met him." He stepped in front of her and crossed his arms. "What did he want?"

Knowing Seth would pester her until she gave him a satisfactory answer, she told him the truth. "We're going to help his aunt *geh* through some boxes in her attic. She asked us to."

"I see." His laconic look changed and his brow knitted. "Is that all?"

"*Ya*, Seth. That's all."

"Gut." He straightened to his full height. "If he causes you any trouble, let me know."

Ivy nearly laughed. "Are you saying you'll protect me from Noah?"

"That's exactly what I'm saying."

This time Ivy couldn't hide her smile. While Seth was tall and broad-shouldered, he also had a baby face that made him look even younger than his years. In her mind he was her pesky brother, not her protector. "Noah's a . . . friend." He wasn't even that, truth be told. More like a well-known acquaintance."

"What kind of friend? A close one?"

"Seth, what is all this about? We're going to *geh* through some boxes Cevilla has in her attic, and then Noah is going back home to Iowa. End of story."

"So you two have another long-distance relationship."

Another? Ivy froze. "I . . . I don't know what you're talking about."

"What about the guy you met in Michigan?"

Now Ivy was uneasy. How did Seth know about John? She hadn't told anyone in Birch Creek about him, not even Leanna. She'd even asked her cousin in Michigan to keep the news about her dating John to herself. It was a secret she'd wanted to savor for a while before she brought him up at home. Which ended up being a good thing, since it all turned bitter in the end.

"It didn't take much to put two and two together. You made a point of checking the mailbox yourself for months after you got back from Michigan." He shrugged. "You also got mopey when nothing came for you."

Ivy had to give Seth a lot of credit for figuring it out. But that was all she was going to give him. This was going beyond the annoying-younger-brother routine. "It's none of *yer* business," she snapped. "And there isn't any *mann* in Michigan."

"Because now there's Noah."

Ivy was losing patience. "Seth, stay out of *mei* business. I don't need you or anyone else looking out for me." She gave him a small shove, and he stepped out of her way.

"What are you getting so mad about?" he said, sounding a bit upset. "I'm just looking out for you."

She ignored him and went upstairs. Why did he suddenly feel the need to poke into her personal life? As she told him, she didn't need anyone protecting her. She was fine on her own.

But when she walked into her bedroom, she couldn't help but look at her nightstand. Once again, John had come to mind. Yet instead of feeling longing or pity for herself, she felt annoyed. How long was she going to carry a torch for a man who had no interest in her? Why was she even saving the one letter he'd sent her, the one filled with broken promises? She yanked open the drawer, took out the letter, and ripped it into tiny pieces before tossing it into her trash can.

"Good-bye, John," she said, satisfied to finally put that part of her life behind her. She was finished pining for John King—for good.

Chapter 2

Dear Noah,

I realize you are a busy man, but I believe you are also a man of your word. The contents of those boxes in my attic aren't going to sort themselves. I expect you to be here within the month. It's high time you kept your promise.

Love,

Aunt Cevilla

As Noah drove back to Cevilla's home, her letter burned a hole in his pocket. He'd received it in the middle of November and had felt properly chastised. It wasn't that he hadn't wanted to help his aunt, but this had been a particularly busy and successful year for him, and he couldn't get away until now. Even November had been busy, even though auctions typically started slowing down then because of inclement weather. So it wasn't until now that he'd been able to carve out time to make good on his promise.

A promise he was suddenly looking forward to. He let the horse leisurely guide him back to Cevilla's. The prospect of finding some good stuff in the attic intrigued him, although he also had to wonder what his aunt was up to. Cevilla could be sneaky when she wanted, yet this time she didn't seem to be bothering with subtlety. It wasn't as if she hadn't been trying to fix him up for the last ten years. His being a thirty-two-year-old bachelor had people worried, including his parents.

He wasn't worried, though. He had his job, and that's where his commitment lay. Although he had to admit he was anticipating this break from work and travel.

He turned into the driveway and put Cevilla's buggy in the barn. After he made sure the horse was settled in, he strolled outside. It was a beautiful night in Birch Creek, and even though he stared up at the sky, the same sky that was in Iowa, for some reason he felt different here. He enjoyed his visits to this area, maybe because it was one of the few places he could completely relax.

Not that he could relax for too long. He already had a couple of auctions scheduled for January, even though winter was usually his slow season. But it shouldn't take long to go through those boxes in Cevilla's attic, and he'd made sure he had time to stay a few extra days to visit with his aunt. Not to mention take some time to wind down. He was tired. Overly so. Spending some downtime in Birch Creek was exactly what he needed before he returned to Arbor Grove to be with his parents and siblings for Christmas.

He took one last look at the beautiful sky and then headed toward the house. He made note of how neat Cevilla's home was on the outside, and he knew from experience it was tidy on the inside. He also knew the community helped her with shoveling snow and, in the summer, lawn maintenance. Birch Creek was a place where people definitely took care of their own.

He went to the front porch and touched the old hickory

rocker there. He'd told Cevilla it needed to be inside, but she insisted on keeping it on the porch, even in the winter. "That's where *mei vatter* always had it, on the porch," she said. "He made it with his own two hands, and *nee* snow or windstorm or rain is going to affect it. It's been through some tough winters. Just like the rest of us." She was right. The rocker was a little weather-beaten, but it still looked good and sturdy.

He knocked five times on the front door and entered the living room, his signal to Cevilla that he was home. She was sitting in another rocker, an early twentieth-century model that had been her stepmother's. It was the one piece of furniture she'd asked for after Glenda died. Little did she know at the time that her stepmother had a stash of stuff that now almost filled Cevilla's modest attic.

She was sitting by the woodstove, her hands flying with a crochet hook and some bright yarn that didn't look particularly Amish. "Who's that for?" he asked, lowering himself onto the lumpy couch across from her.

"For an English friend in Iowa," Cevilla said. "Her granddaughter is having a *boppli*. Her first great-grandchild."

He nodded. "I didn't think it was for anyone here. Not with those colors."

"Sometimes I like to do something different. Variety is the spice of life, after all." She lifted her head from her work and peered at him over her silver-rimmed glasses. "Did you talk to Ivy?"

Noah nodded. "She'll be here in the morning. We'll knock out those boxes real quick for you."

Cevilla smiled. "*Gut*. And it's about time," she said in a voice so low Noah barely heard it.

"I've already apologized, *Aenti*. Three times." He smirked.

"Besides, it's not like those boxes have been in your way up in the attic."

"*Nee*, they haven't. But it's about time, that's all."

"I have the feeling you're up to something other than getting *yer* attic cleaned out."

"Who, me?" Cevilla's eyes widened, and she batted her eyelashes at Noah. "I would never do anything sneaky. And what would you even think I was going to do?"

"Oh, I don't know." Noah curled his fingers and examined the nails. "Set me up with Ivy?"

"Ivy Yoder is a lovely *yung* woman, and don't you forget it."

"She is nice." He had to agree with her. Ivy was cute too. Definitely cute. He'd thought that the first time he saw her. He wasn't blind, and he noticed pretty girls like Ivy. And she was so tiny, much shorter than him, which had made her even more noticeable. But he hadn't given her a second thought. He wasn't interested in dating or marriage, at least not seriously.

He did have an occasional thought about settling down, though. He'd spent the last decade of his life building his business, and while he loved his work, sometimes traveling didn't appeal. Then there were those times when he saw his friends and classmates in their twenties and thirties with their families established, and as far as he could tell, happily so. It made him wonder if he was missing something.

He dismissed those thoughts. He was here to relax, not spend time musing about his life. Which was a good one, anyway. "At least you're finally getting *yer* attic project done."

"Thanks to you and Ivy." She went back to her crocheting. "You better get on upstairs to bed. I have a feeling she'll be here very early in the morning."

"Why do you say that?"

"She gets up nice and early. All the Yoders do."

He stood and stretched. It had been a long bus ride from Iowa, and he was pretty tired. "I'll see you tomorrow, then." He leaned down and kissed her on the cheek. She didn't look up from her crocheting. "'Night," he said.

"*Gute nacht*, Noah."

He went upstairs to the spare bedroom and quickly got ready for bed. He had drawn the quilt up to his chin, his feet pressed against the baseboard of the old bed, when it started. The ringing. The light-headedness. The churning stomach.

He bolted from the bed and turned on the light. The ringing had stopped. So had the light-headedness. Now everything was normal, except his heartbeat. This was the third time he'd experienced these strange symptoms. The first time he thought he had the flu. That was a little over a year ago, and he'd forgotten all about it until about two weeks ago, when the ringing and dizziness hit him again. Yet he still chalked it up to coming down with something.

His heart rate slowed. He must be more tired than he thought. That was the only explanation that made sense. His auctioneer business was a one-man show that required a lot of hours, and he'd been working six days a week for several years straight. Of course, he took Sundays off. That was mandatory. Still, his mother had warned him more than once about working too hard. Noah had always thought she was overreacting. But now he was beginning to think she might be right.

He turned off the light and slid back under the quilt. When he closed his eyes, he half expected the light-headedness and ringing to start up again. When they didn't, he finally relaxed.

He closed his eyes, and for some reason Ivy's pretty face came into view, taking the rest of his worry away. If he had to spend a few days in an attic with someone, he was glad it was her.

Cevilla put down the baby afghan she was working on, stared at the staircase, and sighed. She made it a policy not to worry, but when it came to her favorite nephew, she couldn't help it. He looked tired. More accurately, he seemed exhausted. Not that he would admit it to anyone. He had given her his bright smile when he arrived, telling her he was good. He was happy. Everything in his life was perfect.

She knew better. No one's life was perfect, and in Noah's case, something was going on. Not that she expected him to talk about it with her. Noah, while a kind, friendly man, was also very private, so she hadn't pressed the issue. If he wanted to talk, he would. Until then, she'd keep at least a short-term eye on him. That was one reason she was glad she'd agreed to take Glenda's stuff. It presented an opportunity to have Noah under her roof for at least a few days.

And a lot of stuff it was. Now she understood why her stepmother's family wanted to be rid of it after the death of Glenda's sister, who had originally inherited it all. Cevilla had known Glenda was a collector. Cevilla also loved her as deeply as she'd loved her own mother, which was why she trusted Noah and Ivy to take this task seriously. Noah had the appreciation for antiques and old things, and Ivy understood sentimental value. They would make an excellent team.

Cevilla pulled a few more inches of pink yarn free from

the ball. With so many babies being born in Birch Creek, she had difficulty keeping up with the afghans. But she'd had a few months' respite and decided to make this one for her English friend's great-grandchild back in Iowa. Every new Birch Creek baby, however, would get a Cevilla Schlabach afghan. Now that Emmanuel Troyer, the former bishop, was unlikely to return after almost three years, she wasn't surprised that Birch Creek was flourishing in all ways—spiritually, financially, and now with a population boom. She smiled. The oppression the community had been under for years was finally lifting.

She wanted the same for Noah. And of course, for Ivy, whom Cevilla saw as a surrogate granddaughter of sorts. The pretty, petite young woman would be a catch for any man, and Cevilla firmly believed the right man was Noah. All she had to do was put them in proximity of each other, and Glenda's boxes were the exact tool to bring the two together. Cevilla smiled. Yes, this was the perfect plan.

But her smile faded as she thought about Noah. "Help him, Lord," she whispered. "Whatever he's burdened with, please make it light. And," she said, unable to help herself, "let Noah and Ivy see how perfect they are for each other. If it's *yer* will, of course. Amen." Satisfied, she went back to her crocheting. But she couldn't help glancing at the staircase and saying an extra prayer for the man she loved as if he were her own son.

Chapter 3

"Why don't you take some of these donuts to Cevilla?" *Mamm* asked as Ivy slipped on her gloves.

Ivy paused and looked at the pile of donuts that remained on a plate from breakfast. They were as hard as hockey pucks, which was the only reason they hadn't been eaten. When Judah suggested they use them on one of the larger frozen ponds later for a hockey game, her father had given him a stern look. He hadn't reached for one of the donuts, though. No one had. "Maybe next time," Ivy said, giving her mother an encouraging smile.

"Next time they'll be better." *Mamm* frowned at the plate of powdered-sugar rocks, and then threw them in the trash. "Phoebe's shown me how to make these several times. I don't know why I can't manage them myself."

Ivy tied the bow of her black bonnet under her chin and gave her mother a quick hug. "Everything else you make is delicious." Well, except for that fruitcake she once made. That would have made a good doorstop.

"Then why am I a failure at making donuts?"

"We can't be *gut* at everything." Ivy started for the front door, but then she turned back to her mother. "Besides, a few failures make us humble."

"Very true." *Mamm* wiped her fingers on her apron. "Humility is important."

"*Ya*, that it is. I'll see you later."

"Are you taking the buggy?"

"*Nee*, I thought I'd walk." Although it was cold outside and there was still a dusting of snow on the ground, the sun was out, and Ivy was in the mood for a walk.

Outside, she blew out a breath, a big white puff filling the air. Relief washed over her as she thought about the torn letter in the trash can in her room. She'd done it. Cut the strings to the one and only romance she'd ever had. Yet despite the relief, there was a twinge of disappointment, mostly regarding her own judgement. She believed everything happened for a reason, and for some reason of his own, God didn't want her and John to be together. *I'd been so sure of the opposite.* She blew out another breath. None of that mattered anymore. She was letting go of John and moving on. She tucked her chin inside her coat and headed for Cevilla's.

Half an hour later, she'd wished she'd brought her scarf. It was colder than she thought it would be. Her toes in her boots were also chilled, but at least it was a beautiful morning to be outside. Several buggies and two cars had rolled past her as she walked, and she'd waved at all the drivers before turning down the short, dead-end road with only Cevilla's house on it. "I like the privacy," Cevilla had explained one time when Ivy stopped by for a quick visit. "I'm away from all the noise of life."

Considering how quiet Birch Creek was anyway, she wasn't sure what noise Cevilla was referring to, but Ivy didn't question it. The woman had her ways, and they had suited her fine living alone all these years. As Ivy walked up Cevilla's gravel drive, she paused and looked at the house. Cevilla had bought the land when she arrived in Birch Creek twenty years earlier, had hired local Amish to build it, and unlike all the Amish houses in the area, elected to keep it small. Just big enough for one or two guests and to have church as long as the weather was pleasant enough to have fellowship outside. Her barn was bigger than the house, and that's where she hosted the service when it was her turn.

Cevilla had never been married. She was also in her eighties, even though she didn't look like it or act like it. Quirky and spry, even while using the cane she now depended on, Cevilla was an interesting and highly independent woman. And while she and Ivy weren't close, they were friends. But Ivy had to wonder if that friendship was based on the fact they were both unmarried—and at the rate Ivy was going, she would continue to be.

Ivy also wondered if she was glimpsing her future in Cevilla—unless she left Birch Creek, something she seriously considered when she met John. But even then a part of her had hoped to convince him to move here if their relationship resulted in marriage. Birch Creek had had its share of troubles in the past, but she loved it here. She didn't want to live anywhere else.

She brought her glove-covered hand to her cold chin. She had to remind herself that life wasn't only about getting married and having kids. Cevilla was a prime example of that. She was content and lived a full life. Ivy could do the same. And someday the desire for a husband and children would wane. She would find satisfaction in being the best aunt she could be. She was already an honorary aunt to Malachi and Hannah, and once Karen and Adam had their own *kinner*, she would be a blood aunt.

Yes, she could be like Cevilla. She could be alone and be happy. Because she was never really alone. She glanced at the sky. *I've got you, Lord. That's more than enough.*

Her spirits boosted, she went to the front door and knocked on it five times before walking inside. It was a signal Cevilla insisted on. "I'm too old to bounce up and get the door," she said. "This way I'm sure I know the person on the other side."

Once in the living room, Ivy saw Cevilla waving around a feather duster without making contact with any furniture. "Do you need some help?" Ivy said as she pulled off her gloves and boots.

"*Nee*. I'm just trying to swat the cobwebs away." She stopped and looked at Ivy. "Look at those rosy cheeks! Is it that cold outside?"

"*Ya*."

"Don't tell me you walked over here."

"*Ya*," she repeated before moving closer to the small stove in the corner of the room. She remembered when her father insisted Cevilla replace her woodstove with this gas one. "It'll be easier for you to manage," he'd said as he moved it into place.

"I don't need easier," Cevilla had insisted.

Her father looked at her with the same immoveable expression Ivy was familiar with whenever he stood his ground. "You'll thank me in the future."

"Well, you are the bishop now," she sniffed, not looking at him. "I can't really argue with you."

"Try to remember that."

Ivy had no idea if Cevilla ever thanked her father, but Ivy was grateful for the heat that warmed her cold fingers now. Maybe walking over here hadn't been the best thing. Then again, a little cold never hurt anyone.

Cevilla tossed the feather duster onto her coffee table. "Noah's upstairs."

"He's started already?" Ivy was surprised. She had assumed Cevilla would want them to work on the project together from the beginning.

"He better not have. I told him he could *geh* up there and rearrange the boxes, but that's all. *Nee* opening them until you arrived." As Ivy untied her bonnet, Cevilla added, "Just leave *yer* things on the couch. I'll hang them up. *Geh* on upstairs."

Knowing better than to protest, Ivy did as she was told. She could see pull-down stairs from the attic at the end of the upstairs hall. Now she would find out how compliant Noah was with his aunt's demands. Demands that were a little ridiculous, but not anything Ivy wouldn't agree to. She didn't mind humoring the woman.

She climbed the stairs, stopping at the top and peeking around the attic. Boxes of every size filled the room, and she didn't see much space to move around. She spied Noah immediately. He was bent over, dragging a large box by the plain wooden bench in front of the one small window in the attic. Ivy cleared her throat, not wanting to startle him.

He turned around, his lips curving into a smile. "*Gute morgen.*"

"Morning." She climbed into the attic and looked around. "Seems like we have our work cut out for us."

"*Ya*. It's a lot of stuff."

She turned to him. He was still slightly bent because of the lack of head space in that part of the attic. "Now that I'm here, we should get started." She shivered. The attic was chillier than she'd expected. She was surprised Cevilla hadn't offered her tea.

Well, at least she had on a sweater, but the next time she came up here she would at least wear her scarf.

He nodded, and then tilted his head. "Are you cold?"

She hugged her arms around her. "*Ya.* A bit. It's pretty cold outside."

He kept looking at her, and then he walked over, blew on his hands, and cupped her cheeks. "Better?"

She almost gasped. What was he doing, touching her this way? She looked up and searched his face, but all she saw was genuine concern. Did he even realize his gesture was more than a bit . . . intimate?

Then she felt the warmth of his hands soak into her chilled skin. His palms were huge and covered her cheeks completely. For a second she forgot her surprise and just let herself enjoy the warmth of his skin on hers.

"Better?" he asked again, his voice unaffected, as if he were warming up a kitten or puppy instead of a woman.

That made her gain her senses. "I'm fine," she said, moving away.

"*Gut.* Wouldn't want you to get too chilled." He turned slightly and gestured to a stack of boxes to his right. "How about we start with these?"

She nodded and walked to the boxes, still reeling a bit at the strange exchange. She knew Noah was a bit different from anyone she'd ever met, and friendly, but she hadn't expected him to be *so* friendly. And she was paying way more attention to the warmth in her cheeks than she should. Telling herself he was just being nice, she focused on the task at hand—a very large task, she gathered from the number and sizes of the boxes surrounding them.

Noah brought a box down from the first stack and tore off the tape that held it closed. He crouched and started to paw through it, although gently, she noticed. Then he closed the flaps. "Doilies. A whole box full of doilies."

Ivy opened another box, whose tape was already loose, and pulled out a delicate filigree crocheted doily. She examined it in the sunbeam coming through the attic window. It really was beautiful. She kneeled and sifted through the contents. "*Ya*," she said. "Only doilies."

"Anything else?" Noah appeared at her side, and then crouched down.

"Not that I can see." She carefully went through the layers. "Oh wait."

"What is it?" He was practically resting his chin against her shoulder as he peered into the box.

Ivy frowned. Noah needed a little lesson in personal space. She nudged him with her elbow as she pulled out a large crocheted tablecloth.

"Hey," he said, moving back and rubbing the spot on his chest where she'd jabbed him. "You could hurt someone with those," he said, pointing at her elbows. "They're little, but deadly."

She glanced at him. For someone who was silver-tongued at the auctioneer podium, he didn't seem to have much of a filter. "Here," she said, shoving the off-white tablecloth at him.

"What do you want me to do with this?" He held it up.

"I don't know. You're the one who wanted to know if there was anything in the box other than doilies." She got to her feet, and even then she was barely taller than him as he remained in a crouched position. She also noticed they were at eye level. This was the first time she could remember being at eye level with any man, and that had to be the reason she couldn't move. She could only stare at Noah and the play of light on his face.

Like the rest of him, his face was long. He also had an angular chin, and she could see the faint shadow of dark whiskers on it. There was a cleft there, too, beneath a full bottom lip. Her gaze drifted upward, past his mouth, his sloped nose, and finally landing on his eyes. They were a hazel-green color, and right now they seemed to be shifting shades in the sunbeam. They were also narrowing.

"What are you looking at?" he said, tilting his head to the side.

"Uh . . ." Words. Where were her words? She'd never been at a loss for them before. She was quiet and a bit introverted, but she wasn't shy. At least she hadn't thought she was until this moment.

"Ivy? I asked you a question."

Yes. Yes he had. And he deserved an answer. Why couldn't she give him one? "I, uh . . ."

"Is there something on *mei* face?" He wiped one hand over his forehead, cheeks, and jaw. "There. Did I get it?"

"Um, *ya*. It's gone." She cringed inwardly at the lie, but she couldn't admit she was staring at him, at his eyes that were so surprisingly beautiful, which was a bit unfair since he was a man. She blinked, her thoughts clearing, and her interest in Noah's eyes disappeared as fast as if she'd been dunked in a bucket of ice water.

"What was on *mei* face?" He ran his hand over his jaw again.

She didn't respond. Instead, she turned around and started rifling through the box with the tablecloth, even though she already knew its contents.

Noah moved to the other side of the attic. He set the tablecloth on top of one of the other boxes, and then scowled. "Please don't tell me this attic is filled with fifty boxes of doilies and tablecloths."

"What if it is?" Ivy said, sounding a bit snappish. She tempered her next words. She wasn't irritated with him. She was annoyed with herself. "Maybe Glenda made all these. Maybe this is what she treasured."

But Noah didn't answer. Instead, he sat down on the bench. "If it's just crochet stuff, I don't know why I have to be here."

"How did you know it was crochet?" Ivy asked. Her father and brothers couldn't tell a crochet hook from a knitting needle.

"Just like I know the sweater you're wearing was knitted by hand."

He was right. She'd bought it from Abigail Bontrager, who was an excellent knitter and weaver.

"And like I also know this"—he picked up a doily from the box—"isn't crochet."

"It's not?" She went to him and examined the doily. It looked similar to the other ones.

"*Nee*. It's tatting."

"What's the difference?"

"The tools used. Crocheters use hooks and tatters use shuttles." He picked up another doily, which was a light pink, and held one in each hand. "See how uniform the lace is with this one?" He nodded at the white doily. "The pink one has more variations, because of the tension of the thread."

Ivy was impressed. "I didn't know you were an expert at this."

He put the doilies back in the box. "I'm definitely not an expert. I just know enough to be dangerous. And to make a lopsided tablecloth." He grinned, but his amusement quickly disappeared. "It would be one thing if these were antique lace, but they're clearly made of inexpensive yarn. If these boxes are full of crochet and tatting, I'm not sure why Cevilla needs us both to help."

His disappointment was obvious to Ivy. "What were you expecting?"

"Some antiques." He stood and wandered around the attic, ducking his head when he walked past a low spot. "Pictures, mirrors, jewelry, stamps, silver . . ." He turned and looked at Ivy again. "Glenda was English, so I was sure she had some of those items here. I didn't realize she was interested only in doilies and tablecloths."

"We still have a lot of boxes to inspect," Ivy pointed out.

He suddenly squeezed his eyes shut, as if it pained him to be here—a complete shift from the way he looked a moment ago. Then again, maybe this was how he'd felt all along, that he was wasting his time here.

"I can do this myself," Ivy said, a little annoyed that he was so shallow. She hadn't expected that from him. Cevilla wouldn't be happy, but Ivy wasn't going to spend hours with Noah if he didn't want to be here.

He opened his eyes, his surprise evident. "Why would you do that?"

"Because you seem disappointed by what we've found so far."

He shook his head. "I'm not." Then he paused. "Okay, maybe a little. But like you said, we have plenty of boxes left to *geh* through. And even if all we find is a bunch of yarn goods, I made a promise to *mei aenti*. I won't *geh* back on that."

Well. That was admirable, at least.

He went over to another one of the boxes and crouched in front of it. He tore off the tape and peered inside. "Guess what I found," he said, staring inside the box.

"What?" Ivy could feel her curiosity rise. She hurried to him and looked over his shoulder.

"More doilies!" He grinned and picked up a handful. Then he dropped them back inside the box, his smile dimming as he leaned back on his heels. "*Aenti* Cevilla was so insistent on me going through these boxes that I thought she wanted me to appraise the contents."

"Then appraise the doilies."

"They aren't worth anything, other than sentimental value."

Ivy pulled a box on the floor near the stack toward her. It was smaller than the other boxes they'd gone through. "Then they're priceless," she said, as she tugged on tape that seemed more stubborn than the rest.

"To someone, *ya*. But they're not collectable. Or even salable."

"Does that matter?" Was this tape made of cement? Noah had made opening the other boxes look like a piece of cake. "You can't put a dollar amount on emotions."

"I do it all the time."

She glanced up at him. Again, he was being genuine, not insulting.

"People sell their treasures for a variety of reasons." He got up and knelt beside her. "It's *mei* job to make sure they get a fair price. It's also *mei* job to let them know when an item doesn't have monetary value." He put his hand over hers, making her jump. "Let me open it," he said.

Did he assume she couldn't open a simple box? Without thinking, she nudged him with her elbow again. "I've got it."

"Ow!" he said, rocking back as if she'd stabbed him with a hot poker.

"I didn't nudge you that hard." She couldn't help but smile a bit. "Don't be such a *boppli*."

"I'm telling you, *yer* elbows are sharp. Maybe you should use them to open up that box."

She chuckled, and that gave him enough of an opening to take the peeled-up part of the tape from her and rip it off. "There," he said. "Just like a Band-Aid."

As the morning wore on, they went through two stacks of boxes. They weren't all filled with doilies, but according to Noah, they hadn't uncovered anything of real value either—just mostly English clothing ranging from the 1940s to current times. Ivy reached into one of the boxes and pulled out a man's hat. She handed it to Noah.

"A fedora." He examined it. "Probably from right after World War II." He put it on his head and lifted his chin, pulling down the brim. "How do I look?"

The hat was strange, nothing like the Amish hats familiar to her. Noah's hair came down past his ears, and the hat made it stick out on the sides. But she had to admit he looked pretty good in it. "It suits you."

He took it off and put it back in the box. Then he looked around at the boxes they'd opened. Now the cramped attic had become even more crowded. "We have to do something with all this before we can open any more boxes."

As if on cue, the sound of heavy footsteps on the attic stairs made Ivy turn to look. Unlike Noah, Cevilla practically stomped when she walked, and she added another thump with every use of her cane. "I'm going to have to get a cowbell or something," Cevilla said, stopping at the top of the stairs and putting her hand on her chest. She heaved a dramatic breath. "I'm too old to be climbing a mountain to come get you two for lunch."

It was lunchtime already? She hadn't realized they'd been up here for nearly three hours. And why hadn't Cevilla simply called up the attic stairs?

"I made pimento cheese sandwiches," Cevilla said.

"*Mei* favorite." Noah walked over and put his arm around her shoulders. "You're so *gut* to me, *Aenti*."

"Of course I am." Her wrinkled face looked stern. But a smiling glint shone in her pale-blue eyes behind her silver-framed glasses, as well as a touch of softness Ivy had seen only when Cevilla was around her nephew. It was clear they loved each other very much.

"I'm starving." Noah headed to the top of the stairs, and then looked over his shoulder. "Are you two coming?"

"In a minute." Cevilla turned to Ivy. "I need to speak with you first."

Noah paused, but then he shrugged and went downstairs.

Cevilla stepped toward her. "I want to tell you how much I appreciate you helping me with all this." She looked around the attic and sighed. "It's overwhelming, but I knew you and Noah would make a *gut* team."

"Why do you think we do?" It was a question Ivy had been wanting to ask ever since last year when Noah told her about Cevilla's request.

"You both have an appreciation for things other people tend to discard."

"But I'm not an antiques expert. I don't even know much

history, although I do like to learn about it. And so far all we've found is crocheted items and a few clothes."

Cevilla peered at her. "You do understand the intrinsic value of things, though. And that's more important than head knowledge." Cevilla sneezed. "Dust," she said, waving her hand in front of her nose. Then she sneezed four more times. "Goodness!"

"We should get you out of here," Ivy said, putting her hand on Cevilla's shoulder and guiding her to the stairs.

Cevilla sniffed. "*Ya*, before Noah eats all the sandwiches. I wouldn't put it past him."

Chapter 4

Noah's mouth watered at the sight of the sandwiches on a large platter in the center of Cevilla's kitchen table. He was hungry. Starving, actually. Cevilla ate light for breakfast, and Noah had missed the eggs, sausage, and toast he usually had. When he could, he'd add gravy and biscuits to the mix, but that was usually when he went out for breakfast. Which was frequently since he didn't enjoy cooking.

He eyed the sandwiches again. He'd have to control himself not to eat three of them, although he noticed Cevilla had made extra.

Buzzing suddenly filled his ears, making him grimace. It was preferable to the piercing hum that had hit him while he was upstairs. That sound was new. And unnerving. He'd also never had this issue two days in a row. He'd hit the hay early again tonight. In fact, he'd sleep three days in a row if he could just get rid of the strange noises in his ears.

He heard Cevilla and Ivy coming down the stairs. "You didn't eat without us, did you?" his aunt called out before she entered the kitchen.

Noah understood what she said, but it sounded like she was

talking underwater. "Of course not," he said, making sure his tone sounded light.

"*Gut.* Because I made an extra sandwich for Ivy." She winked at him as Ivy came in behind her. "The *maedel* doesn't know when to stop eating."

"I think you have me confused with Leanna." Ivy went to the kitchen sink and turned on the tap.

"I also made banana cream pie."

Noah's mouth watered more, and for a second he forgot about the buzzing. His aunt made the best banana cream pie he'd ever had, and that was saying something considering how much he traveled and how many Amish homes and restaurants he'd eaten in.

"Did I ever tell you how I won the pie contest for six years in a row in Arbor Grove?" Cevilla said as she moved to the table. "Until Rose Jantzi cheated."

"Cheated?" Ivy responded. Then she looked at Noah and returned his knowing smile, cluing him in that this wasn't the first time she'd heard this story, either.

"She was dating the judge on the sly." Cevilla leaned down and spoke in Ivy's ear. "I'm sure her banana cream pie wasn't the only thing that got first place that day."

"*Aenti,*" Noah said, but he couldn't hide his laugh. He adored his aunt, and her humor, along with other things about her. She was quirkier than any of his other relatives, and he didn't know whether that was because she'd been raised from the age of six by an English stepmother, or if she was just born that way. But in a family of staid, follow-the-rules-without-fail Amish family members, she was a breath of fresh air.

He walked over to the sink, where Ivy was now washing her

hands. "You'll have to excuse *mei aenti*. Sometimes she gets a little . . ."

"Cheeky?" Ivy grinned.

"To say the least." He smiled back. Ivy had a round face with a small nose that upturned at the end and blue eyes clear as antique glass. Underneath her *kapp* he could see her pale-blond hair, and her skin was an appealing pale-peach color. Her cheeks had been apple red when she came upstairs this morning. Which was why he'd thoughtlessly warmed them with his hands. He realized as soon as he did it that he'd overstepped, but he couldn't pull away. It was her fault for walking over here in the winter.

He moved away from the sink, having already washed his hands. He had to give his aunt credit. If he were looking for a girlfriend or even a future wife, Ivy fit the bill, at least physically. No, more than that. He could see how much she liked his aunt, and that meant a lot to him. It didn't surprise him that they were friends. Cevilla never let age get in the way of her social life.

Ivy held her wet hands over the sink and looked around. Realizing what she needed, he found a dish towel behind him. "Here," he said, handing it to her.

Ivy dried her hands and gave him a quick smile, and then she hung the towel on a hook. "Excuse me," she said, brushing past him.

Without thinking, he touched the place where she'd elbowed him. Twice. It was only when she walked away that he noticed the buzzing was still in his ears. While he was looking at her, it had faded into the background.

She pulled out a chair and sat down, her back straight and her hands in her lap while Cevilla poured glasses of iced tea. "Noah," Cevilla said, motioning to him. "Come sit down."

Again, the words were muffled yet clear enough for him to make out. He nodded and sat down next to her, across from Ivy.

"I thought you might have started eating already," Cevilla said, looking at him. "You never could resist pimento cheese sandwiches."

Suddenly his stomach rumbled. From the way both she and Ivy were looking at him, he assumed it was loud. "I was waiting on you two slowpokes."

"I beg *yer* pardon." Cevilla sat down and sniffed. "I am not slow."

"I'm just teasing," he said, wondering for a moment if he'd gone too far. Then his aunt smiled, and he knew he was still in her good graces. He glanced down at the antique wood table, noticing as he always did the pits and divots in its finish. He'd bought it for her two years ago after seeing it up for auction in Shipshe. He was stunned that no one had bought it, but he knew Cevilla would love it. When he told her the story behind the purchase, she said, "Then God intended for me to have it."

They prayed, and finally he could dig into one of the sandwiches. He also added a few carrot and celery sticks to his plate. The lunch, like Cevilla's breakfast, was a little sparse. He'd be hungry a short while later. Maybe he'd volunteer to cook after all. He wasn't a bad cook. He'd had to learn out of necessity because he lived by himself. He was fairly sure Cevilla wouldn't mind if he made a meal or two. A rib-sticking, man-size meal.

He glanced at Ivy, expecting her to take delicate bites of her sandwich. Instead, she took a big bite. "Delicious, Cevilla," she said after swallowing. Then she took a gulp of tea.

Noah continued to watch her, growing more amused as she polished off the sandwich. When she set down her empty glass, he couldn't help but say, "You must have been hungry."

Her eyes widened a bit, and he wondered if he'd said the wrong thing. "Um, *ya*," she said, putting her hands in her lap. "I didn't realize I was eating so fast."

"*Nix* wrong with a healthy appetite." Cevilla was cutting the crusts off her bread. For a woman who was so laid back with everything else—including dusting, he gathered from the amount of dust floating around in her attic—she was finicky with her food. "Is there, Noah?"

"Um, *nee*," he said, surprised at her question. And he believed that. He'd much rather be around a woman who enjoyed food than one who picked at it. Then again, it wasn't as though he spent a lot of time taking women to supper. For years that was because he was traveling and busy building up his business. Now he couldn't try to date anyone even if he wanted to. It wouldn't be fair to the woman involved.

After he ate another sandwich and the rest of the rabbit food, he said, "We should get back to work upstairs."

"What's *yer* hurry? You've got all afternoon." Cevilla took a sip of tea.

"The faster we work, the faster we'll get *yer* attic back to you." He glanced at Ivy, who was nodding.

"I thought we could play a game of Dutch Blitz first," Cevilla said. "*Nee* need to work on a full stomach."

Noah looked at Ivy again, and he saw the glint of sadness in her eyes. It mirrored his own feeling. It was clear Cevilla was lonely and trying to stretch out the time he and Ivy were here as long as possible. That led to a feeling of guilt. He'd been so sure his aunt was working a matchmaking angle, but she just wanted some company. "I'm okay with playing a game," he said to Ivy. "Do you have somewhere you need to be this afternoon?"

"I was going to *geh* to Schrocks'," Ivy said, putting down her napkin. "But I can do that tomorrow."

"Noah can take you," Cevilla piped up. "Surely you weren't going to walk there and then carry groceries home in the snow."

"I wasn't going for groceries." Ivy explained how her job had ended at Miller's Bookbinding. "Leanna mentioned Aden might be looking for someone to work at the store, so I planned to talk to him today."

"Oh." Cevilla glanced at her plate. She gave one of her uneaten carrots a push. "Then you should get the attic finished quickly."

Ivy met Noah's eyes for a brief moment, and then she looked at Cevilla again. "I'm sure it can wait. Leanna said he was only thinking about hiring someone else."

"It's also snowing," Noah added, catching on to what Ivy was doing.

"And you're right," Ivy said. "I did eat faster than normal, so it would be *gut* to let *mei* lunch settle. I'd be happy to play a game of Dutch Blitz while we wait."

"Excellent," Cevilla said in English. She still slipped into it over the years, and Noah attributed that to her English upbringing. "I'll get the cards."

"I'll do the dishes." Noah stood.

"I'll help," Ivy added.

They carried the dishes to the sink, and Noah turned on the tap while Ivy took the plates to the trash can and scraped off what few crumbs were left. The sink was filling with soapy water by the time she returned. "*Danki*," he said when she handed him the plates.

"They weren't that dirty."

"*Nee.* Not that." He lowered his voice. "Playing the game. You've made her happy."

"I love Dutch Blitz, so it wasn't a hard decision to make."

She made what she'd done sound simple, but she'd put her job hunt aside to help him keep Cevilla company. That was no small gesture.

He washed the dishes while she dried. They made quick work of the task, and as he was putting away the clean dishes, Ivy wiped and dried the table. She came back and rinsed the dishrag.

"Were you really going to walk to the grocery store in this weather?"

"It's not that far."

"How far, exactly?"

She bit her lower lip. "About a fifteen-minute walk."

That wasn't too bad. "And how long to get to *yer haus* from there?"

"Uh, forty-five minutes."

He glanced at the window. Snow was falling. It wasn't thick, and it was intermittent, but still . . . When he went outside to feed the horse this morning, it was cold. "I'll take you," he said, not liking the idea of her walking in the snowy cold.

"I'll be fine. I like a brisk walk."

"So do I, but not when it's twenty below."

She smirked. "It's not that cold."

"It'll feel like it by the time you get back home." He went to the small, gas-powered refrigerator and opened it. "Just as I thought. More bird food in here." He turned to her. "I have to get some groceries anyway. A *mann* can't exist on carrots and celery alone."

"Noah, you really don't have to—"

"Found them!" Cevilla came into the room waving a deck of cards. "Took me a while to remember where I put them." She looked at the table and then at the two of them. "You do make a *gut* team," she said, grinning widely.

Noah shifted on his feet. Okay, maybe his aunt wasn't just lonely. He glanced at Ivy, who looked up at him. If she was uncomfortable at Cevilla's claim, she didn't show it.

"Do you like to play Dutch Blitz?" Ivy asked him.

He was terrible at Dutch Blitz, but he wasn't going to admit it. "*Ya*. So be prepared to lose."

"*Nee*," she said, lifting her chin. "I'm prepared to win."

He watched her walk away and smiled to himself. He could think of worse things to do than spend the afternoon losing at cards to his aunt and Ivy Yoder. Then he stilled. The buzzing was gone. Completely gone. He wasn't sure when it disappeared, but he didn't care. He almost leaned against the kitchen counter with relief. Hopefully this little problem would be gone completely after a few good nights of sleep.

"Noah," Cevilla said, tapping the cards. "We're waiting on you."

With a grin, Noah went to the table. "Let the game begin."

After they finished playing Dutch Blitz—with Cevilla thoroughly winning the game—Noah started for the stairs only to have his aunt stop him. "Wait for Ivy."

"I won't open anything, *Aenti*—"

"Wait for Ivy."

Noah merely nodded, and Ivy watched the exchange with

a bit of discomfort. What did it matter if Noah went upstairs without her for a little bit? It wasn't as if they had to open each box together. Sometimes Cevilla was more *seltsam* than quirky.

Ivy followed Noah upstairs and into the attic. She blew out a breath. Their task looked even more overwhelming than it had this morning because the boxes they'd opened were spread all over the floor. She walked over to one. "What are we going to do with all this stuff?"

Noah rubbed his chin with the top of his forefinger. "Cevilla already said she didn't want to keep the doilies."

Ivy nodded. She'd brought up the doilies to Cevilla during the card game, asking why Glenda had so many. "She went on a crochet spree when she retired," Cevilla explained. "She liked making doilies because they were quick to crochet and could be given as small gifts. Guess she went a little overboard with them."

"Someone will have to sort through them and figure out which ones are worth saving," Noah said, picking up a doily from one of the opened boxes.

"That someone being me."

He lifted his brow in innocence. "You know more about doilies than I do."

She tilted up her chin. "Because I'm a woman?"

He put the doily back. "*Nee*, because as you said before, you can't put a price on sentimental value. I'm leaving it up to you to decide what's valuable. Then we'll pack them up and . . ." He frowned. "If this was Iowa I would know where to send them. A couple of the women in our district recycle old fabric and yarn work and sell it to tourists. They make some beautiful items."

"Maybe we could ship what we have to them."

"Certainly we could send them some."

Ivy looked at all the doilies. They'd already opened five boxes of them, and there had to be hundreds to go through just from those. They couldn't send all of them away. "I'll take two of the boxes," she said.

"Are you sure?"

"*Ya*. I've got some space in *mei* bedroom." She'd figure out what to do with them later. She was intrigued by the idea of recycling them, although she wasn't that good with a needle and thread. Abigail Bontrager, however, was. Ivy would ask her if she had any ideas.

"That sounds like a plan." He turned around and started opening another box.

Ivy sat down on the small bench. Although it was cloudy outside, she could still see the dust motes dancing in the light from the window. After they were done sorting through Glenda's stuff, Ivy vowed to give this room a good, thorough cleaning, especially now that she knew the dust made Cevilla sneeze.

While Ivy sorted through the doilies, Noah looked through a box full of postcards and souvenirs from various places around the country. That seemed to interest him, and they worked in silence for a while.

"Ivy," Noah said.

She looked up from the two piles of doilies she was working on. The "keep" pile was getting bigger and bigger. She was having trouble deciding which ones to discard, but at least a few were too stained or too wonkily made to even consider keeping.

"*Ya*?" she said, looking at another doily and trying to figure out which pile to put it in. This one was rather pretty, made with an antique-colored yarn instead of the stark white most of the other doilies were.

"Do you think *mei aenti* is trying to get us together?"

Ivy's head shot up. Noah's expression was unreadable, as if he'd just asked her for the time instead of what she thought might be Cevilla's matchmaking intentions. "I, uh . . . I don't know." But she did know. Cevilla wasn't being subtle about making sure she and Noah were basically glued together while Ivy was here.

"I'm pretty sure she is." He tossed a postcard back into the box.

"Oh." She wasn't sure how to respond to that. But her face did, and she was sure her cheeks were bright red, because they felt like they were on fire.

"But you don't have to worry about that happening. I'm only interested in getting the attic cleaned out. I'm not interested in you."

"Oh," she repeated, uncertain what else to say. How was she supposed to respond to that kind of rejection? And now that she thought about it, it stung. "That was rude," she said, the words slipping out.

Noah's expression immediately turned contrite. "I'm sorry. That didn't come out right." He scrubbed his hand over his face. "I don't mean I'm not interested in you."

"What?" Now she was confused. Was he interested? Is that why he had warmed her cheeks that morning? And why she caught him looking at her a few times while Cevilla was beating them at Dutch Blitz? She assumed his first gesture was because he had a bit of a personal space issue, and the second . . . Well, she was used to people staring at her because of her small size. But was there something more to it?

"I mean, I don't think you're *uninteresting*." He paused. "I'm digging a deeper hole for myself, aren't I? Sometimes I stick *mei* big foot in *mei* big mouth. What I mean is—"

"Noah." She softened her tone, wanting to put him out of his misery. "I understand. And so you won't worry, let me say I'm not interested in dating either."

He took a take a step back. "*Gut*—"

Some of the boxes—and Noah—tumbled to the floor.

"Noah!" Ivy jumped up from the floor, dodged two large boxes, and went to his side. "Are you okay?"

He sat up, looking a little dazed. Then he squeezed his eyes shut.

"Noah?'

"What in the world happened here?"

Ivy looked over her shoulder to see Cevilla walking toward them. She hadn't heard the woman come up the stairs. "The boxes fell," Ivy said, turning her attention back to Noah.

His eyes were open now, and his expression was clear. "I'm fine," he said, scrambling to his feet. "Somehow the boxes missed me."

"What a relief." Cevilla tapped her cane on the wood floor. "That's enough work for one day."

Now that she knew Noah was all right, Ivy looked around the attic. It was an even bigger mess than before, and she hadn't thought that was possible.

"I'll stack the boxes again." Noah reached for one of them, but he was blocked by Cevilla's cane.

"You'll do *nee* such thing." Cevilla pulled back her weapon, but she still held it out as if she were ready to intervene if he disobeyed her. He looked behind him before stepping back this time.

Cevilla turned to Ivy. "We can tackle this tomorrow. Noah can take you to the Schrocks' before driving you home."

Ivy glanced out the window. The snow had stopped falling, and a sliver of sunshine pierced the cloudy sky. "That's not necessary."

"It is," Noah and Cevilla said at the same time.

Knowing she couldn't argue with them both, she nodded. "I'll *geh* downstairs and get *mei* boots and coat on." As she walked toward the attic stairs, she heard Cevilla speaking in a low voice.

"Take the quilt from *mei* bed, Noah. It's nice and warm."

A short time later she was bundled up in a thick quilt and Noah was driving her to the Schrocks'. Although the quilt was toasty warm, she started to take it off. "This really isn't necessary."

"Do you always refuse when someone tries to do something nice for you?" Noah asked.

Ivy glanced at him. He was staring straight ahead, holding the reins loosely in his hands. Cevilla's horse knew its way around Birch Creek as well as any human. "I haven't really given it much thought."

"I don't mind taking you to the Schrocks' and to *yer haus*, and Cevilla gave you that quilt for a reason. Enjoy the ride and stay warm."

Ivy sat back and didn't say another word.

Chapter 5

After Noah and Ivy left, Cevilla went back upstairs. Her knees complained loudly as she made her way up into the attic. She'd have to put some of that arthritis salve on them tonight. It was an old family recipe going back two generations, and it worked better than any of the fancy creams and ointments she'd bought from drugstores over the years. She hadn't gone up the stairs so many times in one day in a long, long while. But a little knee pain was worth seeing Noah and Ivy working together.

Her suspicions had been confirmed—her nephew and that sweet girl did make a good pair. And she hadn't missed the stolen glances Noah gave Ivy over lunch and while they were playing Dutch Blitz. She wondered if he even realized he was paying that much attention to her. Noah was an intelligent man, but not exactly a whiz when it came to women. The card game had been a last-minute thought, and a smart one at that. "You're a genius, Cevilla," she said, stretching her back. "An absolute genius."

She looked around the attic and saw all the work Noah and Ivy had done. They'd unpacked quite a few boxes, but they had many more to go through. Little did Cevilla know she'd be dealing with so many of her stepmother's belongings when she agreed to let Glenda's family send her some boxes. If she were a younger woman, she'd do the sorting herself. But that wouldn't be nearly as much fun as watching Noah and Ivy fall in love. Because she was certain they would. She was rarely wrong about these things.

Cevilla glanced around the room one more time and spied a box different from the others. It was bent and smashed, with a large water stain on the side, and it was separate from the rest of the boxes, hidden in a darkened corner. She sighed and turned away. She needed to deal with what was inside, but she couldn't bring herself to open that box now. "Someday," she said. She'd been saying someday for sixty-four years now. What was another day, or month, or year? It wasn't as though the box was going anywhere.

She turned to go downstairs, but then she took one last look at the old box, remembering what it represented. She blinked the sudden moisture from her eyes. "Someday," she whispered again, and headed downstairs.

The ride to the Schrocks' passed quickly, and by the time they arrived the sun had disappeared and the snow had started falling again. Cold air hit Ivy as she took off the quilt and got out of the buggy. "I'll make this as quick as I can," she told Noah.

"*Nee* hurry. Like I said, I need to do some grocery shopping."

Noah pulled away to park the buggy and Ivy went inside. The store was empty of customers, which wasn't a surprise considering the weather and that it was nearly closing time. "Hello?" she called out.

"Just a minute." Aden Troyer called from the back of the store where the office was. A few seconds later he was walking toward her. "Hi, Ivy. You came just in time. I was about to close up."

"How's Sadie doing?"

"Fine. She's resting right now." He smirked. "She's not too happy that she can't spend all her time here. But Patience told her to get as much rest as she can."

Patience was Birch Creek's midwife, and Sadie was expecting her baby in a couple of months.

"Leanna mentioned you're considering hiring someone on," Ivy said as she lifted her gaze to Aden's. "I'm interested in a job since the Millers are moving away."

"It's only part-time."

"Part-time is fine."

He gave her a crisp nod. "All right, then. You're hired."

Ivy's jaw dropped. "Like that?"

"Like that." His lips curved into a grin above his rust-colored beard. "Sadie and I have known you for years. We trust you. Besides, you've just made *mei* job easier. Now I won't have to conduct any interviews." He held out his hand. "Congratulations."

Out of the corner of her eye, she saw Noah pushing a grocery cart down the canned goods aisle. She hadn't heard the door's bell when he entered. His shoulders were slumped slightly since the cart was on the low side, which was the perfect height for her. She faced her own challenges because of her short stature, but she hadn't thought about Noah having difficulty because he was so tall.

She turned back to Aden. "When do you want me to start?"

"How about after the Christmas holidays?"

"That'll be fine. I'm working on a project for Cevilla right now. I'll be finished with that way before then."

"I'm glad I'm not interfering with that," Aden said. "I want to stay on her *gut* side."

"A wise decision." Noah pushed the buggy toward them and cracked a smile at Aden. "It's always important to be on the positive side of *mei aenti*."

"I didn't realize you were in town, Noah," Aden said, moving to stand behind the counter.

"Just got here yesterday." Noah placed the items from his cart on the counter.

"In time for the snow, I see."

The men made small talk as Aden tallied up the groceries on the simple cash register and then placed them into plastic bags. Ivy noticed how at ease Noah was with Aden. He seemed at ease with everyone, which was probably part of the reason his auctioneering business was so successful.

After he paid Aden, Noah gathered his groceries, one large hand easily grabbing the handles on all three bags.

"See you here after Christmas," Aden said to Ivy as they started to leave.

"Danki." After Ivy walked out the door Noah was holding open for her, she climbed into the buggy and looked at the quilt. Remembering what Noah said, she wrapped it around herself.

Noah got in on the other side and put his bags on the buggy floor. Once they were on the road, he said, "I take it you got the job?"

"I did. I start after Christmas." She smiled, relieved at her success.

"Congratulations. We'll be finished with the attic well before then, of course."

"Not if you keep knocking down boxes."

Noah glanced at her with a raised brow, and she chuckled. "I'm kidding."

He gave her a wry smile. "I promise to watch myself up there from now on. It's such a cramped space, though."

A short while later Noah pulled up in front of her house. "You're right, you don't live that far from *mei aenti*. I didn't pay that much attention when I came to see you last night. Still," he said, turning to look at her, "if it's this cold out, don't walk. Especially if it's also snowing." Then he paused before saying, "Although I think you're going to ignore what I just said."

She should be annoyed by his concern, but she found it a little . . . charming. That didn't mean she needed him—or anyone else—hovering over her, though. "Of course I will."

"For a small thing, you sure are stubborn."

Ivy hesitated. Should she be insulted? But one look at his gorgeous eyes told her he wasn't making a dig at her height or her character. Only stating a simple observation. She relaxed. She was starting to realize she had no reason to be touchy around him. He was just different from any man she'd ever met, and in a good way.

She shrugged off the quilt, and an instant chill went through her. It had been nice and cozy riding in the buggy, wrapped in a faded, well-worn quilt that still kept in the warmth as they passed the countryside frosted with snow. Noah hadn't talked too much. He seemed fine to drive in silence, and that hadn't bothered Ivy. It was . . . comfortable. Like Noah. She felt at ease around him, which was nice. "I'll see you tomorrow," she said, stepping out of the buggy.

He leaned forward and called after her. "'I'm glad you got the job, Ivy."

She smiled, feeling warm again even as she stood in the cold evening air. "Me too."

Ivy again walked to Cevilla's on Friday morning, and she arrived even earlier than she had the day before. While Noah was in the barn feeding Cevilla's horse, she accepted the cup of tea the older woman offered. "Are you sure I can't get started right now?" Ivy said.

"Noah will be finished soon enough. Then you two can work to *yer* hearts' content."

Ivy pondered what Noah said yesterday, about Cevilla trying to put them together. Now the woman's strange demands were starting to make sense. Why else would she insist on her and Noah working so closely together? Ivy should explain there was no interest in romance on either side, but as Cevilla spooned a small amount of honey onto her toast, Ivy kept quiet. If it made Cevilla happy to think Ivy and Noah might get together, Ivy wasn't going to spoil that for her. Not now. Cevilla would find out soon enough anyway, once they were finished with the boxes in attic and she and Noah parted as friends.

"*Gute morgen*," Noah said as he entered the kitchen, his gaze landing on Ivy. "You're here early."

"I wanted to get started as soon as possible."

"That's the spirit," Cevilla said. She looked up at Noah. "Don't you appreciate a woman with a *gut* work ethic?"

"Uh, sure." Noah winked at Ivy. "Speaking of work, we better get to it."

Ivy followed Noah upstairs, and this time she remembered to take her scarf. She wrapped it around her neck and looked at the boxes that had scattered on the floor with Noah's tumble.

"Hopefully there isn't anything breakable in them," he said.

"Surely they would have packed the breakables safely."

"You never know. I've seen people toss antique glassware into a box without any paper or protective wrapping. I can't imagine what they're thinking when they do that."

"I'm sure that's not the case here." She ripped off the tape on one of the boxes, now an expert at opening them. "Oh," she said, peering inside.

"Let me guess. Doilies."

"I think you'll like this better." She pulled out a small hand-carved, wooden clock. It was lying on top of a thick, yellow fleece blanket.

"Now, that's more like it," he said, moving over to her, his eyes sparking with excitement. "Can I see it?"

"Sure." She carefully handed him the highly detailed clock, and he examined it. Its face was in the center of a carved house, complete with shingled roof and chimney. In a tiny hole an even tinier white bird with a red beak was perched between two pairs of open shutters, each with a dancing couple dressed in old-fashioned clothes. Simple roman numerals were painted on the plain clock face.

"Definitely a cuckoo clock." He turned the clock around and turned a small knob. Nothing happened. "Probably broken," he said, gently turning the clock over.

"I'm sure Leanna Raber could fix it," Ivy said. "I can't think of anything she can't repair."

"She's the tall *maedel*, right?" He crossed the room and set the clock on the bench beneath the window. "I think *Aenti* told me she worked in a mechanic's shop."

"She *is* a mechanic. A very *gut* one." Ivy steeled herself, prepared for what she typically heard from people who didn't know Leanna very well—that only men should be mechanics, that now that Leanna was married she should have a proper job more suited to a woman, and other wrong assumptions.

But all Noah said was, "We should drop it off at her shop, then."

Ivy smiled. "I can do that on *mei* way home. Her workshop is right by *mei haus*." Before Leanna and Roman married, Leanna set up her own workshop on her family's property. Now she split her time between the Rabers' shop and her own, where she usually worked only on small projects friends and family brought by. Ivy turned her attention back to the clock, pleased that Noah was open-minded about having Leanna look at it.

"I hope she can fix it, because this is definitely something we can sell. We just have to make sure Cevilla doesn't want to keep it."

Ivy looked at the clock again. It was nice and unusual. As she continued to gaze at it, she realized how much she liked it. Maybe if Cevilla didn't plan to hang on to it, Ivy could purchase it from her. *But where would I put it?* Mei *bedroom?* No, that wouldn't be the right place for it. That kind of clock needed to be on display for people to enjoy.

"You seem pretty interested in the clock." Noah moved to stand next to her.

She lifted her gaze. His black hair was a bit disheveled today, but she didn't mind. Actually, he looked a little handsome with messy hair. *Wait . . . what?* She froze. Since when did she start noticing how Noah looked?

"Ivy?"

Embarrassed, she hurried toward the clock and picked it up, pretending to be completely interested in it and not confused about the path her thoughts had traveled. She touched the tiny bird's beak and calmed herself. There was nothing wrong with noticing Noah was handsome. It didn't mean she liked him, or would fall in love with him, or something ridiculous like that. She carefully set the clock back on the bench and faced him. "*Ya*," she said, looking at him squarely. "I like it a lot."

He tilted his head to the side and looked at her for a moment. Another strange jolt hit her, but then she immediately ignored it. She walked back to the box where she'd found the clock and knelt. Best to focus on the task at hand, the reason she was there in the first place, instead of admiring Noah's tousled hair. "I wonder what else is in here?" she said, a little bit too loudly.

Noah didn't seem to notice the volume of her voice as he crouched behind her, peering over her shoulder. He was so close she detected the scent of . . . lemon? She hadn't noticed that yesterday. Then again, for some reason she was noticing small details about him today. When his arm reached around her to get something from inside the box, his chest pressed against her back for a split second. She held in a surprised gasp.

"Look at this." He pulled out what looked like an ornate bracelet.

The shiny stones on the bracelet made Ivy forget about his proximity. The bracelet was gold, with a rectangle-like box on top surrounded by pearls. She scrutinized it more closely and realized what the item was. "Is this a watch?"

"*Ya.*" He stood up, and she followed suit, turning to face him. "And I think these are sapphire," he said, pointing at the square boxes on each side of the watch face. "I'm sure this is real gold and these are real pearls. The only thing I'm unsure about is how old the piece is."

"It sure is fancy." Ivy glanced at her wrist. She couldn't imagine wearing anything like this, and she thought the watch was rather gaudy. But Noah seemed fascinated with it, turning it over in his hand and peering closely.

"I'll need to look up more information on it," he said. He glanced at her. "Where's the nearest library?"

"Barton."

"It has computers, right?"

"Of course. Are you allowed to use them?"

"Only for work. Our bishop gave me special permission." He took the watch and carefully set it on the bench next to the cuckoo clock. "He wasn't all that eager to grant it, but I keep *mei* word and only look up items to learn their history and value."

Ivy eyed the watch again. She definitely preferred the modest beauty of the hand-carved cuckoo clock. "I can't imagine Cevilla would want to keep a watch like that."

Noah shrugged. "Maybe it has sentimental value. Or maybe she'll want it if it's worth a lot."

Ivy frowned. "Cevilla's not interested in money."

"I know. But sometimes people do unexpected things when it comes to valuable items. I've seen it happen over and over. It's not bad—as long as money and possessions don't have a hold on you."

Ivy had seen that happen firsthand. Emmanuel Troyer had abused his power as bishop and hoarded the community's money. His greed had become his downfall. When he left and her father became bishop, her father made sure the community fund was available to everyone. And he'd made it clear that if anyone wanted to know how much was in there, he would show them the bank statements. No one had ever asked, though, which proved they trusted him.

She turned and saw Noah crouched in front of the box. "This whole thing is full of watches and clocks." He pulled out a simple, silver woman's watch with a stretch band. "This one isn't worth much. They still make this type of watch now." He put it back in the box and pulled out a man's watch. "Same with this one. It looks like a lot of typical watches are here, along with a few wind-up alarm clocks." He stood. "Whoever packed this box didn't do a very *gut* job of protecting them, though. Just covered them with an old blanket. Which is better than *nix*."

They sorted through the rest of the clocks and watches. Noah set aside two small clocks and three watches he wanted to research, and he put the rest of them back in the box. He pulled a black marker out of his pants pocket and started writing on one of the box's top flaps and its side. "We need to do this from now on so we know the contents of all the boxes we've opened. That will save us time down the line."

Ivy pulled open another box and found it was full of English clothes Glenda—or maybe her younger sister—would have worn more recently. She decided to make more piles of the clothes, organizing them by type. When she was through she had four neat stacks of shirts, slacks, skirts, and jeans.

"Those we can donate to a local thrift store," Noah said. "As long as they're in *gut* shape."

"They are, and there's one in Barton." She stood and arched

her back. Noah had found another box full of souvenirs, which he claimed were, while interesting to look it, basically worthless. He marked the box and set it to the side. Ivy heard his stomach growl.

"Lunchtime already?" she said with a grin.

He looked sheepish. "Can't help it. I've got a big appetite."

She had noticed that yesterday at lunch. "What time is it?" she asked.

"Depends on what clock you're looking at." He went to the bench and pointed at the cuckoo clock. "This one says four. This watch says twelve. This alarm clock says—"

"I get it," she said, chuckling.

"And *mei* stomach says it's time to *geh* get something to eat." He walked past her and headed down the stairs.

Ivy started to leave, but then she spied a box in a dark corner of the attic. She moved closer and peered at it for a moment. It was different from the other boxes—smaller, dented on one side, and had what appeared to be a water stain.

"Are you coming?" Noah asked from the bottom of the attic stairs.

"*Ya.*" She looked at the box again, wondering what was inside. It was so beat-up. She shrugged. She'd find out eventually.

Cevilla directed Noah to pour apple cider into the glasses she'd set out. "I'm glad you picked that up yesterday from the Schrocks'," she said as she set a platter of sandwiches on the table.

Noah was too. He loved apple cider, and when he saw it in the store, he couldn't resist. He also couldn't resist the chocolate cake on a shelving unit near the front of the store marked Amish Baked Goods. Cevilla didn't have much of a sweet tooth, but Noah did, and he didn't hesitate to pick up the cake. He'd cut himself a big piece last night after supper—and right before another painful bout of buzzing in his ears. He was starting to get concerned about that, since he'd had a good night's sleep the night before. After eating the cake he'd gone to bed early enough to surprise Cevilla. Early enough to surprise himself.

Now he felt well rested, and so far, no humming or buzzing or ringing. He hoped that would be the end of it now that he wasn't so tired. Besides, he had other things to focus on, especially now that they had finally uncovered something interesting upstairs. He had started to think the only things Glenda had been interested in were doilies and tablecloths and cheap souvenirs, but some of the clocks and watches got him excited. He agreed with Ivy that the sapphire-and-gold watch was too much—he could tell she thought it was ostentatious by the way she looked at it. And it was, in a ridiculous way. But that had been the style in the nineteenth century, which made him even more eager to find out about it. If it ended up being a valuable piece, he'd ship it to an English friend of his who dealt with estate and antique jewelry.

Ivy appeared, and after they said grace, they started to eat. Cevilla had made, of all things, peanut butter and jelly sandwiches. Last night they had eaten chicken noodle soup, which had been light on both the chicken and the noodles. He needed more sustenance than that. Tonight he was definitely making supper himself.

"Did you find anything interesting this morning?" Cevilla asked as she cut the crusts off her bread.

"Some clocks and watches." Noah stuffed half a sandwich into his mouth. At least the jelly was good, obviously homemade, and it tasted like rhubarb. "I need to look up some of the items so I can find out more about them. Ivy said there's a library in Barton. I thought I'd *geh* tomorrow."

"What's the rush?" Cevilla put down her knife. "Tomorrow's Saturday, and the Yoders are hosting church on Sunday. I'm sure Ivy is busy helping prepare for that."

"I don't need Ivy to *geh* with me," Noah said. He glanced at Ivy from across the table, hoping she didn't misconstrue his meaning. He knew he'd stepped in it yesterday when he talked about his aunt trying to get the two of them together. He hadn't meant to be rude, but he wanted to be forthright. She didn't have to worry about anything romantic happening between them. He had zero intention of letting that occur.

Ivy gave him a small smile, which made her plump cheeks rise and her blue eyes crinkle at the corners. Cute. She was also smart. And nice. But just because Ivy Yoder was cute and smart and nice didn't mean he was interested.

"I do have to help *Mamm*," Ivy said.

"See? End of discussion." Noah reached for his apple cider. "Just give me the directions to Barton and I'll *geh* myself."

"But you can't!"

Both Noah and Ivy stared at Cevilla. The woman rarely lost her composure, but now she looked genuinely upset. "Tomorrow is *mei* visiting day and I have plans with Rhoda Troyer. I'll need the buggy." She straightened in her chair. "You won't be able to *geh* until Monday."

"I could drop you off at Rhoda's and pick you up later," Noah said, hoping she would relent. If not, and if she wouldn't let him unpack more boxes by himself, what was he going to do all day? He'd be bored out of his mind after five minutes without something to work on.

"You'd have to take a taxi to Barton, Noah. It's too far away for a buggy ride," Ivy said quietly. "I thought you knew that, Cevilla."

"I most certainly do," Cevilla said, shooting Ivy a look. She tilted up her chin. "I have a solution to our problem."

Noah frowned. "I don't see a problem here—"

"I haven't been to Barton in ages. There's a great Mexican restaurant I want Noah to try."

"Mexican?" Noah lifted a surprised brow. "I didn't realize you liked tacos."

"I don't. But I do enjoy a burrito occasionally. Now, stop arguing with me and eat *yer* peanut butter and jelly. We'll *geh* to Barton on Monday. You, too, Ivy." She cleared her throat. "There. I'm glad that's settled."

Noah and Ivy looked at each other in confusion. Sometimes his aunt had a way of making him feel like a six-year-old boy who'd been caught with his hand in the cookie jar. Ivy looked perplexed as well. It was one thing to have stipulations about how she wanted the boxes in the attic managed. Noah humored her about that because it was her stuff, and it wasn't that big of a deal to go through it with Ivy. In fact, having another person dive through clothing and doilies made the job easier. But to order his and Ivy's time outside the attic job? That wasn't quite fair.

He opened his mouth to say exactly that, but then he caught Ivy's small shake of her head. Fine. He'd keep his thoughts to himself. But he still didn't appreciate his aunt's bossiness.

Ivy didn't say much while they worked in the attic for the rest of the afternoon, only to comment on some more of the items they'd unboxed—a few pocket mirrors, some broken toys from the 1970s, and, of all things, twenty unopened packages of panty hose. Ivy discreetly added those to the box for the thrift store.

After they were finished for the day and Noah was handing Ivy her coat, he said, "I'll talk to *mei aenti*. You don't have to *geh* to Barton with us on Monday."

"I don't mind going." Ivy slipped her arms into her coat. "I like Mexican food anyway. And I'm interested in finding out more about the clocks and watches."

They still had two stacks of boxes to go through, and they had to get rid of the items they'd unpacked before they had room to open them. "We could take those clothes to that thrift store in Barton," he said.

"*Ya*. We should also take all those empty boxes we broke down to a recycle place. There's one near the library."

"*Gut* idea. That will make more room in the attic so we can *geh* through the last two stacks of boxes without tripping. Or falling." He looked down at her, seeing a light sprinkling of freckles across the bridge of her small nose. Cute, like the rest of her. *Wait*. He frowned. He was noticing her cuteness a little too much lately.

"Is something wrong?" she asked.

He shook his head. "*Nee*. Of course not. Everything's fine." He pushed his thoughts about how adorable she was to the side and said, "*Danki* for understanding."

"Understanding what?"

"*Mei aenti*." Good. Bringing up Cevilla squashed any kind of admiration for Ivy. He was still annoyed with his aunt for manipulating them. "Although some days I don't understand her myself."

Ivy grinned. "That's what makes her so interesting. Monday should be fun."

"It will be something," Noah muttered. Things always were when it came to his aunt Cevilla.

Ivy picked up the cuckoo clock from the mudroom bench and opened the back door to go. The sun had been out today, warming the cold air a bit. Still, Noah said, "I'll drive you home."

"That's okay. I'll walk."

"It's *nee* bother—"

"Noah, really. I'm fine. I like to walk. Like I said before, I don't live that far. And it's not snowing." She tucked her chin into her scarf and hugged the cuckoo clock to her chest. "Will I see you at church on Sunday?"

"I'll be there." He made sure never to miss a service, even when he was out of town, unless there weren't any services on that particular Sunday. When that happened, he read his Bible and spent time in prayer. One thing he did struggle with was letting go of work on Sundays. He was supposed to focus on God and rest, but he found himself thinking about his job even when he wasn't working.

Come to think of it, he hadn't thought about work too much the past couple of days. It had been a relief too.

After Ivy left, he closed the door, stepped into the kitchen, and saw Cevilla sitting at the table with a basket of stationery supplies. She stopped writing and said, "You're not supposed to be here."

"That's news to me."

She frowned. "Don't be a smart aleck. Why aren't you driving Ivy home?"

"I offered, but she wanted to walk."

"Humph. You should have tried harder." She touched the tip of her pencil to her tongue. "Do I have to do everything?" she mumbled.

"Everything what?"

"Never mind." She started writing again.

Noah sat down at the table, his foot tapping against the floor. After a few minutes he said, "Do you mind if I make supper tonight?"

"Not at all."

He watched her again, her head bent as she scribbled her pencil across the paper. Then his thoughts turned to tomorrow. "What am I supposed to do with myself while you're gone all day?"

"Hmm." She turned and looked at him. "Clean the barn?"

"It looks pretty clean to me."

"*Ya*, Freemont and his *buwe* did a *gut* job. They made quick work of it a few days ago."

Noah was glad to hear that. He'd enjoyed getting to know Ivy's parents a little bit the other night when he was waiting for her. It was clear Ivy came from a good family, and Noah was happy to see his aunt was being well taken care of by her community when he wasn't there. Cevilla had always been naturally good at taking care of herself, but it put his mind at ease to know she had support when she needed it.

"What about the gutters?" she said, putting down the pencil. "You could check on those."

"All right, but cleaning those out will take me only half an hour at most. *Yer haus* isn't that big."

She started to fold the letter. "Here's a novel idea. You could just rest."

"There's Sunday for that. Trust me. I get plenty of rest."

"Do you?" Her gaze narrowed as she peered at him over her glasses. "You're able to let *geh* of *yer* work and *yer* troubles?"

That wasn't true, of course, but it didn't keep him from nodding. His foot tapped faster. She was getting close to prying. He gave his aunt a lot of leeway, but if there was one thing he would stand firm on, it was talking about anything too personal. Like how even though he was successful, he often wondered if all the hard work was worth it in the end. Yes, he had a good business, which he'd invested a lot of time, energy, and even money in. But he was also on the road a lot, and it wasn't as satisfying as it used to be.

Then there was the humming and buzzing and ringing in his ears. Right now he could barely hear it, but it was still there, and he was growing more concerned. Sleep didn't seem to be the answer. He'd definitely make a doctor's appointment when he got back to Arbor Grove. And he definitely wasn't about to burden his aunt with his problems. He rarely talked to anyone about anything that bothered him, and he liked to keep it that way.

Cevilla slid the letter into an envelope. "Clamming up, I see." She reached into the basket for a pen and started writing down the address. "I'm sure you'll find something to do tomorrow," she said, almost as if she were talking to herself. "Something . . . or someone."

Wonder who that someone is? Noah grimaced and didn't bother answering her. She was dropping enough hints about him and Ivy. He wanted to tell her not to waste her time, but he doubted she'd listen to him anyway.

He got up from the table, put on his winter wear, and went outside. He always welcomed fresh air. The sun was dipping low in the horizon, and he realized he'd have to start on supper soon. Time seemed to slip by fast while he was working in the attic. *Cooking. Never imagined I'd be thinking about that.* But he had to admit he was looking forward to puttering around in the kitchen. Hopefully Cevilla would like what he cooked. More importantly, he hoped it would be edible.

He took in a deep breath of crisp air and realized the noise in his ears had finally ceased. He relaxed, relief flooding him. "Whatever this is, Lord," he whispered, looking up at the wintry sky, "please make it stop . . . for good."

Chapter 6

Ivy spent most of Saturday helping *Mamm* clean the house, while her father and brothers cleaned out the barn in preparation for tomorrow's church service. It was another sunny day, but chillier than the day before. While Ivy scrubbed the wood floors until they gleamed, her mind was on her conversation with Leanna yesterday. Ivy had dropped off the cuckoo clock at Leanna's workshop on her way home, and her friend had been impressed with it.

"It's really nice," she'd said. She turned it over and twisted the knob a bit. The clock didn't respond.

"Think you can fix it?"

"I'll sure try." She set the clock on the counter. "When do you need it by?"

"*Nee* rush. After Christmas should be fine. Cevilla says she's not in any hurry. She might keep it rather than sell it."

"I'll see if I can get it done before then." She ran her finger across the edge of the counter and grew silent.

Alarms went off in Ivy's head. Leanna was rarely silent. "What's wrong?"

"*Nix.*" Leanna didn't look up. "*Nix* is wrong."

"You're a terrible liar." Ivy walked around to the other side of the counter. Behind them was Leanna's workstation, and the scents of oil and grease and metal hung in the air. She took Leanna's hand, knowing without looking that her friend's fingers were stained with grease. She didn't mind. "Tell me what's going on."

Leanna lifted her gaze and looked down at Ivy. "I'm . . . expecting."

Ivy drew in a sharp breath. That was the last thing she expected to hear. "That's . . . that's wonderful." Why did her voice sound so flat? And why was she feeling the sharp pinch of envy in her heart? She tried to ignore it, but it kept growing as Leanna went on.

"I haven't even told Roman yet." She squeezed Ivy's hand. "You're the only one who knows. Except me, obviously." Her shoulders slumped. "I don't know what to do," she whispered.

Hearing the uncharacteristic fear in Leanna's voice pulled Ivy to her senses. This wasn't about her. This was about her friend. "You should tell Roman, Leanna."

"I know. But I'm so worried. I don't know anything about being a mother. Well, I know some things. Not enough, though."

"Have you and Roman talked about having *kinner*?"

Leanna bit her lip and nodded.

"Did you tell him you were afraid?"

She nodded again.

"What did he say?"

Leanna squeezed her hand again before letting it go, her cheeks taking on a rosy glow. "He said he loved me."

Another stab of envy hit Ivy. Did Leanna have any idea how

wonderful it was to be married to a man who loved her so much? "You'll be a great mother."

"You think so?"

"Aren't you *gut* at everything?" Ivy said, managing a smile.

"I'm not *gut* at housework. Or cooking. Or—"

"Leanna." Ivy put her hand on her friend's arm. "Don't be afraid of this. You've got plenty of people to help and support you . . . especially me."

Leanna burst into tears, and then she leaned over and hugged Ivy. "I don't even know why I'm crying," she said as she pulled away.

"Happy tears, I hope." Ivy's smile widened, and despite her negative feelings, she experienced some genuine joy for her friend.

"Definitely."

Ivy tossed the sponge into the bucket and sat back on her heels. She'd meant what she told Leanna. She wanted to be there for her friend. But thinking about it even now, she could feel another twist of envy coming on. *Lord, shouldn't I be over this by now?*

Mamm walked into the room carrying a basket full of fresh, stiff-from-the-line laundry. "Karen's bringing one of her orange bliss cakes over in a little while. She also asked if we could help her put some ribbon around the jars of jelly she made to sell at Schrocks' for Christmas."

Ivy stood. The area by the front door had needed particular attention, but she would use a mop for the rest of the wood floors in the house. "When did you talk to her?"

"Yesterday, while you were at Cevilla's." *Mamm* paused at the base of the stairs. "How are things going with cleaning out the attic?"

"*Gut*. Glenda collected a lot of things, so there's plenty to *geh* through."

"And . . ." *Mamm* paused. "How do you like working with Noah?"

Ivy also paused. She enjoyed working with him. Other than the personal space issues, which she now found more quirky than annoying, he was the perfect gentleman. She admired his knowledge and enthusiasm for antiques, and of course there was his devotion to his aunt.

Not to mention he was handsome. And a bit charming.

Great. She was back to that again—and reminding herself that thinking Noah was handsome and charming didn't mean anything. "I like it . . . well enough."

"Just well enough?" *Mamm* leaned forward, her expression expectant.

"*Ya*." Ivy picked up the bucket. "We should have the attic cleaned out within the week."

"What does he plan to do after that?"

She shrugged and turned toward the kitchen to empty the bucket and fill it with fresh water. "Go back to Iowa, I guess. We haven't talked about it."

"What do you talk about, then?"

Ivy glanced over her shoulder, now realizing what her mother was getting at. "We talk about Glenda's stuff," she said, telling the truth. "That's all."

"Oh." Her mother looked a little deflated. "Well, at least you have another week together. Working together, I mean."

Before Ivy could respond *Mamm* hurried up the stairs. Honestly, how could her mother think there was anything between her and Noah? How could anyone think that? Her mind went back to when he told her he didn't find her interesting. She'd thought he'd been a little rude, but when he explained, she understood. She didn't find him interesting either. Not romantically. Regarding him as handsome and charming didn't count. But leave it to her mother—and Cevilla—to think otherwise.

Frustrated, Ivy turned her focus back on finishing the floors.

By the time Karen arrived with her cake and boxes of jelly jars in tow, it was late afternoon, and Ivy's emotions had simmered down. "I'll start supper while you two work on the jars," *Mamm* said, taking a large stockpot from one of the lower kitchen cabinets.

Karen sat down and started pulling jars out of one of the boxes while Ivy made her a cup of hot tea. Karen took out a roll of festive red ribbon and a pair of scissors. "I thought this would help entice the English customers to purchase my jelly."

"I'm surprised you made it this year." Ivy pulled out a chair to sit down, and then she took some of the ribbon and circled a jar lid with it.

"Adam insisted I didn't have to, but I enjoy doing it." She lined up the jars on the table.

"When are you planning to *geh* to Florida?" *Mamm* asked as she carried carrots to the counter.

"Florida?" Ivy was holding the scissors, having stopped mid snip. "You're going to Florida?"

"*Ya.*" Karen looked a little sheepish as she glanced at their mother over her shoulder. "I hadn't told anyone about it yet."

"Sorry." Now it was *Mamm*'s turn to look uncomfortable. "I'll just be over here chopping carrots and keeping *mei* mouth shut."

"She can't keep a secret at all," Karen whispered.

Ivy leaned forward. "Was Florida a secret?"

"Adam and I have decided to visit Sarasota in March. He hasn't been there in several years, and I haven't been at all. But he still has to tell Jalon he's leaving for a week." She glanced at the forest green ribbon in her hand. "We thought we better *geh* now, before . . ."

"Before what?"

Karen glanced at *Mamm*, and then averted her gaze from Ivy.

A knot formed in Ivy's stomach. In an even lower whisper she said, "Are you expecting?"

Karen shook her head. "*Nee*, not yet." She mouthed her next words. "We're trying."

This time it wasn't a twist or pinch of envy. It was a full-on wave. Sisters no longer sharing everything about their lives when one of them married was one thing. But now Karen had more in common with their mother than she did with her. Karen and her husband were trying for a baby. Leanna was pregnant, and Ivy was sure that after their talk yesterday, she had told Roman. Her best friend and her sister were moving on with their lives, doing things Ivy wanted to do. Having things Ivy wanted to have, even though she had spent years denying she wanted them.

The wave turned sour. She wanted to jump up from the chair, run to her room, and have a good cry. Alone. Like she'd be for the rest of her life.

"Ivy?" Karen asked.

"What?" Ivy spat out the word.

Karen frowned slightly. "Can I have the scissors, please?"

Ivy swallowed the bitter lump in her throat and handed Karen the scissors. She couldn't run upstairs and cry. She had to sit there and smile, hide her envy and resentment and pretend to be happy for Karen. At least she didn't even have to pretend very hard. Underneath the layers of pain, she knew she was happy. She just couldn't feel it right now.

For the next few minutes they worked on the jars without saying anything. The only sound in the kitchen was her mother's knife against the cutting board.

"I'm sorry I didn't tell you about our trip," Karen finally said, sounding apologetic. "We've been so busy these past few months with the harvest and the farm. I know we haven't spent much time together."

"It's okay." Ivy tied a neat bow around another jelly jar. But inside she was in turmoil.

"Are you angry with me for not telling you?"

Ivy glanced at Karen's worried expression and chastised herself. This was ridiculous. She couldn't spend the rest of her life upset every time someone got married or had a baby. She had to come to terms with being single. Pressing her emotions down, she took her sister's hand. "*Nee.* I'm not angry. I hope you two have a wonderful time on *yer* trip."

Karen smiled, a relieved look on her face. "We will. I've never been to the ocean before. Adam's been telling me about it, and it sounds wonderful. I'm excited to see it."

"I would be too," Ivy said.

Karen's eyes lit up. "Why don't you *geh* with us?"

Ivy stilled. The last thing she wanted was to be a third wheel around Karen and Adam. But she had another reason not to go. The idea of traveling was more appealing than doing it. She wasn't as adventurous as Karen, and she definitely wasn't a free spirit like her traveled friend Leanna. It had been hard enough to leave Birch Creek and spend those weeks in Michigan helping her cousin. And if she hadn't gone to Michigan, she wouldn't have met John. And if she hadn't met John, she wouldn't have had her heart broken.

She shook her head. "I can't. I'm starting a new job at Schrocks' after Christmas. It wouldn't be right to ask for vacation time right away."

"You're going to work for the Schrocks?" *Mamm* asked. "When did that happen?"

Ivy couldn't believe she'd been so distracted that she'd forgotten to tell her family she'd found a job.

She explained how she applied with Aden the day before, leaving out the part about Noah taking her there. If *Mamm* knew Noah had driven her somewhere—at least other than home—Ivy would never hear the end of it. Not even someplace as simple as the grocery store.

"Congratulations," Karen said. "Maybe next time we'll have a chance to *geh* on a trup together."

"Maybe next time," Ivy said. She looked at Karen and smiled. "You can always send me a postcard."

Karen smiled back. "I'll do that."

Once they finished decorating the jelly jars, Ivy helped Karen pack them carefully in the boxes. She hugged Ivy goodbye. "Don't tell *Mamm* what we talked about," she said in her ear. "She won't leave me alone about wanting *grosskinner*."

Ivy couldn't help but laugh as she handed one of the boxes to her sister. Karen's comment made her feel better. At least she wasn't the only one *Mamm* was pestering. She picked up the other box of jars and followed her into the living room. Karen balanced her box in one hand and opened the front door. To Ivy's surprise, Noah was standing on the porch. He shuffled his feet.

She peeked around him. The sky was a dusky gray, the setting sun hiding behind a swath of winter clouds. But she didn't see Cevilla's buggy in the driveway. Had he walked?

"Hi," Karen said. She gave Ivy a questioning glance.

Ivy almost sighed out loud. Was everyone going to give her weird looks every time Noah came over? "Karen, this is Noah Schlabach. Cevilla's great-nephew."

"Oh, right. I thought I'd seen you before." She gave Ivy another look, which now mirrored the nosy one *Mamm* had given her earlier. Oh great, now her sister was wondering what was going on between her and Noah. "I didn't realize you were coming over," Karen said.

Ivy lifted her gaze to Noah's face. "Neither did I," she said. He pressed his lips together and gave a little shrug.

"I better get back home and start on supper." Karen passed another look between Ivy and Noah. "I'll see you in the morning, Ivy."

"Tell Adam I said hi," she replied.

Karen nodded.

"Can I help you with that box? It looks heavy," Noah said.

"No. I'm fine. I just have to carry it to *mei* buggy. But *danki*." Karen slid past Noah to make her way home.

He looked down at Ivy. "I don't suppose you'll let me carry that for you, either."

"Nope—"

But before she could slide by him, he artfully took the box out of her hands. With a satisfied smirk, he took it to Karen's buggy.

Ivy crossed her arms over her chest as he walked back up the porch steps. He stopped at the middle one and mocked her stance, including tilting his head to the side the same way she was.

She dropped her arms and laughed. She couldn't even pretend to be annoyed with him.

He walked up the rest of the steps and paused in front of her, slipping his hands into his coat pockets. "I hope you don't mind a surprise visit."

"Not at all." Ivy opened the door wider. After he was inside she added, "What brings you by?"

"Well, I cleaned the gutters, I cleaned out the barn even though I didn't need to, I shoveled the snow, and I fixed a broken board on *Aenti* Cevilla's porch—and I had all that completed by ten this morning." He shrugged again. "I didn't realize how quiet it is around *mei aenti*'s *haus* when she's not home. I finally went for a walk, and when I ended up here, I thought I would stop by and say hi."

"So you're here because you were bored?"

"Exactly." He grinned.

She laughed again. "That makes sense. Why don't you stay for supper? *Mamm* always makes plenty."

He turned serious. "I don't want to impose. I'm sure Cevilla will be expecting me home. She should be getting back from Rhoda's anytime now."

"And I'm sure Cevilla will be fine making dinner for herself."

"I did leave her a note to let her know I was going for a walk." He looked at the fireplace in the corner of the living room. "That fire looks like it's getting low. Want me to get more wood for you?"

She was about to tell him no, since it was Judah's job to keep enough firewood in the house. But Noah seemed antsy, so she said, "*Daed* would appreciate it." Not to mention Judah. "Let me get *mei* coat and boots. I'll come out and help you."

A few minutes later they were outside near the firewood

pile. It was covered with a tarp to protect the wood from rain and snow. As she pulled on her gloves, Noah reached up over her head and removed it. He was standing very close behind her, but instead of being concerned, she was relaxed. Proximity didn't mean anything to him, and she found herself not minding that he was so close to her.

She grabbed a couple of pieces of wood and turned to take them into the house. As she walked away she felt something hit her shoulder. She craned her neck and saw streaks of snow on her dark-blue coat. Ivy turned to see Noah standing there, looking up at the sky and whistling.

"Did you just throw a snowball at me?"

"Who, me? I'm Mr. Innocent." He turned around and faced the woodpile. "I'm just over here getting firewood like a *gut bu*."

Ivy set down her logs. She grabbed a handful of snow and started packing it between her hands. "You do realize turnabout is fair play, right?"

Noah kept his back to her and didn't say anything.

As soon as she had the snowball ready, she whizzed it at him, hitting him dead center in the back.

He turned around and looked down at her. "You do know this means I must return the favor." He knelt and gathered more snow. Ivy did the same.

"You also realize," he said as he walked toward her, "that when I was a kid I was the best baseball pitcher in *mei* district."

That took a bit of the fun out of the game. She took a step back. Surely he wouldn't throw a snowball at her as hard as he would if he were pitching a baseball?

He paused and looked at her for a moment. Then he tilted his head. "You seem worried." His expression had turned serious.

"You just told me you were an ace pitcher. Of course I'm worried."

His hands dropped to his sides. "Do you really think I would hit you hard with a snowball?"

Now that he said it out loud, she realized her concern was ridiculous.

"I would never do that to you, Ivy." He started toward her again, his long legs closing the gap quickly. "I would never hurt you." He dropped the snowball, his expression even more serious.

"I know that." And for some reason, she did. She felt safe with Noah. It was odd, considering they didn't know each other very well. But deep in her heart she knew he wouldn't cause her harm. In fact, she was sure he didn't have a mean bone in his body.

"We should get inside," he said. "I'll *geh* get another load of wood."

Ivy nodded, and then she bent over to pick up the wood she'd put down. She lifted it up, turned, and tripped over her own two feet. The wood went flying out of her arms, and she fell facedown in the snow. Before she could stand up, she felt herself being lifted gently to her feet.

"Are you okay?" Noah turned her around in his arms. He kept one hand at her waist while he brushed snow off her face with the other. They were so close she could see how long his eyelashes were, smell the scent of lemon drops on his breath, notice how soft his lips looked. The word *handsome* entered her mind again, and this time she didn't push it away. She barely noticed the cold on her face as he wiped the top of her cheek with his thumb. Butterflies started to swarm in her stomach.

Then she came to her senses. This was Noah, and handsome

or not, he didn't understand personal space. "I'm fine," she said, moving out of his grip.

He easily let her go. "Are you sure?"

"Positive." She was fine. A little embarrassed by her clumsiness and still a little breathless from being so close to him, but her mind had been filled with marriage and babies and . . . other things, which explained why right now she felt a sudden jolt of . . . something.

"Hold still." He brushed his fingers across her chin. "You had a little more snow there. I think I got it all."

Her skin tingled from his touch. "*Danki*," she said, surprised at the softness of her voice.

She thought she saw his eyes change color, but as soon as they did he bent down and picked up the two logs she'd dropped.

"You get inside and get warm," he said. "I'll bring the rest of the wood."

She was about to protest, but he was already heading to the woodpile.

Once inside, she slipped off her coat and gloves and hung them on the peg rack near the front door. She removed her boots and then walked to the fireplace, took the poker, and started shifting the almost-spent logs to make room for the new ones. Curls of smoke rose while sparks popped in the fireplace.

The front door opened and closed behind her, and she turned. Noah was carrying a large pile of wood—bigger than her father or brothers could have carried. He slipped off his boots with ease and went to the fireplace, kneeling with the wood still in his arms. He stacked the logs in the curved iron firewood rack, and then started placing fresh ones in the fire.

Ivy couldn't help but watch. She had assumed that because

he was so thin and lanky, he wasn't as strong as her father and brothers. Even her youngest brother, Judah, was sturdy because of all the farm work he did. But Noah was handling the heavy wood as though it weighed next to nothing.

Moments later the living room was flooded with warmth. *Mamm* entered and said, "Oh. Goodness. I didn't realize we had company."

"Noah stopped by," Ivy said, not sure how to explain why he was here.

"I can see that." *Mamm*'s brow lifted.

"He, uh, got more wood for the fireplace." Not much of an explanation, but it was all she could think of at the moment.

"Oh, that's wonderful." *Mamm* looked up at Noah. "I hope you can stay for supper."

"I already invited him," Ivy blurted. Why she said that, she had no idea.

"Oh, really." *Mamm* looked at Ivy with that same knowing, annoying expression, and Ivy suddenly wished she hadn't invited Noah to stay, much less told her mother she had. Now *Mamm* probably thought there was something between her and Noah for sure. From the way she was looking at Noah, then back at Ivy, then back at him again, Ivy was certain her mother was reading more into their acquaintance than there was. Ivy would make sure to set her straight later.

"We're having beef stew, homemade biscuits, and apple pie for dessert." *Mamm* smiled. "I hope you brought a big appetite."

"I always have a big appetite." Noah winked at Ivy. "Just ask her. She's seen it firsthand."

"Oh, really," *Mamm* said again.

"I think we should wash up after getting the firewood," Ivy

said, desperate to get away from this situation. "I'll show you where the washroom is."

After they'd both washed their hands, they went into the kitchen. Her father and brothers were already seated at the table, and *Mamm* was setting an extra plate where Noah would sit. Judah and Ira already had their heads bowed in anticipation of prayer—not because they were eager to give thanks, but because they were hungry. They always were. But Seth kept his eyes on Noah. Which Ivy thought was odd, because normally he was just as eager to start eating as their brothers were.

They all bowed their heads in silent prayer, and after they gave thanks, *Mamm* passed out bowls of stew. As they ate, the conversation flowed smoothly, with mostly Noah answering questions about his auction business. Ira seemed particularly interested, especially in the traveling aspect of it. "Don't you get tired of moving around?"

"Sometimes. I'll admit it gets to me, especially if I've been gone a while. It's *gut* to be home after a long trip. But I don't like to keep still for too long, so soon I'm on the road again. I meet new people and see new places. Can't ask for a better job."

Ivy thought about Karen and Adam going to Florida, and again about Leanna's travel. She didn't have their adventurous spirits, and she definitely wasn't as adventurous as Noah. This was where they were very different.

"All this sounds so fascinating," *Mamm* said. "Doesn't it, Ivy?"

Ivy fought not to roll her eyes. Her mother wasn't being subtle. In fact, she was rivaling Cevilla for being obvious. She glanced at Noah, hoping he didn't notice. But he was on his second bowl of stew, which *Mamm* had enthusiastically provided. She'd even buttered a biscuit and handed it to him as their discussion turned to the church service the next day and their preparations.

When they'd finished eating, two of the boys left the room to care for more outside chores. "You can have your dessert once you're finished," *Daed* said.

Seth lingered for a moment, giving Noah another narrowed look.

Ivy frowned. Surely he wasn't being the overprotective younger brother with Noah. Noah was the most nonthreatening person she'd ever met. She thought about how gently he'd removed snow from her face. Her cheeks tingled.

"I can help clear the table," Noah said.

"You'll do *nee* such thing." *Mamm* shooed him out of the kitchen. "*Geh* with Freemont to the living room and finish *yer* conversation. We'll bring dessert and *kaffee* to you in a minute."

When the men left, *Mamm* came up alongside Ivy. "He's very *schee*, isn't he?"

Ivy wasn't about to admit she'd been thinking the same thing lately. "He's tall," was all she would say.

"*Ya*, but I don't think that's a problem. Do you?"

"Why would it matter to me if he's tall?"

Mamm let out an exasperated sigh. "I give up, Ivy. *Geh* put the *kaffee* on."

Noah and her father were deep in conversation when Ivy brought the pie and coffee. She set the tray on the coffee table, and then went back to finish cleaning the kitchen while her mother joined the men. By the time she was almost done, Noah had walked in.

"Delicious pie," he said, carrying the tray with all the soiled dishes to the sink. "*Danki* for inviting me for supper. Everything was *gut*, and this was much better than sitting at home by myself waiting for Cevilla to come home. But I better get back soon or she'll think I walked myself right out of Birch Creek."

Guessing that her parents had excused themselves for the evening, and that *Mamm* had gladly agreed when Noah offered to take the tray to the kitchen, Ivy said, "I'll walk you out." She folded the kitchen towel she was holding and put it on the counter. After all, seeing him to the door was the polite thing to do.

When Noah was about to walk down the front porch steps, he turned. "See you tomorrow, Ivy."

"See you tomorrow."

He skipped down the porch steps, his hands stuffed into his coat pockets again. She watched him leave, glad he'd stopped by. She'd enjoyed spending time with him tonight. Noah had been a good distraction, keeping her mind off what she finally realized was really bothering her about Leanna and Karen.

She shivered and pulled her sweater closer around her body. Once her sister and best friend had children, they would have even less time for her. That was the bitter truth. And she couldn't admit that to anyone, especially them. It wasn't their fault that she felt alone. It was something she'd have to deal with. Something she'd have to pray about.

But tonight she'd had Noah, and he would be around for a little while at least. Knowing that cheered her spirits. She was glad they were becoming friends. Because right now, she could use one.

When Noah arrived home from Ivy's, Cevilla was in the living room. She had a cup of tea and a piece of toast on a small plate on the end table. When Noah walked in she gave him a stern look. "Where have you been?"

He hesitated. He hadn't planned on ending up at Ivy's, but being bored out of his mind after doing the few chores Cevilla had around the house, and knowing he would have to deal with his aunt's wrath if he dared go upstairs and even look at the attic, he'd decided to take that walk. He'd wandered for at least an hour and found himself in front of Ivy's house. It dawned on him that he could just walk past it, but for some reason he felt compelled to at least stop by and say hello. He hadn't expected to be invited to stay for supper.

He also hadn't expected to be so close to her. When he saw her fall, he instinctively picked her up. She was light, and he knew when he set her on her feet he should have taken a step back. When he was younger his mother had tried to teach him not to stand too close to people. "It makes them uncomfortable," she said. He tried to be mindful of that, and most of the time he was. But sometimes he forgot. With Ivy, he hadn't forgotten, but for some reason he hadn't wanted to let her go. At least not right away.

"Noah?"

He looked at Cevilla. *"Ya?"*

"It's a simple question. Where have you been?"

"Ivy's," he said, folding himself onto the couch across from his aunt. "I've been at Ivy's."

Cevilla's face lit up like a Roman candle. "Oh my goodness. I can't think of a better way for you to spend a Saturday afternoon than with Ivy Yoder," she said, her voice coming out in a sweet-sounding gush.

Noah leaned back against the couch. Normally he could think of a dozen better ways to spend his Saturday, but none of them came to mind. "I wasn't there the whole afternoon, and actually I spent the time I was there with her *familye*," he said, hoping to set her straight. He didn't bother to tell her about how soft Ivy's cheeks felt as he brushed the snow from them, or that she had a nicely shaped mouth. Hold on. Why was he noticing her mouth? He shouldn't be noticing anything about her.

But something about Ivy Yoder was begging to be noticed.

"And what did you do over at Ivy's *haus*?"

"I had supper, talked to Freemont and Mary." And got the oddest look from Ivy's brother, Seth. Noah had no idea what that was about. The kid looked like he wanted to smash a snowball in Noah's face. Or smash something else. "Then I came home," he continued. "Simple as that."

"Then I don't have to offer you anything to eat." She peered at him. "How are you feeling?"

"Feeling? Why would you ask me that? I feel fine."

"Always *gut* to check how someone feels." She picked up her tea and took a sip. "Tomorrow we'll be leaving bright and early to *geh* to the Yoders' for service."

"Understood." Even though he had just eaten a little over an hour ago, the walk home had made him hungry again. He thought about the ham, cheese, and fresh bread he'd bought from Schrock Grocery and decided to make himself a sandwich before he hit the hay. He stood up from the couch . . . and the room began to spin.

"Noah?"

He could hear Cevilla's voice, but she sounded far away, as though she were calling to him from a tunnel. He closed his eyes and felt like he was riding an out of control merry-go-round. *Oh God, what is happening?* He fell back on the couch.

"Noah," Cevilla said, sounding more urgent. "Talk to me."

Then, just as quickly as the dizziness came on, it disappeared. He opened his eyes. The room was still. He looked at Cevilla and saw the worry there. "I'm fine," he said, his voice shaky.

"You are not fine." Cevilla started to get up. "There's something wrong. Something has been wrong. I've had a suspicion—"

"I'm tired," he said, gathering his composure. "That's all."

Cevilla stayed in her chair. "Maybe you should see a doctor."

"*Aenti*, I appreciate *yer* concern, but I'm fine." He wasn't about to tell her he'd been thinking the same thing. He didn't want to worry her. He stood up from the couch, waiting for the room to spin again. When it didn't, he turned to Cevilla. "See? I'm perfectly fine. I'm going to eat a sandwich before going to bed. I'll see you in the morning."

"Noah—"

"*Gute nacht, Aenti.*" He hurried to the kitchen before she could ask him any more questions. But instead of making a sandwich, he leaned against the counter. Okay, that was new. He'd never had that kind of dizziness before. He stilled again, waiting to hear buzzing or humming or the piercing sounds. He only heard the tick of Cevilla's clock above the sink. He also didn't feel dizzy or even light-headed. Yet he was unnerved.

"Tired," he whispered. "I'm just tired." He skipped the sandwich and quietly went straight upstairs, stepping softly so his aunt wouldn't turn and see him. He needed another good night's sleep. That was all.

But once he was in bed, he remained wide awake. His fists clenched as he waited for the dizziness to return. He wasn't sure how long he laid there, tense under one of Cevilla's decades-old quilts, preparing for his world to literally turn upside down.

Without intending to, his mind wandered to Ivy. He closed his eyes. Remembered how she looked and felt when he'd brushed the snow off her. His fists relaxed. He thought of how she was standing on tiptoe as he walked into the kitchen after he talked to Freemont and Mary, and how he had to resist the urge to reach over her and help her out. Or just pick her up and . . .

He felt himself drifting off to sleep, only slightly aware that the humming in his ears had returned.

Chapter 7

Church service went off without a hitch on Sunday. Ivy had noticed her father was always more comfortable holding church service at their place than any other home in the district. Ivy also noticed he was settling in with his preaching. She was learning a lot from her father, even though he initially hadn't wanted to be the bishop. He spent a lot of time reading the Bible and preparing his sermons, taking the job seriously. It was all paying off for him and the community.

Fortunately, her mother had been too busy with church preparations to quiz Ivy about why Noah had come over the day before.

Once the service was over, community members staying for lunch moved from the barn to the Yoder house. Ivy buzzed around the kitchen with other female members of the community—*Mamm*, Karen, Phoebe, and Phoebe's mother, Rose, along with a few other older women. They set out the potluck meal on the Yoders' large, rectangular kitchen table. The fare was abundant—thick slices of home-baked bread; Swiss, cheddar, and muenster cheese slices; and trail bologna and ham along with lettuce, sliced tomatoes, and mustard and mayonnaise. One large bowl held pretzels and another pickled eggs and pickled beets. They also had peanut butter spread and loaves of banana bread for a sweet treat. Ivy and Karen put on two pots of coffee and placed several large pitchers of water on the table.

As everyone filled their plates and dispersed throughout the house to eat, Ivy poured herself a mug of coffee and slipped out the back door, leaving her coat behind. She breathed in the cold air and took a sip. The sky was overcast today, and she suspected it would start to snow any minute. But she needed a bit of a break from all the activity in the house. Apparently so did some of the younger members of the community. Several *kinner* were chasing one another around the backyard, most of them Phoebe's younger brothers. Their father, Thomas, was standing watch nearby and talking to Adam. Three of the boys were playing catch with a baseball on the other side of the yard.

"Busy morning, I'd say."

Ivy turned around at Noah's voice. "*Ya.* I just needed some fresh air."

"Me too."

They stood in silence for a moment, watching the children. "Have you ever wanted *kinner*?" she asked, genuinely curious.

He glanced down at her, a surprised expression on his face. "I thought about it once or twice. When I was younger and still working for *mei vatter*." He took off his black jacket and put it around her shoulders. It swallowed her, but its heavy warmth was welcome. She hadn't planned to stay outside long, but she wasn't in any hurry to go back inside.

She curved her hands around the warm mug. "What does *yer daed* do?"

"He runs a harness shop. The only one in Arbor Grove, so he does *gut* business."

"And you used to work for him?"

Noah nodded, crossing his arms over his chest. She tried not to notice the way his white long-sleeved shirt tightened over his biceps, but it was hard to avoid. He looked exceptionally nice in his church clothes. "Until I was twenty. I was expected to take over the business. But it was just *Daed* and me in the shop, except for the customers who came in to give and pick up their orders. I thought it was pretty boring, to be honest."

"Is that why you became an auctioneer?" She turned and leaned against one of the chairs on the back patio.

"Kind of. I've loved going to them ever since I was a little *kinn*. The crowds, the sound of the auctioneers' voices, the excitement of bidding and selling. I did a little auctioneering when I was a teenager, but *nix* serious. I thought I'd end up making harnesses for a living." His arm shot up as a baseball came sailing toward them. He caught it without hesitation, and then he threw it back to one of the boys.

Ivy looked at the back window. If Noah hadn't caught the ball, it likely would have crashed through the glass. "*Danki*," she said, looking back up at him.

"*Nee* problem. Anyway, when I was twenty I decided I needed a change. I'd been thinking about auctioneering for a while, but I was a little scared to take the plunge. Finally, I realized it was now or never. If I didn't at least try, I'd regret it." He turned and looked down at her. "The rest, if you'll pardon the pun, is history."

She grinned. "*Gut* history, I'd say. You seem very successful."

The light in his hazel-green eyes dimmed a bit. "Sometimes

success comes at a price." He shrugged. "It's pretty cold out here. I'm going inside. You should come with me."

She took off his jacket and handed it to him. The last thing she wanted was her mother—or Cevilla, God forbid—to see her wearing Noah's jacket. He took it without a word and then opened the back door for her. Once they were in the kitchen, she set her coffee mug on the counter and asked, "Have you eaten?"

"Of course." He grinned. "I was the first one at the table. I better *geh* check on *Aenti*, though, and make sure she did more than just sniff the food. I've never seen anyone eat as light as her."

"She is getting older," Ivy said, her tone gentle.

"I'm pretty sure she's going to outlive us all." Noah smiled and then went into the living room.

Ivy nibbled on a piece of cheese while she helped her mother and the other ladies clean the kitchen. She'd eat some more later, but right now she wasn't that hungry. An hour later everyone had gone home, including Noah and Cevilla, but not without Cevilla reminding Ivy in no uncertain terms that they were all three going to Barton tomorrow morning. Ivy chuckled as she hung a dish towel on the hook near the sink.

Her father came into the kitchen, took a glass from the cabinet, and poured some of the water left in one of the pitchers. "*Yer mamm*'s got a bit of a headache," he said. "I'm going to need *yer* help Tuesday night."

"Sure. What do you need me to do?"

"We decided this afternoon to hold a school board meeting here, but I didn't realize *yer mamm* had already made plans to *geh* to Naomi Beiler's. Seems some of the women are getting together to make Christmas cookies. They're going to pass them out in the two nursing homes in Barton. Since she won't be here, I'll need you to whip up a little snack and make some *kaffee*."

"I'll be glad to."

"*Danki*. I better get this to *yer mamm*."

Ivy made herself a sandwich, decided what she would serve the school board on Tuesday night, and spent the rest of the day relaxing with a book, an activity she enjoyed on Sunday afternoons. She ended up falling asleep while she was reading, but she still went to bed early. There was no way she would be late for tomorrow's trip. She'd never hear the end of it from Cevilla if she were.

The next morning after breakfast, a dark-green four-door car pulled into Ivy's driveway. She quickly put on her boots, coat, and black bonnet, and then slipped on some gloves. "I'll be gone to Barton most of the day," she told her mother.

"Be careful." *Mamm* paused and then smiled. "Enjoy lunch with Noah."

Ivy regretted telling her about this outing over sausage sandwiches a few minutes ago. She needed to learn how to keep her mouth shut. Then again, her mother would have noticed the taxi when it came.

"It's not just lunch, *Mamm*. And it's not just Noah. I told you, we're all three going to the library to do some research on some items we found in Cevilla's attic." Well, Noah would be doing the research. She would probably be perusing the fiction section. Maybe she'd find the sequel to the book she'd almost finished reading yesterday.

"If you say so." *Mamm* smiled again and went back to kneading her bread dough.

Ivy started to say something else, but then she shook her head. What was the point? Her mother was as stubborn as Cevilla.

When Ivy got to the car, she saw that Cevilla was in the front seat, which gave her no choice but to sit with Noah in the back. What a surprise. She opened the door and slid in next to him.

"*Gute morgen*," he said with his usual bright and friendly expression.

"*Gute morgen.*"

She'd been intrigued by what he'd said about his auctioneering business yesterday, and more than a little impressed. Here she was not wanting to venture beyond Birch Creek, and she still didn't. But he had left a steady family business to strike out on his own, which she thought was admirable.

She was about to ask him a little bit more about how he started his auctioneering business, but before she could, Noah leaned back against the seat and closed his eyes. Actually, he squeezed them shut, which made her wonder if he was okay. Then he relaxed, and it wasn't long before she heard him softly snoring. She was amazed at how fast he'd fallen asleep.

Ivy didn't have to worry about silence in the car. Cevilla kept up a steady chatter with the taxi driver, who seemed to know Cevilla well. Then again, everyone in Birch Creek knew Cevilla Schlabach.

A short while later they arrived in Barton. Noah's eyes opened as Cevilla directed the driver to stop at the recycling place. Noah dropped off the flattened boxes he'd put in the trunk of the car at Cevilla's. After that, they stopped at the thrift store to drop off several bags of both vintage and more recent clothing, and then headed for the library.

When the driver pulled in front of the library's entrance, Noah scrambled out and opened the door for Cevilla, and then he held out his hand and helped her out of the car. Ivy joined her while Noah paid the driver, and they walked into the library. It wasn't too crowded, and Noah signed up to use the computer while Cevilla and Ivy went to look for novels. After Ivy found two, she sat down at a table and started to read. She'd been tempted to go sit next to Noah since she was curious about how he did his research, but she didn't want to bother him—or give Cevilla false hope.

Cevilla soon sat down across from her with a magazine in her hand, but Ivy noticed she'd also picked out several Christian romances.

Before long Noah sat down in one of the chairs next to her.

"I found what I was looking for." He was grinning.

Ivy glanced up at the clock on the wall. They'd been there only half an hour. "That was quick."

"It actually took longer than I expected to get to the information I needed, especially about that watch with the sapphires. And then I got a little sidetracked. Did you know Rolex was the first company with movements that allowed the rotor to move three hundred and sixty degrees?"

She shook her head. "I had *nee* idea. Who's Rolex?"

He chuckled. "A watchmaker."

"So that watch was made by Rolex?"

"*Nee*, that was just a bit of trivia I came across while I was researching. Anyway, that watch is definitely from the nineteenth century. It's also worth a lot of money."

"That old thing?"

Both Ivy and Noah turned and looked at Cevilla. She licked her thumb and turned the page of the magazine in her lap, not looking up from her reading. "If you're talking about that gaudy blue crystal watch, it's not worth anything."

Noah's forehead furrowed. "*Aenti*, it's a rare, valuable watch."

"It's a fake trinket." Cevilla finally looked at him. "Glenda liked sparkly things. But *mei vatter* didn't have the money to buy her expensive jewelry, so everything she wore was costume."

"Maybe the watch is a *familye* heirloom?" Ivy said.

Cevilla laughed. "If it was, her *familye* wouldn't have packed it in those boxes. They definitely would have kept it." She looked down at the magazine.

Noah looked at Ivy and shrugged. "I'm going to give it to *mei* friend for an appraisal anyway."

"Suit *yerself*," Cevilla commented, again without looking up. "Waste of time and money if you ask me, though."

"Did you want to look for any books?" Ivy asked Noah, trying to defuse the situation a bit.

He glanced at his aunt again, a touch of annoyance in his eyes. Then he turned back to Ivy. "Nah. I'd like to get back to the *haus* and work on the boxes in the attic some more. We might find more interesting items there."

Cevilla tossed her magazine on the table. "We can't *geh* back now. It's not lunchtime yet. I promised to take you two to The Dancing Taco."

"The Dancing Taco?" Noah and Ivy said at the same time. Ivy didn't know such a place existed in Barton.

"Okay, maybe that's not the name—although it would be a rather nice one, don't you think? In any case, I can't remember what it's called right now. I just know where it is."

"Why don't we have lunch at home?" Noah suggested.

Cevilla shook her head. "Because I want tacos."

"I thought you liked burritos," Ivy said.

"Same thing, right?"

It was Noah's turn to shake his head. "Actually, they're not—"

"Let's check out." Cevilla pushed herself up out of the chair and snatched her cane. "We can take a walk around town until the restaurant opens."

"Are you sure?" Ivy said. Although it was a nice day—warm enough that the small amount of snow that fell overnight had already melted. December was turning into a bit of a topsy-turvy month weather-wise. But it was still cold, and they had at least ninety minutes to kill before eleven o'clock.

"I'm sure," Cevilla insisted. "I might walk a little slower than you two, but I won't slow you down. Now, let's *geh*."

Ivy and Noah looked at each other and both shrugged. He leaned close and whispered, "You know it's pointless to argue with her."

"I know." She grinned at Noah and he smiled back.

After they checked out, Noah offered to carry their books in the bag Ivy had brought while they meandered toward the town square. Cevilla pointed out the Mexican restaurant, which was on the other side of a crosswalk—and definitely not named The Dancing Taco. "Pancho's Cantina," she said. "I was close."

"Not close at all." Noah rolled his eyes.

"Let's walk down the opposite side of the street," Cevilla said, barging forward. But she slowed her steps soon after. "You two *geh* on ahead," she said, motioning with her cane.

"We don't mind walking with you," Noah said.

"I told you I wouldn't slow you down, and I meant it. Now *geh*."

"Is it *mei* imagination or is she bossier than usual today?" Noah asked Ivy.

"I heard that, nephew."

Noah chuckled and quickened his steps. Because of his long legs, it didn't take him any time to pass Cevilla. Ivy had to rush to keep up, and after a few minutes she said, "I think I'll stick with Cevilla."

"Sorry." He shortened his stride and glanced down at her. "You can't wait for Cevilla, by the way. Don't you know she wants us to walk together?"

"I figured." She couldn't help but smile. "She's relentless."

"That's Cevilla." He put his hands in his pockets. "Nice day for a walk, though. The temperature has warmed up a bit."

"I hope the ice doesn't melt on the pond."

"The ponds are frozen over already?"

"Not all of them. Just the shallower ones." She told Noah about Leanna's pond on her brother Jalon's property. It was lovely and private, and Phoebe's father had built a couple of wood benches last fall and put them nearby. His children liked to swim there in the summer and skate in the winter.

"You like to ice skate, then," he said.

"I do. I'm not very *gut* at it, though."

"I'm a terrible ice skater. Two left feet. Two big left feet. I've always wanted to get better, though."

They walked past a couple of buildings, and then Ivy glanced behind her. Cevilla was still walking, but she wasn't that far behind them. Ivy was pretty sure she could easily outwalk them at this pace, even with her cane.

"Have you eaten at Pancho's Dancing Taco Cantina?" Noah asked with a wink.

Ivy laughed and shook her head. "I've been to Barton more times than I can count, but I don't usually visit any of the restaurants. As I mentioned last week, I do like Mexican food—although I admit it's not one of *mei* favorites."

"Mine either. Although I do like chips and salsa."

"Maybe we should have said something to Cevilla."

"Do you want to be the one to tell her? I figure I can eat anything anywhere for one meal if it makes her happy."

"Me too."

They had walked a little farther—stopping from time to time for some window shopping with Cevilla still lagging well behind them—when Ivy saw an English woman hauling a big box from a car parked in front of one of the storefronts. Noah rushed ahead. "Let me get that for you."

"Thanks." The woman handed the box to Noah, who still managed to hang on to the book bag. "It's not that heavy, but it's cumbersome. You can just set it inside there on the left, by the window."

Ivy moved to hold the door open as Noah carried the box inside. The building consisted of two storefronts on the first floor and what looked like office space or apartments on the second. The storefront on the right had a For Lease sign in the window.

The woman lifted another box out of her car, this one smaller. She was on the tall side, but she was still much shorter than Noah. When he came out of the building, Noah offered to carry that box too. "That's all right," she said. "This one just has yarn in it."

"Please," Noah said. "I'll take it in for you."

The woman relented, and she followed behind Noah. "Thank you," she said to Ivy. "I've got some coffee ready. Would you two like a cup?"

"Did someone say coffee?" Cevilla smiled as she arrived behind Ivy and Noah. "I'd love some."

A few minutes later they were all inside, clearly in a shop of some sort. Several boxes sat on the floor and empty metal shelves sat against one wall. A small counter on the left side had a coffeemaker and a stack of Styrofoam cups on it. The woman walked over and filled three of the cups. She gathered them up and handed them to Ivy, Noah, and Cevilla. "I hope you don't mind it black," she said. "I forgot to bring cream and sugar this morning when I left my apartment."

"I'll take coffee any way I can get it," Noah said, taking a sip and setting the book bag on the counter.

Ivy took only a small sip of hers. She didn't really like drinking it this late in the morning. It was delicious and warm, though.

"I'm Noelle O'Bryan," the woman said, holding her hand out to Noah. "Thanks again for your help."

"Glad to do it." He shook her hand, and then she greeted Ivy and Cevilla. She was a strikingly pretty woman, with shoulder-length black hair that hung in curls around her flushed face. She wore a pair of dark-framed glasses, and she wasn't wearing any makeup except for on her lips, which were a dark shade of red. But the color wasn't gaudy or stark. It looked nice with her slim jeans, crocheted poncho, and dangly earrings.

"I've been impressed with how friendly people are around here," Noelle said.

"Where are you from?" Cevilla asked.

"Wisconsin. I moved here about a week ago." She gestured to the almost-empty store. "I'm hoping to make a fresh start here with my dream business."

"Which is?" Cevilla leaned against the counter and set the coffee on it, untouched.

"Welcome to Noelle's Yarn and Notions," she said, beaming. "At least it will be when I get everything set up. It's mostly for knitters and crocheters, but I'll have some fabric and sewing notions here too. I'll also be giving a few classes once I'm established."

"Sounds wonderful," Cevilla said.

Soon the two women launched into a conversation about crocheting. Ivy glanced at Noah, who was nodding at all the right places, but by the way the toe of one shoe was bouncing on the cement floor, Ivy could tell he wasn't all that interested. "I'm going to show Noah the fountain in the town square," she told Cevilla after deciding she needed to rescue him.

Cevilla grinned. "That's an absolutely wonderful idea. I'm surprised I didn't think of it myself. You two run along. I'll stay here and rest these old legs. You don't mind, Noelle, do you?"

"Not at all." She pulled a chair from behind the counter and placed it near Cevilla. "I need a break from all the moving anyway."

"*Geh* on," Cevilla said, shooing Noah and Ivy with her hands. "Don't rush back."

When Ivy and Noah stepped out of the store, Noah touched her on the arm. "*Danki*," he said. "I don't think I could have listened to another minute of yarn talk."

"That's what I thought." She looked up at him. "I do want to show you the fountain, though. It probably won't be on because of the weather, but it's lovely year-round."

"Lead the way."

Chapter 8

Would you rather have some tea?" Noelle said as she pulled up a stepstool across from Cevilla.

Cevilla shook her head. "I'm not thirsty, but thank you." And she wasn't, despite being slightly winded from her walk from the library. This matchmaking business was wearing her out. But seeing Noah and Ivy together was worth it. She'd have plenty of time to rest once those two were married off.

Noelle nodded and sat down on the stool. "I'm eager to get my store together. Just talking about crocheting with you makes me want to get out my hooks right now."

Cevilla smiled. "It's nice to see someone passionate about their work."

"I've been crocheting and knitting since I was a child. It's always been a hobby, though. I used to be a paralegal."

"You worked in a law office?"

She nodded. "That's where I met my late husband."

Cevilla's heart pinched. "I'm sorry for your loss."

Noelle averted her gaze. "Thank you. It's still hard to talk about. Patrick and I were married only a year when he was diagnosed with cancer." She looked back at Cevilla, her large brown eyes filling with tears. "Two years after that he was gone."

"You decided to move here to escape the memories."

"Not at first. I couldn't even go through Patrick's closet for a year after he died. But eventually I knew I had to move on. It was what he wanted. He knew I'd always had a dream to open my own shop in this part of the country, and he made sure I had the resources to do it." She sighed and looked around the store. "I just wish he were here to share it with me."

Cevilla's heart went out to the young woman. She couldn't be more than thirty, and she had already been through so much.

Noelle slapped her hands against her knees, her face brightened. "Enough of that. Tell me about that couple who just left. They're an interesting-looking pair."

"They are, aren't they?" Cevilla smiled. "They're truly perfect for each other, if I do say so myself."

"Seeing people in love gives me hope." Noelle smiled. "That's something else Patrick wanted for me. I'm still not ready, but at least I'm a little more open to the idea."

"That's the spirit." Cevilla leaned forward. "And when you are ready, God will send you the right man. I'm sure of it."

"I hope so. He sent me Patrick." Noelle stood up and went to the counter. She pulled out a white grocery bag of yarn. "I've got at least thirty of these scrap bags at my apartment. Would you mind winding these into balls for me? I need to bring in one more box."

"Of course." Before Cevilla started working on the yarn, she watched Noelle head out the door. She closed her eyes and said a prayer for the woman. "Give her peace in her heart, Lord," she whispered. "And while you're listening, give Noah and Ivy a little nudge in the right direction too." She opened her eyes and grinned. Love was definitely in the air.

The square wasn't far from Noelle's store, and when Ivy and Noah arrived there, he said, "You're right. This fountain is impressive."

"Years ago someone donated funds to the town and stipulated that the fountain be built with them," Ivy explained.

"Is it a memorial?"

"*Nee.* Just a nice fountain—with no water in it right now." She sat down on its edge.

"It's Tuscan style. That's interesting." Noah walked around the structure, which was two tiered and made of sand-colored marble. At the top was a sculpted flower. "Very nice. Do people ever use it for a wishing well?"

Ivy glanced at where coins would be under water in much warmer weather. "Yes, but that seems like a waste of money to me."

"You don't believe in wishes?" Noah sat down next to her.

"*Nee.* Do you?"

He shook his head. "If I need something, I pray about it. Although God doesn't always answer the way I expect." He stared at the fountain and grew quiet.

His words brought John back to mind, for some reason. How many times had she prayed to hear from him after she returned from Michigan? God's answer had been silence, both from John and from him.

"If you could wish for something, what would it be?" Noah asked.

Ivy paused. At one time she would have wished for John. But now that she was thinking about him, she felt no longing or regret. Just . . . nothing. She smiled. She felt nothing when she thought of John. She was finally free of him.

"That must be a *gut* wish you're thinking about."

She turned to Noah. "I think the one thing I wished for has already come true." She laughed. "That really sounded corny."

"I think it was sweet." He glanced at the fountain again. "I'm glad you're happy, Ivy."

"Are you?" Ivy asked without thinking. For some reason, she really wanted to know.

An uncertain expression crossed his features, only to quickly disappear. "Sure," he said, rising from the fountain's edge. "I'm happy." He glanced down the street. "I see some people walking into the restaurant."

"It's eleven o'clock already?"

"Time flies when you're talking about wishes and yarn." He held out his hand to her. "We should get Cevilla."

She looked at his hand. Large, strong. A tingle went through her. Tentatively, she slipped her hand into his. Naturally it engulfed her much smaller one, but it didn't feel strange or make her uncomfortable. His palm was smooth and warm. An unexpected feeling of security came over her, and for some reason she didn't want to let go.

He gently pulled her up and then quickly released her hand. "Ready?"

She nodded as he slipped his hands into the pockets of his navy-blue coat. Which of course he would do. He'd given her a friendly hand up. Nothing more.

But if that was the case, why did the butterflies show up

again? And why was she feeling something different—and far more pleasant—than she ever had with John?

As they headed back to Noelle's, they discussed how they would organize the rest of the items they'd already unpacked. "I talked to Abigail Bontrager yesterday after church," Ivy said as the morning sun hid behind a fluffy cloud. "She said she'd take some of the doilies. She has some ideas how to repurpose them."

Noah nodded. "That's a *gut* idea. I've seen people do that at craft shows. They use them to cover lampshades, or they'll put them in a nice frame for a simple wall decoration. I even saw some appliqued on a quilt once."

"See? Doilies aren't useless."

"I never said they were." He peered down at her. "I said they weren't monetarily valuable."

She smirked. "Not everything has to be."

"As you've stated." He gently nudged her shoulder with his elbow. "And like I said, I agree with you." His expression turned serious. "You can't put a price on the best things in life—faith, *familye* . . ." He glanced down at her. "Friendship."

Ivy smiled. "Very true."

"I'd still like to *geh* through a few more boxes today, if we can get Cevilla to go home after lunch," he said. "If you have time."

"I do." She paused. "Are you eager to get back to Arbor Grove?"

He paused. "*Ya.* I have some Christmas shopping to do. Plus I have some indoor auctions in January to get ready for." They stopped in front of the yarn store, and he stood in front of her. He leaned forward slightly, enough that it was easier to look him in the eyes. "But I've enjoyed *mei* time here too. A lot."

Before she could say anything, he straightened and opened the door for her.

"Back already?" Cevilla said in English as Ivy and Noah walked into the shop.

"It's lunchtime," Noah said, responding in kind.

"Right. So it is." She turned to Noelle. "Thank you kindly for the visit. And good luck with your business. I'll make sure to send my friends your way when you open."

"Thank you." Noelle grinned. "I should be ready in a couple of months. I'm going to take some time off around Christmas to visit my family back in Wisconsin."

The three of them walked to the restaurant, Cevilla moving a little more slowly this time. When they walked inside, the scent of cumin and chilies was in the air, along with festive Mexican music.

"Table or booth?" A young girl with straight black hair, olive skin, and wearing a bright yellow shirt embroidered with pretty flowers picked up menus from beside the hostess stand.

"Booth," Cevilla said without hesitation.

When they got there, Cevilla sat down first, and then she put her cane across the rest of the booth seat.

Ivy smirked at Cevilla's obvious ploy. Without a word she slid into the opposite seat, and Noah slipped in beside her. Once they were both seated, Cevilla moved her cane.

Noah dove into the chips and salsa as soon as they were on the table, and Ivy began telling Cevilla about the rest of their plans for Glenda's things, at least what they'd unboxed so far.

"*Mei* friend Carl will evaluate the watches and clocks," Noah added, scooping up a large dollop of salsa on a huge tortilla chip. "Except for the cuckoo clock, assuming it's not repaired by the time I leave. We'll have to catch that another time. But once we learn their value, we can sell the rest right away if you want."

"Whatever you think is best," Cevilla said, breaking a chip in half. She dipped one corner into the salsa.

"What would you like to do with the proceeds?" Noah asked.

"We can discuss that later." Cevilla picked up her menu. "Lots of Spanish on here," she said, peering through her glasses.

Ivy glanced at Noah, who was smirking as he picked up his water glass. "Were you expecting French?" he asked.

Cevilla stared over the menu. "Very funny."

Their waiter appeared and took their orders. Ivy opted for a cheese quesadilla. Noah ordered a combination meal and Cevilla a single burrito. The food was delicious, making Ivy realize she liked Mexican food more than she'd thought, and Cevilla kept them entertained with stories about Noah's family. "I remember the time *yer vatter* and three of his friends snuck out of the *haus* to *geh* night fishing."

"*Daed* did that?"

"*Ya.*" Cevilla smiled, her eyes taking on a faraway look. "He had his rebellious moments when he was younger."

"I can't imagine that. He's a stickler for rules now."

"Probably because *mei bruder* caught him and took him to the woodshed. I don't recall him trying to sneak out again."

After they finished lunch, Cevilla was fine with calling for the taxi, which picked them up promptly. When they arrived home, Cevilla announced she was going to take a nap. "Too much activity today," she said, sounding genuinely weary. She turned and headed for her room. "You two don't work too late."

Noah nodded and then turned to Ivy. He gestured to the stairs. "Shall we find what other treasures await?"

She grinned. "By all means."

John King finished wrapping the oak chest of drawers with clear packing wrap and then moved it closer to the front of the warehouse. His employer, Dienner Furniture, had been doing excellent business selling and delivering Amish furniture all over the country. The Dienners didn't make the furniture. They contracted with local craftsmen to create the custom pieces, which were then sold to the general public. John was in charge of the warehouse and had been for the past five years. It was good, steady work, and with the way the business kept growing, he was sure he'd have a job for a long time to come.

"Got this shipment ready yet?" Mark Dienner, the owner's son, entered the warehouse. Mark and John had been friends since they were kids. Mark usually traveled with the English driver they hired to deliver the furniture.

"Almost. Two more pieces to wrap up, and then we can get everything loaded." He wiped his forehead with the back of his hand. The warehouse wasn't heated, and it was cold enough that snow had started to fall, but he'd been working hard.

"*Gut.*" Mark pushed his hat back from his forehead and stroked his beard. "I've got a favor to ask you."

"*Geh* ahead." John started to pull out one of the two end tables that would be going in the shipment this afternoon.

"We just got a big order in for some custom shelving. It's not due to be delivered until late January, but that's the same week Katherine and I are visiting her family in Tennessee. Could you help with the delivery?"

"Sure. Where's it going?"

Mark glanced at the paper in his hand. "Barton, Ohio. Some yarn store or something."

John paused before nodding again. Ohio. He hadn't purposely thought about Ohio in over a year.

"*Danki.*" Mark turned and left.

John wiped his forehead again. Guilt churned in his stomach as he was reminded of the biggest mistake he'd ever made. He'd had the start of a wonderful relationship with a pretty, petite woman named Ivy Yoder. Although their time together while she was visiting family in Michigan had been short, it had also been sweet. He thought about the promise he'd made in the only letter he'd written to her. A promise he broke soon after.

He shook his head. He should contact her and explain. At least write her a letter. He'd tried a couple of times over the past year, but he always chickened out. She'd written several letters to him, which he threw away without reading. Because if he'd read them, he would have had to respond, and it was easier not to. Not to mention cowardly. But he'd moved on with his life, and by now he was sure she'd moved on with hers. Explaining why he'd cut off contact with her would just open wounds that needed to remain closed.

He returned to wrapping the end tables. He had no idea where Barton was. Not that it mattered. It wasn't as though he was going to try to track down Ivy while he was in Ohio. The past needed to stay in the past.

Noah opened one of the boxes and pulled out a stack of magazines. He shuffled through them briefly. "Fire starters," he said, dropping them onto the floor.

Ivy went to them. They were ladies' magazines and she picked one up. "I think some women would find these useful."

"They're from the seventies and eighties," he said. "Everything in them is dated."

She thumbed through the one in her hand. Only the recipes would be of interest to Amish women, and she didn't see that many of them. She tossed the magazine on the pile. "Let's open another box."

They opened two and found them filled with magazines as well. "Magazines and doilies. Apparently, that's what Glenda collected the most."

"Don't forget clothes. We've found a lot of clothes."

Noah sat down on the floor and rubbed his neck, and then closed his eyes. He squinted them just as he had in the taxi that morning, as if he were in pain.

Alarmed, Ivy kneeled in front of him. "Noah? Are you all right?"

He opened his eyes halfway, his lips curving into a partial smile. "Fine," he said. "Right as rain." He rubbed his eyes. "There's a lot of dust up here."

She rose and put her hands on her hips. "That's it. Tomorrow I'll start cleaning."

"*Gut* idea." He scrambled to his feet. "We can start by getting rid of these magazines. Maybe have a bonfire with them—"

"Wait. It seems wasteful to burn them."

"Let me guess. You have an idea of what to do with them."

"Not yet, but let's hang on to them a little while longer."

He leaned over and looked at her. "Ivy Yoder, I had *nee* idea you were a pack rat."

"I'm not," she said, lifting her chin. "I just don't like throwing things away if they have a purpose. I'd like to try to find a way of recycling them."

His expression grew serious. "You're right, of course." He put the magazines back in the boxes and shoved them against the wall.

Pleased, Ivy turned and spied the dilapidated box she'd noticed the other day. She was walking over to open it when Noah said, "Let's call it a day."

"All right. After I open this one box."

"Nah. We've got all day tomorrow."

She glanced out the window. The sun had started to set, and she hadn't realized how late it was getting. It seemed as though she and Noah had just started working on the attic a short while ago.

"I'll drive you home," he said.

"You don't have to do that."

"Fine." He went to the top of the attic stairs. "I'll walk you home, then."

"Noah—"

He held up his hand. "*Nee* arguments." Then he faced her. "I want to take you home, Ivy. Walk or ride, it's *yer* choice."

She looked at him, trying to discern his intentions. She'd never met a man like him. Then again, it wasn't as though she had a lot of experience. John had been affectionate with his words, but not with his actions during the short time they dated in Michigan. Noah was the opposite. He'd stayed close to her side while they worked this afternoon, and then there was the split second of holding hands at the fountain in Barton. But everything he said to her was with the same tone and expression he used with everyone else—friendly and genuine. She had to stop speculating about whether there was something more between them. He'd made it clear to her and Cevilla that there wasn't.

For the first time, that disappointed her.

"Ivy?" He waved at her. "Have you decided?"

"Walk," she said. She didn't want him to go to the trouble of hitching up the buggy. And the fact that walking would give them more time together had nothing to do with her decision.

Nope. That had nothing to do with her decision at all.

Chapter 9

Noah didn't mind walking Ivy home, but he had another reason to do it other than to keep her company. The buzzing was back. It started in the Mexican restaurant, but at that time it was barely noticeable. Then while he was unpacking the magazines, the buzzing increased. Now it was loud and painful. Maybe he could walk it off.

And maybe getting rid of the dust in the attic would help. Or maybe he needed to go to bed early tonight.

But for the first time, he was thinking none of those things would work.

Cevilla, of course, couldn't hide her glee when he poked his head through the open door to her bedroom and told her he was walking Ivy home. "Don't feel like you have to rush back," she said, sitting up in her bed faster than Noah thought she could move. "I'm still full from lunch, so I was planning on a light supper."

He got the hint, and he knew he'd be making himself something more substantial to eat later on. He didn't mind. What he minded was the buzzing, and now humming, echoing in his ears. It had never been this bad before.

He was still trying to deal with it as he and Ivy stood by

Cevilla's front door. He felt a tap on his arm and looked down. Ivy was talking, but he couldn't hear her. God, he couldn't hear her. He shut his eyes again, praying for the pain and noise to go away.

"Noah?"

Her voice sounded far away, much as Cevilla's had yesterday. But at least now he could hear her. And if he could hear her, he could pretend the noise didn't bother him. "Sorry," he said. "Do you need something?"

"*Mei* coat. Would you mind getting it for me?"

Noah had hung her coat on a high peg, and she couldn't reach it. "Sure," he said, making a note to hang it lower next time. He handed it to her. "There you *geh*." His own voice sounded muddled. What was happening? He shoved down the rising anxiety and forced a smile. "Ready?"

"*Ya*." She looked at him oddly, but he quickly opened the door for her.

As soon as he stepped out on the porch, the buzzing was gone. So was the pain. *Thank you, God.* Now all he had was a mild headache, and he would take that any day over the weird and frightening symptoms he'd been experiencing.

Still, he couldn't get his thoughts off what happened. What kept happening. He couldn't chalk it up to fatigue anymore. Perhaps it was some kind of strange bug he couldn't shake.

"Noah? Is everything okay?"

Her words brought him out of his thoughts, and he realized they were halfway to her house and he hadn't said a word. When he glanced down at her, he saw the odd look again. He didn't blame her. He excelled at conversation, and he rarely remained quiet for long. It had bugged his parents that he was so talkative, though he'd managed to channel that trait into his business as an auctioneer. But here he was with Ivy, a woman he found easy to talk with, and he hadn't spoken at all. He felt the need to apologize, but how did one say sorry for being quiet?

"I can walk myself home next time," Ivy said. "I shouldn't have put you to the trouble."

"It wasn't any trouble. I've just . . . I've got a bit of a headache."

"Oh." She frowned. "*Mei mamm* makes a ginger-peppermint tea that does wonders for headaches. I'm sure she won't mind making you some when we get to *mei haus*."

"That's all right." He didn't want to put her or her mother to any trouble. "I'm sure it will *geh* away soon. Don't worry about it."

They walked a little farther, and Noah could see the Yoders' house in the distance. He tried to think of something to say, but all he could focus on was the pulsing pain in his head, which was now traveling to his left ear. When they arrived at her house, he barely paused to say, "I'll see you in the morning."

"*Ya*. See you then."

He watched her walk to the porch, and he was suddenly filled with regret. They didn't have much time left to spend together, and he found himself looking forward to being with her. It was true that he was eager to get back to Iowa. Well, maybe eager wasn't the right word. He had responsibilities he needed to take care of. But for some reason the thought of leaving Birch Creek in the next couple of days gave him pause. He'd miss his aunt, of course. He always did. And now he realized he'd miss Ivy too.

He glanced down at his hand, remembering how her small palm fit in his. He'd assisted her up from the fountain on impulse, and he wasn't sure if she was going to take his offer. As soon as he felt her soft skin against his, he felt something definitely not defined as friendship. Which was why he immediately let her go and stuck his hands into his pockets.

Noah turned and headed back to Cevilla's. The strange symptoms were wreaking havoc on his sanity, at least where Ivy was concerned. That, and he was getting caught up in Cevilla's matchmaking game. But he had to collect his senses. Ivy was a friend, and he didn't want to spoil that because of some spark of attraction. Seriously, who wouldn't be attracted to Ivy Yoder? She was cute and nice and sweet . . .

No, she was more than that. She was beautiful. She had a heart bigger than any woman he'd ever met. She even cared about wasting some old magazines, which he would have thrown away in a heartbeat. She was special. No doubt about that.

And he had no doubt that she lacked romantic feelings for him.

As he walked home, the headache continued, but at least the pain didn't increase. When he arrived at Cevilla's, he found her snoozing in her living room chair. He frowned. She'd already taken a nap that afternoon, and now she was asleep again. She really was worn-out from the day's activities. Next time he'd make sure she didn't walk so far. The weather was too cold.

He lightly touched her shoulder, and she lifted her head, her eyes bleary. "Huh . . . what?"

"You were asleep, *Aenti*."

"Was I?" She blinked and looked at the project in her lap. Her crochet hook had fallen to the floor.

Noah picked it up and handed it to her. "You should *geh* to bed," he said.

"I will in a little while." She took the crochet hook from him, studied his face for a moment, and then frowned. "You don't look well."

"I'm—"

"Fine. I know. You're also stubborn." She jammed the hook into the half-crocheted afghan. "If you're not going to talk to me about how you feel, then tell me about you and Ivy. You got to spend a lot of time together today."

"We did. And we made some more headway in the attic."

"How are you two getting along?"

"Fine," he said. More than fine, at least in his estimation. Not that it mattered much in the long run.

Her eyebrows lifted. "Just fine? Is that all?"

He crouched down in front of her so they could be at eye level. "She's nice, *Aenti.*" That was an understatement. "But if you're hoping for a love match, you might as well give up now. I'm . . . not interested."

"How can you not be interested in Ivy?" Cevilla glared straight ahead as if she'd been personally offended. "She's a wonderful *maedel.*"

He couldn't hide the truth. "I agree with that."

Cevilla swung her gaze back at him. "Aha! Then you *are* interested in her."

He rubbed the back of his neck. He should have known Cevilla wouldn't make this easy for him. He also knew it was because she loved him, and he couldn't be angry about that. Still, he had to make her understand she was wasting her time. "*Aenti*, please, listen to me for once. I'm fine being single. *Mei* business keeps me occupied, and I'm not interested in giving that up. It wouldn't be fair to Ivy or any other woman for me to be on the road all the time."

"Are you truly happy being on the road? Does auctioning fulfill that emptiness in *yer* heart?"

Noah blinked. *How did she know about that?* Lately he'd realized something was missing, something undefinable. But now that Cevilla had labeled it, he knew she was right. Some small part of him felt empty. Yet was a relationship the way to fill that empty place? He hadn't given any real thought to marriage or family since . . .

He pushed those thoughts to the side. "I'm happy with *mei* life the way it is. *Nee*, better than fine. I'm content. Isn't that what matters?"

Cevilla started to speak, but then she closed her mouth. "This is unexpected," she said, almost mumbling the words.

He didn't know what she was talking about, but he rose to his feet, eager to end the conversation. "I'm going to cook up a ham steak and some potatoes. Do you want some?"

She waved her hand, not looking at him. "I'm not hungry."

"I'll make you some toast anyway."

She didn't respond, just stared at the fire in her gas stove. Noah looked at her for a long moment and then shrugged and went to the kitchen. He searched the drawers until he found some aspirin and downed two of them with a glass of water.

And hopefully Cevilla's subdued reaction meant his explanation had worked, that it had finally sunk in that her efforts on his behalf were useless. He couldn't deal with her constant matchmaking attempts, not when he was already confused about his feelings for Ivy. He'd been truthful with Cevilla when he said he was happy. He was happy. Other than the weirdness in his head and ears, his life was good.

Except for the emptiness.

Shaking off the thought, he started to cook his supper. Feeding his stomach would get his mind off his troubles, and hopefully the aspirin would do the trick for his headache.

Cevilla was confused. Deeply confused. *Lord, did I hear you wrong?* She'd been so certain that he'd given her his approval about a Noah and Ivy match. And Cevilla had done everything she could to get them together, shy of locking them in a room and throwing away the key until they fell in love. Even Noelle, a perfect stranger, had assumed they were together. Which was easy to do. Noah and Ivy got along very well. They were at ease with each other. They seemed to have been friends for years.

And there lay the problem. Not only had Noah stated he wasn't interested in Ivy romantically, but Ivy didn't seem interested in Noah either. It was clear they were friends. Now it was clear to Cevilla that that's all they would be.

"Such a disappointment," she said, shaking her head. She'd been so sure these two were meant for each other. When she saw them together, she could picture them as a couple. But the writing was on the wall—and Noah had said as much. He didn't want to get married. In fact, he was clearly married to his work. Which was another problem altogether, but she didn't have the energy to tackle that one now.

She was running out of ways to bring them together. They would be finished with the boxes in the attic soon enough, and Noah would go home. Without Ivy.

"Should I stop meddling?" she whispered. She hated that word, but she had to admit meddling was exactly what she'd been doing. With good intentions, of course, but she was still inserting herself into two wonderful young people's business. Would she have wanted someone to do that to her? Of course not.

She had to accept the truth, not only about Noah and Ivy, but about her role in this scheme. She was trying to force them together, and that clearly wasn't working.

But she wasn't quite ready to give up. Perhaps if she stepped back and stayed out of it, they would see what was in plain sight on their own. Ivy Yoder was the right woman for her nephew. Cevilla was certain of that. He deserved someone like her—kind, sweet, smart, and cute as a teddy bear's nose. And Ivy deserved a loyal, hard-working, determined man like Noah.

Yes, staying out of their business was what she had to do, even though it wouldn't be easy. Cevilla Schlabach wasn't used to staying out of things. But for Noah and Ivy's sake, she would make an exception.

Decision made, she picked up her crochet hook, only to pause again. Something else was going on with Noah, independent of Ivy Yoder. Cevilla had noticed him grimacing a few times since he'd arrived in Birch Creek. He'd also been sleeping more than she'd ever known him do. Now that she wouldn't be so focused on putting him and Ivy together, she would keep a closer eye on her great-nephew. Somehow, she'd get to the bottom of what was bothering him, once and for all.

When Ivy walked in the front door, *Mamm* was standing in the living room next to the window. From the still-moving curtain,

Ivy could tell her mother had been spying. *Mamm*'s next words confirmed it. "I see Noah walked you home."

Ivy rolled her eyes at her mother's knowing smile. Not this again. "*Ya.* He didn't have to, but he insisted."

"He insisted?" *Mamm* got a dreamy look in her eyes, as if she were the one being courted, not Ivy.

Wait. *Courted?* Why would that word pop into her mind? She gave her head a shake and sternly looked at *Mamm*. "I thought you were giving up on talking about this."

"I was." She smoothed her apron. "Then I realized you might need a little push in the right direction."

"And Noah's in that direction."

"He's a nice *mann*, Ivy."

"He is. But, *Mamm*, I think of him as only a friend." *Mostly* a friend. Nevertheless, she was also a little concerned about him. He seemed fine in the attic, but then he'd complained about the dust, and coupled with his quiet demeanor on the way to her house and the headache he had, she wondered if he was coming down with something.

"Friends often become something more," *Mamm* said, her meaning hopeful. "You never know what God has in store."

"Were you like this with Karen and Adam?" Ivy asked, removing her coat and scarf and hanging them on the peg rack by the door.

"I didn't have to be. Karen had liked Adam for years, from the moment she saw him when they were *kinner.* When Adam returned to Birch Creek, I knew they would find their way to each other."

"But you don't trust me to find *mei* own way."

Mamm didn't answer. Instead, she smoothed her apron again.

Her silence hurt. "I'm not going to fall for the first single *mann* who comes *mei* way," Ivy insisted. She cringed inwardly. Hadn't she done that with John? Hadn't she put her hopes and dreams into the hands of a man who had rejected her in the worst way possible—by ignoring her completely? She needed to keep that experience in the forefront of her mind. She wasn't going to go through that pain again. Not with any man, and especially not with Noah. If he rejected her, she couldn't bear it.

"It's not as though you have much of a choice," *Mamm* said quietly.

That stung. "Am I that pathetic?" Ivy asked in a small voice. "Does everyone think I'm lonely and pitiful?" She started to head to her room. She didn't need her mother hurting her like this.

"Oh, Ivy." *Mamm* put her hand on Ivy's arm, stopping her. "*Nee.* Of course not. I'm sorry. That didn't sound the way I intended. *Nee* one thinks you're pathetic or pitiful." She looked away and then again at Ivy. "I just want you to face facts. We don't have single men here in Birch Creek, and Noah is a fine *mann*. A fine *single* man. Couldn't you at least give it a chance?"

"Maybe I should move away," she said, stepping away from *Mamm*. "Then I can date whomever I want. Or not date anyone."

"Is that what you want? To move somewhere else?"

She sighed. She couldn't lie. "*Nee.* I love it here." She looked up at her mother. "I don't want to leave *mei familye* and friends. But the point is, I need to be happy living with myself, *Mamm*. I don't want to date or get married to someone because he's a last resort. That wouldn't be fair to him—or to me."

Mamm touched Ivy's cheek. "You're right, of course. I'm sorry. I just want to see you happy."

"I am happy." And she was, for the most part. She had

something to look forward to—her new job at Schrocks'. She was also enjoying getting to know Cevilla better, despite the woman's unending machinations, which were more amusing and creative than annoying. Even after Noah left, she planned to continue to build their friendship. She even had a few problems to solve—how to get rid of the rest of the doilies and the magazines they'd found in the attic today without just throwing them all away at the dump. Her life wasn't as empty or useless as her mother made it seem.

"I don't have to be dating or married to be happy," Ivy continued, softening her tone. She needed to make her mother understand. "Besides, this conversation is pointless. Noah seems to be perfectly happy being single. And he's made it clear he isn't interested in me. We're friends. Just friends."

Mamm grimaced. "Ivy, I'm so sorry. I never should have pried. And I never should have said what I did." She took Ivy's hand. "I don't know how to explain it. The two of you just seem right to me."

"You and Cevilla have that in common," Ivy mumbled.

"I love you, Ivy." *Mamm* gave her a quick hug, which Ivy returned. "I promise I'll stay out of *yer* and Noah's relationship—"

"Friendship," Ivy clarified.

"Friendship, and I'll keep *mei* opinion to myself about any of *yer* future relationships."

At least her mother was optimistic. Right now Ivy wasn't too optimistic herself. Then again, people were moving into Birch Creek all the time. Perhaps her future husband would arrive at some point. But that possibility didn't change anything. She had to be fine by herself, no matter what the future held. *"Danki, Mamm."*

"I better get the bread out of the oven. Supper will be ready soon."

"I'll be there in a minute to set the table."

"Judah already did it."

Ivy lifted a surprised eyebrow. "I'm sure he didn't like that one bit."

"He didn't, but it won't hurt him to set the table occasionally. Next thing I need to do is teach those *buwe* to cook." She sighed. "It's not as though there's an abundance of *yung* women and girls in Birch Creek, either." She held up her hand as Ivy started to speak. "Don't worry. I'm going to stay out of *mei sohns*' business too."

"*Gut.*" Ivy smiled.

After *Mamm* left the room, Ivy thought about Noah and his sudden headache. Then again, perhaps it wasn't so sudden. She'd have to do something about the dust in the attic tomorrow.

After supper she organized the cleaning supplies she wanted to take to Cevilla's and put them in a bucket by the door. She should have done this before, but in her defense, they'd had too many boxes in the attic to accomplish any cleaning. Now that they'd unpacked almost all of them, and moved out what they could, she had plenty of room to clean. Ivy didn't want Cevilla sneezing, or Noah getting headaches, anymore. She cared about them more than she ever thought she would when she first started helping with this project. And while Cevilla and *Mamm* were disappointed that she and Noah weren't a match, Ivy considered herself lucky. In the process, she'd gained a good friend in Noah and a better friend in Cevilla.

Chapter 10

The next morning Ivy arrived at Cevilla's before breakfast, armed with the cleaning supplies. "Where's Noah?" Ivy asked, taking off her coat in the doorway between the mudroom and kitchen.

"He's upstairs working on the boxes in the attic." Cevilla didn't look at her as she buttered a piece of toast at the table.

"Without me?" Ivy was stunned.

"*Ya.*" Cevilla set the toast on a plate and began to peel a banana.

"I thought we weren't allowed to do that."

"I changed *mei* mind." She pointed at the coffeepot on the stove. "Want some?"

Ivy shook her head, still bewildered. "I'll *geh* upstairs and help Noah." When she headed for the attic stairs, she saw several boxes lined up in the hall and realized Noah must have moved the rest of the clothes boxes down. When she arrived in the attic, she saw he'd also rearranged the boxes so there was more room. "How long have you been up here?" she asked.

"Maybe an hour. I wanted to get up here before she changed her mind." He looked at her and wiped his brow.

"I'm confused," Ivy said. She set the bucket down on the

floor. "Neither of us could be in the attic alone, and now Cevilla's changed her mind?"

"*Ya.*" He lifted one of the boxes. "I have *nee* idea why, though."

"How strange."

"Basically *mei aenti* in a nutshell." He walked over to the stairs. "I'm going to take this downstairs, and then put all those boxes in the spare bedroom. I'll be back in a minute."

"All right." At this point Ivy gave up trying to figure out Cevilla. It was much easier to go with the flow. She was about to start cleaning when she spied the old dented box again. She'd been planning to open it yesterday, but then Noah stopped her and walked her home. It wouldn't hurt to put off cleaning to open one more box.

When she picked it up, the box was surprisingly light. She put it on the bench in front of the window, pulled off the tape—which came off far more easily than the tape on the other boxes—opened the flaps, and peered inside.

With a sigh she picked up a handful of doilies. Unbelievable. Even she was becoming disappointed and overwhelmed with the sheer number of them. She examined the ones in her hand and determined right away that she'd have to discard them. Dark stains were all over the delicate crocheted threads—probably tea and coffee, plus a few purple ones that indicated red wine. One doily was ripped in two. They were damaged beyond repair. She set them aside on the bench and reached for another handful, but then her fingertips brushed against something else in the box. She set down the doilies and looked inside.

Now, this was interesting. She lifted a bundle of letters, neatly tied with a thin red ribbon.

"What did you find?" Noah said, standing behind her.

She hadn't heard him come back up the stairs. He was crowding her again, but she was too interested in what was in front of her to care. She turned to look at him, barely noticing they were only inches apart. "Letters," she said, holding them out to him. "They were under a pile of stained doilies."

"Odd that they'd be stored so carelessly." He took the packet from her and sat down on the bench next to the box.

"Why would you say that?"

"The letters are bundled neatly. And this is *gut* quality ribbon. It's older, but it's not frayed." He looked at the dumpy box. "I would think they would be in a keepsake box."

Ivy nodded. "Or in a trunk. It's like someone just threw them in here." She pointed to the water stain on the side of the box, and then showed him some of the doilies. "These are stained and frayed. And here's one that's actually torn."

"It's almost as if the box was meant for trash, not a storage unit." He set the box on the floor, shoved the old doilies aside, and then tugged on the ribbon. The bow immediately loosened.

"What are you doing?" Ivy asked.

"Seeing who wrote the letters."

"Isn't that an invasion of privacy?"

"I'm not opening them. And it's better to check them this way, instead of bending them back while they're in the bundle." He scooted over and carefully laid the letters on the bench.

She was surprised at how gently he handled this find, even putting the ribbon to the side with a light touch. His fingers were long and slender, but unlike most Amish men she knew, his hands weren't rough and calloused. She knew that firsthand from when he warmed her cheeks that day and when they had briefly held hands by the fountain. Yet his hands weren't pretty either. Masculine was the term that came to mind. And as soon as she thought that, she pulled her gaze away. She couldn't get caught staring at his hands, of all things.

"This is interesting." He picked up one of the letters. "It's from Korea, postmarked 1953."

"Korea?"

He studied the envelope. "That would have been the last year of the Korean War."

She wasn't a history buff, except for what she learned while she was working on the genealogy project. She'd enjoyed that. "There was a war in Korea?"

"*Ya*. North and South Korea fought against each other. The United States was on the South Korean side, and the Soviet Union and China on the North's side. The war was fought over communism . . ." Noah looked down at her. "You're not really interested in those details, *ya*?"

"Not really." She looked up at the envelope. "I can't make out the address on this one."

"Last name is Brown, I think. It's pretty smudged, but I know that was Glenda's maiden name." He held up the letter to the light.

Ivy batted his shoulder. "Invasion of privacy, remember?"

He glanced at her and then stood. "I'll be back," he said, and he headed downstairs, carrying the letter.

Ivy barely heard his footsteps against the attic stairs. For such a gangly, tall man, he was light-footed. Or at least it sounded like it. Ivy looked at the letters again, her curiosity piqued as she noted the Arnold City, Pennsylvania, address on each one. She searched through the box to see if any more letters were in there. All she found was a few crochet hooks, some dried out rubber bands, and a couple of crochet pattern books from the 1960s. She set the hooks and pattern books to the side and threw the rubber bands in the trash can Noah had brought up.

She tapped her chin as she stared at the letters again. Noah had left them on the bench. The doilies in the other boxes had been packed so carefully, but these weren't. Only the letters seemed to have been handled with care, at least with a ribbon keeping them together. Whatever was written on them, they deserved to have a better container than a water-stained box. She searched the attic for something to put them in. Now that they had cleared out a lot of Glenda's stuff, she could see into all the corners of the attic. Maybe Cevilla had something stashed up here Ivy could use.

She hadn't found anything by the time Noah returned, carrying a small wooden box under his arm. "What's that?" she asked him.

"Cevilla said we can store the letters in here. Didn't seem right to leave them lying around in that old box."

Ivy smiled to herself as he put the box on the floor. She didn't reveal that she had been thinking the exact same thing.

Noah handed her the letter. She put it back in the stack and tightened the ribbon, and then handed the whole bundle to him. He put it in the box, latched the lid, and set it on the floor to the side.

"What did Cevilla say about the letters?" Ivy asked.

"Not much. She didn't seem surprised about them, though. She went into her room, brought out the wooden box, and told me to put them in there."

Ivy nodded. Noah went back to opening another box while she picked up the bucket of cleaning supplies. But as she started to sweep the floor with the broom Cevilla kept in the attic, she kept thinking about the letters. She was dying to know what they were about. She remembered Noah telling her that Glenda, Cevilla's stepmother, had been a nurse, but that had been during World War II. Had she also served in the Korean War? Was that even possible? But the letters had to be addressed to her if she kept them. Unless they belonged to a relative with the same last name.

"Is something wrong?"

Ivy looked to see Noah glancing at her over his shoulder. "*Nee*," she said, continuing to sweep. "Just cleaning, that's all."

"You want to know what's inside the letters." Noah smiled as he faced her.

She had no reason to deny it. "Don't you?" She found it hard to believe he wouldn't, considering his curious nature and profession.

He nodded, looking a little sheepish. "I was going to ask Cevilla if we could, but I wasn't sure if you wanted to." He put his hands on his hips. "Might be a *gut* idea if you ask her. She's been acting kind of strange around me this morning."

Ivy nodded, her curiosity truly piqued now. She went downstairs and found Cevilla in the kitchen. Instead of bustling around the way she usually did, she was staring out the window, a pensive look on her face. "Cevilla?" Ivy said, approaching her.

Cevilla turned around. "You're curious about those letters, aren't you?"

Ivy's mouth dropped open a little. "Did Noah tell you that?"

"He didn't have to. I know you well enough." She smiled. "I'm sure it's all right if you read them. The war was so long ago . . ."

Ivy thought she detected a note of wistfulness in Cevilla's voice.

Cevilla put her hand on Ivy's arm. "Read the letters, Ivy. You might find something interesting in them." Then she took her cane and left the kitchen.

Cevilla really was acting odd today. Ivy wondered if she was all right. She was tempted to go after her, but she got the feeling Cevilla wanted to be alone. And if that was the case, Ivy wasn't going to bother her. Still, she paused, second-guessing herself for a minute before going back upstairs and telling Noah what Cevilla said.

"Now I'm really curious." He sat down on the bench and patted the empty space next to him.

"What did you do with the doilies?"

He pointed to the trash can. "Put them where they belong."

Ivy sat down next to him. The bench wasn't all that large, and there wasn't much space between them. Yet she wasn't uncomfortable with the closeness. She was used to it by now.

As she took the bundle out of the box and untied the ribbon, Noah pulled a lemon drop out of his pocket. "Want one?"

She nodded and took it from him, and then she opened the first letter. He popped another drop into his mouth as she started to read silently.

"Out loud, please," he said.

"Oh, sorry."

Dear Bunny,

I can only imagine your surprise at finding this letter in your mailbox. No postage, and dated the day I left you. You're probably wondering why I would write to you before I stepped foot in basic training camp. I've never been good at talking. You know that better than anyone. Remember that day in sixth grade, when the teacher introduced me to the class after my family moved here? The odds were stacked against me. I was the new kid, small for my age, and I had a funny accent. I figured if I kept my mouth shut the guys wouldn't notice me. That didn't last long. By morning recess they were ready to stuff me in one of the lockers.

Then you showed up. Tall, confident, and yes, pretty, even when you were a young girl. And you told them off. A whole group of boys who probably would have beaten you up if there wasn't a teacher nearby. Then again, I figured you could take them.

I was smitten then. I'm definitely smitten now.

I can only imagine the look on your face as you're reading this. It's been seven years since that day on the playground. Seven years of friendship, of playing catch in your backyard, of riding bikes around the neighborhood. Of you sitting in the stands during all my football games, and me going to all your band concerts. Of homecoming dances and proms. Did you really think I asked you only because we were friends? Being there for you when your father died—and you being there for me when my brother didn't come back from the war. And through all of that, through all those years, I wanted to tell you how I felt. But I was afraid. I didn't want to ruin our friendship. Because it was better to have you as a friend than to not have you in my life at all.

You're probably wondering what's changed. Why am I admitting my feelings now? And why through a letter, instead of telling you yesterday when we spent the day together, and you saw me off at the bus station. See, I don't have a problem joining the army, and even though my brother died in battle, I'm not afraid to die for my country. It's why I joined the service instead of waiting on the draft. I don't want my brother's death to be in vain. He was a proud American, and I am too.

But when it comes to laying my heart on the line . . . I'm not so brave. In fact, I'm a coward. I know I'm cheating myself of seeing your beautiful face as I tell you how I feel, on the slim chance that you might feel the same. But I also couldn't bear the pity in your eyes when you, in your own sweet but straightforward way, tell me friendship is all we'll ever have.

I also can't live knowing that, God forbid, if something did happen to me, I was never honest with you. I can't die with a lie between us.

I'd understand if you were angry with me. I also understand if you don't feel the same. I expect it, actually. You're a smart, beautiful woman, and my heart flipped every time you agreed to go out with me, even as friends, when I knew plenty of fellas wanted a chance with you.

So I hope you can find it in your heart to forgive this cowardly hayseed. Even though my future is uncertain, I'm sure of one thing. I love you, Bunny. And I always will, no matter what happens.

Love,
CJ

"Love letters," Noah said.

Ivy caught the disappointment in his voice. "Is there something wrong with that?"

"*Nee.* I was hoping for something more about the war. Something of historical significance."

Ivy sighed. "Noah, these letters have—"

"I know. Sentimental value." He picked up the next one and opened it.

"I thought you weren't interested."

"I never said that." He glanced at her, and then started to read.

Dear Bunny,

I've been in basic training for three weeks, and I have to tell you, it's tough. I can't talk much about what we do, other than learning how to be prepared for war. It wears you out, body, mind, soul. But there's a purpose in it too. Most of us here, even the fellas who were drafted, want to fight. Not because we're eager to get in harm's way, but because we want this war to end. I'm hearing more about the politics about it—the things they don't report in the papers—and I'm wondering if we're doing the right thing by getting into another country's business. But I don't think about it too much. I just do what I'm told and collapse into bed each night.

Now I guess I need to talk about the elephant in the room. I'm guessing since I haven't heard from you after my last letter, you don't want to write me back. It's okay. Actually, it's okay if you forget everything I said in that letter. We can go back to the way things were. We'll be friends, and I promise I'll never make you feel uncomfortable about what I wrote to you. I don't want a bad judgment call on my part to wreck our relationship.

I've gotten a couple letters from Ma, and Richard Johnson sent me a package filled with goodies from his dad's drugstore. The officers let us eat whatever candy and cookies and stuff we get from home before we hit the hay. I've been too tired to eat most nights, but I appreciate Richard thinking of me. He's a nice guy and a good friend.

It's lights out soon, and I'm already yawning. Hope to hear from you soon.

Your friend,

CJ

Ivy read the third one.

Dear Bunny,

I've got three days left here at basic. I should be getting my orders soon. I've never been too smart, so I'm sure I'll be in the infantry, which means they'll send me straight to Korea. Somehow six weeks doesn't seem like enough time to get ready for war, but a part of me is eager to get started on whatever it is they want me to do. We're kept busy here, and the good Lord knows when it's lights out I'm bone tired. But sometimes I can't sleep. And that's when the waiting gets to you. When your mind starts to race and think about the what-ifs. When your chest squeezes at the thought of facing down the enemy, and if you're going to come out of it alive. I wonder if my brother felt that way. He never mentioned anything in his letters. Everything was always good, always fine, always status quo. I can see now why he didn't say anything. I don't say anything either . . . only to you. I guess that's because you're safe.

I haven't heard from you, and for all I know you've thrown my letters in the trash. You did promise you would write, but I guess I messed that up by revealing my feelings to you. I guess you couldn't find it in your heart to forgive me. That's my fault too. So you don't have to worry about me bugging you anymore.

Tell your mother I said hello.

CJ

Ivy put the letter down. "This is sad."

Noah nodded. "I kinda feel sorry for him." He stared straight ahead. "It's never *gut* when someone doesn't keep their word."

"*Nee*, it isn't." She thought about John, and all the letters she'd written to him, only to never hear from him again. At least Bunny—or someone—had read these letters and thought they were special enough to keep. Had John read Ivy's letters? Or had he thrown them away, unopened?

Noah suddenly sneezed. Ivy set down the letters. "I need to finish cleaning," she said, feeling a little guilty that she had abandoned her chore.

"It can wait," he said, reaching for the next letter. Then he sneezed again.

"I don't want you to get another headache." She put the letters back in the box. "We can read them later." She wasn't sure she wanted to, though. So far it looked like CJ was in a one-sided relationship, and she knew all too well how that felt.

For the rest of the morning she cleaned the attic, Noah pitching in by dusting the cobwebs off the rafters. By the time they were finished, there wasn't a speck of dust. After lunch, during which no one mentioned the letters, they found more magazines and inconsequential odds and ends. Then they stacked the last few remaining unpacked boxes against the wall. Noah had broken down the empty boxes and taken them to the barn.

"Looks like we might be finished here by tomorrow," he said.

"*Ya*," she said, her feelings mixed. That might free her up to work earlier for the Schrocks than she'd anticipated. But it also meant Noah would probably be leaving. Other than visiting his aunt, he didn't have another reason to stick around, and she knew he had things to take care of back home. The thought of not coming over here every day, of not seeing Noah anymore, left her feeling bereft.

"I hear there's a school board meeting at *yer haus* tonight," Noah said as they headed down the stairs.

"How did you know?"

He reached the hallway and turned to look up at her. "Cevilla's invited."

"I didn't know she was on the board."

"She's not." He stepped to the side to let Ivy by and then folded the attic stairs and pushed them closed. "Which makes me think she invited herself."

"That wouldn't surprise me."

They went to the mudroom, where Ivy had hung her coat and scarf. She slipped on her boots and was about to get her coat when she felt Noah behind her. He reached up over her head and pulled down her winter garments. She could feel his warmth, smell the scent of the lemon drops he'd shared with her earlier. When she turned to face him, he didn't back away. Instead, he held the coat behind her so she could put her arms in the sleeves. Then he took the scarf and wrapped it loosely around her neck.

"Don't want you to get cold," he said, his gaze meeting hers.

Her breath held. She needed to tell herself once again that he was only being nice, that he always stood too close, that they were just friends. But her head and heart weren't listening to each other.

After a long moment, he blinked, and then he stepped away. "I know you'll insist on walking home by yourself, but I guess I'll see you tonight." He leaned against the mudroom doorway, sliding his hands into his pants pockets.

"Tonight?" She was still having a little trouble catching her breath.

"I'm bringing Cevilla over. For the school board meeting?"

"Ah. Right. I'll see you later, then." She opened the door and stepped outside, the blast of cold air hitting her and finally bringing her back to reality. She chastised herself on her way home. It might be good that Noah was leaving soon, since she couldn't seem to think straight around him sometimes. Those times were becoming more frequent. She had to admit she was getting tired of it all—of policing her thoughts, of her mother's and Cevilla's interference, of the constant reminders of her singleness.

But none of that stopped her from remembering Noah's soft gaze as he wrapped the scarf around her neck, and the shiver that had gone down her spine when he spoke, his voice rich and deep. And she couldn't stop looking forward to seeing him again tonight.

Chapter 11

This was the first time since her father had become bishop that he'd had a meeting in their home. Usually he held them at other people's homes, and no one minded that. But tonight at supper he mentioned he planned to hold more meetings at theirs. "I don't want anyone to get the idea I'm hiding anything," he'd said.

They all knew what was unspoken. Emmanuel Troyer had hidden plenty, and Ivy's father had spent the last three years earning back the trust the former bishop had broken. She didn't blame him for trying to be as transparent as possible.

Mamm had left for Naomi's earlier that afternoon, so in addition to making supper for her father and brothers, Ivy had cleaned up the kitchen and prepared a snack for the board members. Two batches of brownies—one with nuts, one without—had baked in the oven while the family ate their evening meal. By the time the meeting was scheduled to start, she had coffee brewing and a pitcher of water at the ready.

She put the two plates of brownies on the coffee table next to a stack of plates and napkins. Seth had brought out extra chairs and set them up in the living room. The boys made themselves scarce, and Ivy would, too, once the meeting started.

She heard a knock at the door and opened it. Cevilla was standing there, Noah behind her. "It's a cold night," Cevilla said as she marched inside. Noah removed his aunt's coat, and he'd started to sling it over his arm when Ivy reached for it.

"I'll take that," she said. She waited for him to remove his coat so she could hang both of them up in the mudroom.

Daed entered the living room. "Hi, Cevilla. Glad you could join us tonight. Although I'm a little surprised you wanted to come."

"Why? Because I don't have any *kinner* or *grosskinner* attending the school?" She lifted her chin. "I have a viable say in this community's future, Freemont. And these *kinner* are the future. It's about time I participated in some decisions around here."

"Indeed."

Ivy met Noah's smiling gaze. Emmanuel would have never allowed Cevilla to be a part of the school board, and she was glad her father was fine with it. She'd suspected *Daed* had always been a bit amused by her outspokenness, and she was always respectful, which went a long way with him. While Ivy was cleaning the kitchen earlier he'd also said he didn't have the heart or gumption to tell her she couldn't appoint herself to the board or come to the meeting. "Hopefully the other fellas won't have a problem with it either."

Cevilla sat down in the rocking chair near the fireplace as the other members of the school board—Asa Bontrager, Timothy Glick, Thomas Bontrager, and Leanna's brother, Jalon—arrived one after the other. A couple of the men raised their brow at the sight of Cevilla, but if any one of them didn't want her there, he didn't speak up.

Ivy hurried off to hang up the coats and then returned. "Would anyone like some *kaffee*?" she asked.

Jalon, Timothy, and Asa nodded. "Tea, dear," Cevilla said.

"I'll make it."

Ivy turned to see Noah standing by the staircase. She hadn't noticed until now that he'd hung back from the rest of the group. "I can do it," she said, walking over to him. "*Geh* ahead and sit down."

"I wasn't planning on joining the meeting." He reached inside the pocket of his coat and showed her the packet of letters. "I thought we could read these while they're busy talking about school board stuff."

Ivy smiled. "*Gut* idea."

Noah followed her into the kitchen, and she poured the coffee while he made his aunt her tea. When they carried the mugs into the living room, Ivy noticed the fireplace in the corner filled the room with warmth, and Cevilla sat in the rocker like a queen keeping court. She opened her bag and pulled out one of her endless crochet projects—this one looking like, of all things, a doily. Ivy shook her head. She'd had her fill of doilies.

The men looked at Cevilla a bit oddly as she whipped out her crochet hook. Then she pointed at *Daed*. "I suppose we should start this meeting sooner than later, don't you think?"

Daed cleared his throat, something he usually did before speaking in front of a group of people, even one as small as this. "I appreciate all of you coming over on such short notice. I've been meaning to talk about the state of our school for a while now, so I'm glad we were all able to meet tonight."

Noah bent down and whispered in Ivy's ear. "I think this is our cue to leave."

She nodded, and they slipped away to the kitchen. "Do you want anything?" she asked him.

"Maybe a brownie later, if there's any left. They smell really *gut*." He sat down at the table and pulled out the letters while Ivy poured herself a glass of water.

"Do you want to start?" he said, holding out a letter.

"You can."

He nodded, opened the letter, and began to read.

Dear Bunny,

Your letters arrived a few minutes ago.

"Stop," Ivy said, taking the letter from Noah. She read over the sentence. "So Bunny did write him back?"

Noah gently took the letter from her. "Let me finish reading and we can find out."

I'm shipping out in two hours, so I don't have long to write, but I wanted to let you know I got them. I can't wait to read them on the trip. I can't believe they were lost all this time. I gave the cookies you sent to one of the guys who works in the mess hall since I can't take them with me. I'm not happy about that. But I'm happy you wrote me back.

I'll write a longer letter when I'm settled. I miss you so much, Bunny, and I'll be thinking about you every minute I'm gone.

CJ

"Oh, *gut*." Ivy blew out a relieved breath. "I'm glad she didn't ignore his letters after all."

Noah smiled. "Leave it to you to have tender feelings for a couple you don't know who existed a long time ago."

Ivy straightened in her chair, her toes barely touching the floor. "Is there something wrong with that?"

"Absolutely not." He glanced at the letter again. "I'm glad he got a response too. It wouldn't have been fair to leave the poor guy hanging." He paused. "I know what it's like to be . . . disregarded," he said, his voice low and almost inaudible.

That got Ivy's attention. "You do?"

Noah ignored her and picked up the next letter.

Dear Bunny,

Where do I start? I guess at the beginning, right after I finished my last letter to you almost a week ago. I was able to send the letter off in the last mail, but things were a whirlwind after that. I got really sick on the ride over here. I don't know if it was the flu or a real bad case of airsickness, but by the time we got to camp I was dehydrated. So I spent the first three days as an official soldier in the infirmary. I was too weak to write, even. I thought about dictating a letter to one of the nurses, but that seemed too impersonal. I want to say some things for your eyes only. But I'll get to that in a minute.

As soon as I could stand on my own two feet, they sent me to the front lines. That's where I am right now, but that's all I can tell you. I didn't want to tell you even that much, but I know what it's like to wonder. We always wondered where my brother Fred was, and he would never say in any of his letters. That always made us more worried, especially Ma. But I don't want you to worry. I'm fine. I'm going to be fine. God's with me here. I can feel him. Not everyone here believes in God, and

I don't understand that. How do they deal with the fear? The loneliness?

Enough about that. I probably told you too much. Funny how I'm so quiet in person but I can't stop once I start writing. Guess that's why I did okay on my English papers in school. I didn't do great on much else, but I can claim that, at least.

And now—to us. I hope you're smiling right now, because I am. Ah, Bunny. I was so scared I would never hear from you again—especially when I didn't hear from you for so long. They said it was a weird fluke that your letters got lost in the mail. Something about how you make your number sevens. They thought they were ones. I think they weren't paying attention. But that's water under the bridge. I read all your letters, dozens of times. They were what got me through the sickness, and even now I'll pull them out while I'm here and read over them. Because a part of me still can't believe what you wrote. I'm still pinching myself. Because it seems like a dream that you love me too.

Of course, that didn't keep you from taking me to task, asking me why I didn't tell you how I felt sooner, why I kept it to myself. I could ask you the same thing, you know. You could have told me. Then again, it's scary, isn't it? It's hard risking your heart, so I understand why you didn't say anything. I just wish we'd both had a little more courage, because I wouldn't have just given you a hug after prom last year. I would have taken you in my arms and kissed you until the sun came up. That's the first thing I plan to do when I get back home—take you out to Baxter Ridge and hold you close until sunrise. We can plan our future then. When we'll get married. How many kids we'll have. How many grandkids we'll have.

I know, I'm getting ahead of myself. I can't help it.

Thoughts of you and me and the future are swirling around in my brain, and it makes me want to finish up what I'm doing here and get back home. I miss you more than ever, Bunny. I can't wait for your next letter.

Love,

CJ

"He's fallen hard," Noah said, picking up the next envelope.

"I think it's pretty romantic."

"Maybe." He unfolded the letter. "Depends on how Bunny feels."

Ivy took the letter from him. "We should take turns reading them."

Dear Bunny,

I noticed you made sure the number seven was clear on your envelope this time. There wasn't any problem getting it, or the letter before that. And to answer your question—you can write me as much as you want. I'm going to write you every chance I get.

I got another package from Richard. Ma says he's been sending them to all the guys in the neighborhood who are in the service. She thinks it's because he feels guilty since he can't serve because of his bad eyesight. I say he shouldn't feel guilty. He should feel thankful he's not here. But that's all I'm going to say about that.

I liked the poem you wrote me. It was very, very nice. I know you said it was your first poem and that you don't think you'll write one again, but I'll read anything you want to send me. Your poem is special to me. I keep it in my pocket next to my heart. I know it sounds corny, but it makes me feel closer to you somehow. There are things I want you to know, things that the written word can't do justice. Only things I can say to you. I thought writing my feelings would be enough, but it doesn't compare to the words I have in my mind, that I imagine saying to you when we're together. I promise I'll never keep any secrets from you. I will always tell you what's on my heart. And right now, that's my love for you.

Love,

CJ

Ivy sighed. Bunny was a lucky woman to have someone love her as much as CJ did.

"Don't tell me you think the poetry stuff is romantic?" Noah said.

"Of course I do. It's extremely romantic. You have to have a heart of stone not to think so."

He smirked. "I don't think so. But the guy's at war and his sweetheart is thousands of miles away, so I'm not going to judge him. I'll read the next one."

Dear Bunny,

A quick note to tell you I hope you had a good time when you went to Iowa last week. I didn't realize you had family there. I guess the subject never came up between us.

It might be a little longer wait between this letter and my next one. I can't say much more, but just know that I'll write to you as soon as I can. Don't say anything to Ma. I don't want her to worry, because there's no reason to. I'll be fine.

Love,

CJ

Noah was quiet. The reality of the war now intruded on the romance. Ivy looked concerned too. She read the next letter.

Dear Bunny,

You sure got a way with words when you're angry, even in a letter. I guess I deserved it. I wasn't trying to be cagey, but I couldn't give you any more details than I did in my last letter, and like I said, I didn't want you to worry if you didn't hear from me when you usually do. We're back at base camp now. I got a chance to take a lukewarm sponge bath before lights out. I miss hot showers. I also miss Ma's cooking, especially her chicken and dumplings. I'm going to ask her for a huge plate of that when I get home.

I gotta admit I was surprised to find out you have Amish relatives. I didn't realize that's who you were visiting in Iowa. I don't know much about the Amish. They dress a little strange, don't they? And they don't drive cars, but they use a horse and buggy? I don't understand why anyone would do that when it's easier to drive a car. Seems old-fashioned to me. Are they different in other ways?

You know something else I miss? Your blueberry cobbler. I remember when you had me try it because you wanted to enter it in the county fair cobbler contest two years ago. You mixed up the salt and the sugar, and the bottom of the pan was burned almost through. But I ate it anyway, because I could see the light in your blue eyes when you served me a piece. You were proud of that cobbler. Then embarrassed about your mistakes. Remember what I said? I told you mistakes happen, and that I'd be happy to be your guinea pig if you ever wanted to make another one. The offer still stands, by the way. You can make me a blueberry or peach or cherry cobbler anytime. In fact, I'll eat whatever you put in front of me. That's a promise.

I better end this letter. It was lights out thirty minutes ago and I'm writing this under the covers with a flashlight. Hopefully you can read it.

Can't wait to hear from you.

All my love, darling,

CJ

Noah put his hand over Ivy's, startling her. "What is it?"

"Ivy . . . I know who Bunny is."

Chapter 12

"Who?" Ivy asked, eagerly awaiting Noah's answer.

Noah glanced at the letter again. "Cevilla's father moved them to Pennsylvania."

"To another Amish district."

He shook his head. "No. To Arnold City, where he met Glenda. She never became Amish. Cevilla and her father left the church."

Ivy was shocked. Cevilla had never said she'd left the Amish. Ivy had always assumed Glenda joined the Amish through marriage. Although now that she thought about it, the contents of all those boxes gave no indication of that.

"*Mei grossvatter* never talked about what happened. Neither did Cevilla. I only learned about it a few years ago from *mei grossmammi* before she died. *Mei* grandparents were a lot older than Cevilla. Sixteen years' difference, I think. *Mei grossvatter* stayed in Iowa and married *mei grossmammi*, but Cevilla and *mei* great-*grossvatter* left."

Ivy tried to wrap her mind around what Noah was saying. "That sounds confusing."

"It is. I knew at some point Cevilla had returned to Iowa and rejoined our community. *Grossmammi* didn't say when, and I didn't ask. It's as if the years she was gone never happened, and I wasn't about to dig up the past when no one wanted to talk about it. Even when Cevilla told me about Glenda's boxes, she didn't *geh* into detail. I figured whatever had happened to her in Pennsylvania was her secret to keep."

"But these letters are addressed to Bunny Brown," Ivy pointed out.

"Bunny must be her nickname. Like I said, Brown was Glenda's name. Maybe *Aenti* and *mei* great-*grossvatter* changed their name to Brown when they left the Amish."

Ivy looked at the stack of letters. She couldn't believe they belonged to Cevilla, and she hadn't mentioned a word to either of them about it. "Why would she let us read these? They're so personal. And who is CJ?"

"I don't know." He handed Ivy another letter. "Keep reading. Hopefully we'll find out."

Dear Bunny,

Thanks for telling me more about the Amish. I still can't believe you used to be Amish, and that I never knew. One thing I didn't understand was when you said you and your father were shunned. I do understand that they were upset when you left. It's hard to leave family and the people you love. Believe me, I know that as well as anyone. I guess what I can't figure out is why you can go back to the Amish and visit your family but your dad couldn't when he was alive. How can family turn their backs on someone they love? I can't imagine anyone doing anything to me that would make me ignore them for the rest of my life. It doesn't make sense, especially coming from people who are Christians. Maybe you can explain that part to me in your next letter.

I thank God for your letters every day, and that you write to me so often. Even if they're just little notes saying hello, I reread them before my prayers at night. I also replaced the picture in the first letter you wrote with the picture you sent in your last letter. You're so pretty, Bunny. Having you close to my heart makes the distance seem shorter. Hopefully this war will end soon and we can be together and start our future.

Tell your mother I got the cookies she made. I hope she doesn't mind, but I shared them with my buddy Leon. He doesn't hear from back home very much, and the cookies cheered him up a bit.

Love,
CJ

Noah read the next letter.

Dear Bunny,

Now that you explained about how shunning works, I think I understand. Sort of. It's how the Amish discipline those who leave, to convince them to come back. Please don't take offense, but I have a hard time agreeing with that. It seems very harsh and hurtful. So your father was a member of the Amish church, but you're not? That part I did understand—it's like when I became baptized. I had to choose to follow Jesus, and then declare it in front of the church before they dunked me in that old metal water tank Pastor John has had forever.

Was it strange seeing your family again, especially knowing

that they turned their back on your father? I wish I would have been there to help you get through that.

You asked me how things are going here. I don't really want to talk about too many details. I'm fine, and so far the worst thing that's happened to me since that time I was in the hospital was that I twisted my ankle the other day when I stepped into a mudhole. Got real dirty too. I don't think it was just mud in that hole.

My other buddies haven't been so lucky. Leon was wounded in our last fight. I think he'll get to go back home to New York. I'm happy for him. Jealous too. Not of his injury, which is pretty bad. But I can't wait to get home. To see you, hold you in my arms, and kiss you senseless. That's what gets me through, Bunny. Knowing you're there waiting on me.

Lights out is in a few. I got caught the last time I wrote to you after curfew and had to do extra KP duty. I never want to peel another potato.

Love,
CJ

Dear Bunny,

I didn't mean to make you upset in my last letter. I also didn't intend to insult your family. I'm surprised you're not angry with them, though. To be honest, I would be if my family shunned my father or mother. But you're right, I still don't completely understand how that works with the Amish. And I hope you can forgive me for speaking out of turn.

It's nice of you to ask about Leon. He went home yesterday, but not before I told him you're praying for him. He grinned and said to tell you thanks, that no one's ever done that for him before. He's been very resistant with the chaplain here, and we've gotten in a few heated discussions about why he thinks God doesn't exist and why I believe he does. I understand why he thinks like that, though. Especially here. It's hard to understand why God lets things like this war go on. If he loves us, why are we suffering? It even has me questioning sometimes. But then I remember that Bible verse about suffering, about how it hones our faith and belief. I also feel him here, Bunny. Even when I'm terrified and in the middle of fighting, wondering if my next breath is my last, I feel his presence. It's strangely calming, even though the fear is still there. It's hard to explain. I just hope Leon will feel the same thing. I believe he will, if he just opens his heart.

Whew, that ended up being more than I wanted to tell. Don't worry about me here, Bunny. I'm actually a really good soldier. One of the best, the sergeant says. I'm not saying that to brag, just to let you know I'm getting out of here alive, and I'm coming back to you. So pray for me, but don't be afraid. God willing, I'll be home soon.

Love,

CJ

Dear Bunny,

I was surprised to get your letter from Amish country. I didn't realize you were planning to visit there again so soon. Your cousin Maria sounds like a nice girl. She's three years older than you, then? I'm glad to hear you're enjoying staying with her. Are you getting used to being without a car and electricity? The electricity doesn't always work here in base camp, and of course when I'm out in the field, we don't have any. It's pretty amazing at night, especially when it's clear, how many stars you can see. Sometimes there's a lull in the fighting, and I lie back and try to count them. I wonder if you're looking at the same stars back home. I never used to pay much attention in science class when our teachers talked about astronomy. I thought it was boring. But now I think I'd like to learn more about it. Maybe go to college when I get back home. Local college, of course. I'm not leaving Pennsylvania ever again. Folks there say our small town is boring, and I used to think the same thing. Now I know it's the greatest place in the world.

Speaking of the future, I've been thinking about that a lot lately. I know I shouldn't put this in a letter, but if I've learned anything here it's that you can't wait to take a risk. I still regret not telling you how I felt before I left instead of writing it to you. But here I go doing it again. I want to marry you, Bunny. I want us to live in Arnold City and raise a family. And I don't want to wait to do it.

Marry me, darling. Marry me as soon as I get back home. Let's start a new life right away, together.

Love,
CJ

Ivy stopped reading. She always thought Cevilla had been single her whole life. "Did *yer aenti* ever marry?"

"Not that I know of." Noah picked up another letter. "But I'm realizing there's a whole other side to her I never knew about."

Dear Bunny,

I was worried when I didn't hear from you right away. I thought I'd done it again—jumped the gun, wrote what I should have said, didn't wait to tell you to your face. But you made me so happy when you accepted my lackluster proposal. I promise when I get home I'll propose properly. I'll give you the prettiest ring I can find, and I'll make it the most romantic moment of your life. We could invite your Amish family to the wedding, too, if they'll come. I can't imagine why they wouldn't.

I heard from Richard again. It had been a while since he'd written to me. I didn't realize he'd moved to Harrisburg. He said the small-town life wasn't for him. I'm sure he'll be back once he realizes what he's missing. You don't realize what you've got until it's gone. I'm learning that firsthand.

Now on to the hard part of my letter. It's going to be a little while before you'll hear from me again. I can't tell you more than that, but as soon as I can, I'll send you a very long letter. You can keep writing to me, though. I'll get the mail when I'm able to.

I love you, Bunny. Take care of yourself.

Love,

CJ

Dear Bunny,

It's been more than a month since I've been able to write. I thought I would have heard from you during that time. I said you could write to me. Are you upset with me? Did something happen? Richard didn't say anything to me in his last letter about something being wrong back home. Have you gone back to see your Amish relatives recently?

Please write me back. I'm worried about you.

Love,

CJ

Dear Bunny,

I'm in the hospital. Wounded. Four bullet holes, but they didn't hit anything major. Enough for me to come home. Injured my right hand so I'm dictating this to a nurse. Once I'm healed up enough they'll discharge me. I'll get to see you again, Bunny. There's more I want to say, but I'll wait until we're face-to-face.

I need to hear from you, Bunny. Your silence is worrying me. I'm more afraid of that than combat.

Love,

CJ

Dear Bunny,

I'm writing to you from the ship. I got your last letter. I don't understand—you're moving back to Iowa? You're rejoining the Amish? What about us? Were all those words of love just lies? Were you saying you loved me because you felt sorry for me because I was at war?

I won't let you leave me that easily. I'll find you in Iowa, if you're gone by the time I get home. You can't run away from me. I won't give up, Bunny. Not until you tell me to my face that it's over.

And if it's over between us . . . I might as well have died in that war.

CJ

Ivy folded the letter and put it in the envelope. It was the last one. She looked at Noah. "I think we both know how this ended."

"*Ya*," he said quietly.

They sat there, not saying anything for a long time. Ivy still had so many questions. Cevilla had been in love. She'd even come close to marrying someone, at least that's how it seemed from the letters. But what had led her to give that up and rejoin the Amish? And what happened to CJ after that? Did he go see her in Iowa? Had she fallen out of love with him?

"Ivy."

She looked up to see her father in the kitchen doorway. She glanced at the clock. Almost an hour had passed since they started reading the letters. She stood, feeling a little guilty that she hadn't checked on their guests in so long. "Do you need something, *Daed*?"

"*Ya.* We'd like to talk to you."

We? She glanced at Noah, who looked just as curious as she felt. "Um, sure. I'll be right there." Her father left and Noah gathered up the letters.

"I'll wait here," he said.

Ivy paused. Why would the school board want to talk to her? She turned to Noah. "Would you mind coming with me?" She wasn't expecting bad news, but for some reason she wanted Noah to be with her.

"Of course not."

They went into the living room, and Ivy sat down on the edge of the couch next to her father. Asa, Jalon, Thomas, Timothy, and, of course, Cevilla, all looked at her. She folded her hands in her lap, aware that Noah had opted to stand near the stairs.

"We've been discussing various issues," her father started. He cleared his throat, and Ivy looked at him. He seemed uncertain, which alarmed her a bit.

"Mainly the fact that the building is bursting at the seams with *kinner.*" Cevilla picked up her crochet.

"*Ya*," *Daed* said, his brow lifting. "That, among other things. Would you like to take over the meeting, Cevilla?"

"Oh, *nee*," she said, sniffing. "I'm just here as an observer. Don't mind me. Just talk among yourselves."

Thomas exchanged a look with Jalon, and Ivy could see a flicker of a smile on Jalon's mouth. With nine children in school and three who would be attending in a couple of years, Thomas's family was part of the population boom. Ivy's brother Judah was also still in school, but next year would be his last. Asa had two children, Timothy two, and Jalon two. Not to mention all the other babies and toddlers born in the community recently. Whatever the school board had discussed and decided, these children would reap the benefit.

Her father nodded. "*Danki*, Cevilla. Now, because we have so many *kinner* in the district these days, our school building is inadequate."

"That was obvious from the Christmas program," Cevilla interjected.

Which was true. The school children had put on a Christmas program a little over a week ago, and not only were the kids packed into the building, but the parents and families had spilled outside. Several people took turns watching the play and waiting on the playground.

"At the rate *familyes* are multiplying, we might need two buildings," Jalon added.

That brought to mind Leanna and Karen. But this time she didn't feel envy. She looked at Noah, who was leaning against the bannister, listening intently.

"We have plenty of money in the community fund," Asa said. As the district's accountant, he oversaw managing that money. "Enough to easily cover another school building and two teacher salaries."

"*New* teacher salaries," Cevilla added.

For an observer, Cevilla was participating quite a bit. But Ivy wasn't focused on that. "Two new teachers?"

"*Ya.*" *Daed* turned to her. "Sarah Lapp will be resigning at the end of the school year."

No further explanation was given, which meant the obvious—Sarah, who had married a man from Holmes County last year, would be starting her family. God willing, another baby would be added to the ever-growing group in Birch Creek. But Ivy was still wondering why her father wanted her to hear this news now. He could have told her after the meeting.

"I still don't think we should use the emergency fund for this," *Daed* said.

"An overcrowded school *is* an emergency." Timothy picked up a brownie, one of the few left on the plates. "The youngest *kinner* are sitting two to a seat as it is."

Daed rubbed the back of his neck. "I know, and I know we have the money. I just wonder if there's another way to fund it."

Timothy nodded. "We know you're an upstanding *mann*, Freemont, with the district's best interests in mind. But I think we should put it to a vote. Should we pull what we need from the fund or not?"

"If I may." Noah stepped away from the stairs and joined the group. "What if you held an auction?"

"Excellent idea." Cevilla set down her crochet.

"You think we can make enough money to expand the building and hire teachers?" Jalon asked. "All from one auction?"

Noah nodded. "If you have enough donations and bidders.

You would probably want to invite neighboring communities, along with the English. They always enjoy attending Amish auctions. It wouldn't hurt to spread the word around a bit."

The men looked at each other and nodded. "We've never had an auction in Birch Creek," *Daed* said.

"Well, we know why," Jalon added. "Auctions bring in outsiders."

No one had to respond to that. They were all aware of their former bishop's negative legacy.

"Then it's settled." Cevilla adjusted her glasses.

"I wouldn't say it's settled." Asa sat back in his chair and crossed one ankle over a knee. "None of us knows the first thing about running an auction."

"Not to worry. Noah will do it. He's a professional auctioneer."

Ivy shot a glance at Noah, who was looking at his aunt in surprise. "I will?"

"Of course. If anyone can make the Birch Creek School Auction happen, you can."

"Cevilla," Ivy said. "Maybe you could discuss this with Noah later."

"It's all right." Noah grinned. "I can help you with it, as long as you hold it in late February or early March. Since it's still cold at that time, you'll have to hold it inside. Would that be possible?"

"We'll make it work," Timothy said. "I'm with everyone else. This is a great idea. A lot of people in this district would donate items."

"You'll need to talk to them and get a list going." Noah sat down on an extra chair.

Ivy listened as they discussed particulars. She found it interesting, but she was still confused as to why she was there. And she couldn't stop wondering about the letters. She had to force herself not to look at Cevilla.

"Now that we have some of the details about our challenge ironed out," *Daed* said, turning to Ivy, "we need to talk about hiring teachers."

A knot of dread formed in her stomach as she realized why her father wanted her there. She was single, and single women were—

"Have you ever thought about becoming at teacher?" Timothy asked her.

Ivy quickly shook her head. "I wasn't the best student in school."

"Oh, don't be bashful, Ivy. You did very well in all your subjects," *Daed* said.

That was true, but she had to study hard to do so. She'd never cared much about school except for being around her friends. She took it seriously, but she was happy when she graduated.

"I think it's worth considering," Jalon said. "We'll have to hire someone from outside the community for sure, but it would be nice to have a Birch Creek resident as one of the teachers."

"Maybe you could help Sarah out until the end of the year," Asa added. "That way you could get *yer* feet wet and get to know the *kinner* better."

"I'm sure Sarah wouldn't mind." Timothy nodded. "We all know she needs the help."

Ivy didn't know what to say. The knot grew larger. Teaching had never crossed her mind. She couldn't even imagine herself doing it. But that wasn't why her stomach was churning. They had asked her for only one reason.

Because she was single.

Daed looked at Ivy. "What do you say?"

She opened her mouth to speak, but no sound came out. She couldn't bring herself to say yes or no. She was too confused to make a rational decision.

"Oh for heaven's sake," Cevilla said. "Let the poor *maedel* think about it for a little while. You're putting her on the spot."

"Sorry." *Daed* glanced down at his lap. Then he met Ivy's eyes again. "Cevilla's right. Give it some thought and prayer. Get back to us in a couple of days. Is that enough time?"

Would she feel any differently in two days? Two weeks? She had no idea. All she could do was nod.

"Meeting adjourned," Cevilla said, getting up from the chair slowly. "Oh, these old bones are creaking. Been sitting in this chair too long."

Noah jumped up to help her while the rest of the men collected their hats and coats. Feeling numb, Ivy collected the empty Styrofoam cups and the brownie plates and took them into the kitchen. She leaned against the sink. What was she supposed to do?

"This took you by surprise, didn't it?" Cevilla said, entering the kitchen.

Ivy turned around and faced her. "*Ya.* I had *nee* idea they were going to ask me to teach."

Cevilla hobbled toward her. "Don't let anyone pressure you into giving an answer. And don't say yes because there's a need. If you don't feel led to teach, then God will provide the right teacher for the position. Always give God a chance to work." She leaned forward and lowered her voice. "Pray about it. Pray hard, Ivy. Don't make a rash decision." She paused. "I assume you and Noah read all the letters?"

How had she'd known that? "*Ya*. He brought them over tonight."

"I suspected he would. Just as I suspect you two have a few questions for me."

More than a few.

"When you come over tomorrow morning—and please come in time for breakfast—we'll talk." Cevilla took a step back. "Now, where did you put *mei* coat? It's past time Noah and I went home."

As he drove home, Noah's mind spun, and not just because the buzzing in his ears hadn't gone away. It had diminished some when he and Ivy were reading the letters, but he wasn't sure if that was because it had really faded or because he was distracted. Not only by Bunny and CJ's story, but also by Ivy. There was something special about reading the love letters while sitting close to her. They were sharing someone's personal story together. And he was tickled by how taken she'd been by CJ's romantic declarations.

He glanced at Cevilla. He couldn't imagine her being called Bunny. What a nickname. The letters hadn't come up while they ate a hurried supper. He'd ask her about it now, but she started dozing as soon as the buggy hit the road. As a light dusting of snow floated down from the night sky, Noah had plenty of time to think about the day's events. The last thing he expected was to handle an auction for Birch Creek, but now that he was committed, he was looking forward to it. He enjoyed working charity auctions the most, and this one was definitely for a good cause.

Better yet, he would see Ivy again.

There wasn't much left to do in the attic, so his time in Birch Creek was winding down. He'd miss this place, and not only Ivy and his aunt. He'd miss the people here. He'd come to know them a little better during this visit. He could see now why Cevilla wanted to live here. He'd always wondered why she'd struck out on her own and moved so far away, other than the fact that she was the most independent woman he knew. But now he realized how much he didn't know about her, and it was because he hadn't taken the time to learn. He enjoyed spending time with his aunt, but he'd always been thinking about work and the future when he visited with her. How he could keep growing his business. How he could continue to be a success.

He glanced at her again. She had been loved deeply, that much he knew now. Not that it came as such a surprise. CJ, whoever he was, had good taste.

"Are we home yet?" Cevilla opened her eyes and looked around the buggy.

"Almost. Did you have a nice nap?"

She yawned. "It was too short." She shifted in the buggy seat. "*Danki* for agreeing to run the auction. I know I put you on the spot, but that's because I know with you in charge, we'll have the best auction in northeast Ohio. Probably in the whole state."

Noah chuckled. "You have a lot of confidence in *mei* abilities."

"Well-earned confidence." She paused. "Ivy's coming over tomorrow morning."

"*Ya.* We'll finish up the work in the attic for you."

"That didn't take long. You two do make a *gut* team."

Noah nodded. They absolutely did.

"But before you tackle that job, I'd like to speak with you both, and I've asked her to come in time for breakfast."

She turned and looked out the buggy window. He had the winter cover in place, which protected them from the snow and cold air. He knew she couldn't see anything in the darkness, but he didn't push her to say more. He hoped she would shed some light on her past tomorrow. But even if she didn't, he vowed to spend more time with her when he returned to Birch Creek. Quality time, when she talked and he listened. Something he should have been doing all along.

Chapter 13

When Ivy arrived at Cevilla's the next morning, the older woman was seated in the kitchen. Breakfast was already prepared and laid out on the table—pancakes and bacon. Ivy removed her coat and scarf and hung them in the mudroom, kicked off her boots, and then sat down across from her friend.

"Noah will be here in a minute," Cevilla said. "He's finishing up the chores outside."

Ivy nodded. Today they would finish their work in the attic. A sense of sadness had come over her as she'd walked to Cevilla's home. She'd miss coming here every day, and not just because of Noah. "Would you mind if I stopped by next week?"

"Why?"

"*Nee* special reason. Just to visit."

Cevilla smiled, her light-blue eyes growing misty. "Of course I wouldn't mind. In fact, I would like that very much."

Noah opened the back door, and cold air blew into the kitchen. Through the mudroom doorway Ivy could see him shake the snow off his hat. It had started gently falling as Ivy walked over. She'd thought about going back to hitch up the buggy, but then she decided to keep going. She was certain Noah would give her a ride home if it was still snowing by the time they finished their work.

After he washed up and sat down, they bowed their heads and said grace. Ivy glanced at Noah, expecting him to plow into the food the way he usually did at mealtime. Instead, he held back and looked at Cevilla, who also hadn't started eating. She took their cue and put her hands in her lap, waiting for Cevilla to speak.

"I know you both have a lot of questions for me." She sighed. "I never intended for you to open that box. I should have done something with it before you started working in the attic."

"It wasn't a part of Glenda's things?" Noah asked, looking surprised.

Cevilla shook her head. "*Nee.* I brought that box with me from Iowa twenty years ago. When I was packing, I was in such a hurry. I threw a bunch of *mei mamm*'s old crochet on top of the letters. The box was damaged during the trip, though. Why I didn't throw the letters out before I moved, I don't know. I left Arbor Grove for a new start, but I guess I couldn't leave that part of me behind. I also couldn't bring myself to get rid of the letters ever since."

"Why did you let us read them, *Aenti*?" Noah leaned forward. "They were so personal."

"It's time for the truth to come out. It's not that huge of a secret, anyway, at least not in Arnold City, Pennsylvania. No one in Iowa knows about CJ, of course." Her eyes took on a faraway look. "Charles Joseph Manchester," she said in a low voice. "He was decorated in the war, you know. Purple Heart, for the injuries he sustained while saving a fellow soldier. The wounds he got that sent him home. He was a *gut mann*, *mei* CJ."

"What happened between you two?" Ivy asked, unable to stop herself.

"God happened," Cevilla responded. "At least that's the simple answer. I guess I should start from the beginning. After *mei mamm* died, *mei vatter* went into a tailspin of grief. Abel—*yer grossvatter*, Noah—was twenty-two at the time and already courting *yer grossmammi*. After his brother's wedding, *Daed* couldn't take living in Arbor Grove anymore. Too many memories. He was a carpenter, and he decided to *geh* to Pennsylvania to ply his trade."

"But he didn't *geh* to Lancaster," Noah said.

"*Nee*. He didn't want to move to a new Amish settlement. Going to Pennsylvania had been a chance decision. He'd found a map of the United States, closed his eyes, and pointed. Yet what seemed like a whim was also orchestrated by God. I truly believe that, because he met Glenda shortly after we moved to Arnold City." She reached for a napkin and wiped her eyes underneath her glasses. "She loved *mei* father, and he loved her. He was in the bann by then, even though one of the deacons from Arbor Grove had traveled across the country to try to convince him to come back. But by that time we were attending Glenda's Protestant church. *Daed* and I had both become English, to the point that he had changed our names to Brown. Not legally, but that's the way he introduced himself to everyone, and it was how the kids knew me at school and in the neighborhood. Glenda told anyone who asked that her new husband simply had the same common last name she'd had.

"CJ lived two houses down from me. He was shy, and I definitely wasn't. We became friends at school and started to spend time together in the neighborhood. It wasn't until we were in high school that I began to like him in a romantic way. But I didn't want to ruin our friendship by telling him how I felt."

Ivy glanced at Noah. She couldn't help herself. But he was still looking at Cevilla, paying rapt attention to her story.

"When he went off to the war, I was terrified I'd lose him. We were so *yung* back then. I was only seventeen, and he'd just turned eighteen." She picked up a glass of water and took a sip. "I was already half in love with him by then, and I wanted to tell him how I felt before he left, but I chickened out. You can imagine how happy I was when I got his letter telling me his feelings. I could barely contain myself. I wrote back to him that same day. And I kept writing to him. I didn't understand why he wasn't getting *mei* letters, and I felt awful when I read the ones telling me he was afraid he'd made a mistake. But he finally received them, late because of *mei* handwriting." She sighed. "Penmanship was never *mei* forte."

"While he was gone, I went to see *familye* in Iowa. *Mei* cousin Maria would still write to me over the years, even though *mei daed* was in the bann. Father was gone at that point, and it was just me and Glenda. She encouraged me to *geh* back to visit, and as soon as I stepped foot into the district, I felt an overwhelming sense of peace, more than I ever had before." Tears welled in her eyes. "The longer I stayed, the more I realized God had brought me back to *mei* faith and *mei* people, including *mei bruder* and his *familye*."

Ivy nodded. She understood how that felt. Birch Creek was home. While she was in Michigan, she'd felt displaced. Once she returned home, everything felt right. She couldn't see herself living anywhere but here.

"I didn't know how to tell CJ I wanted to return to the Amish. I wanted to *geh* back to the faith of *mei* heart, and I knew

I couldn't ask him to become Amish. He wouldn't do it. He was also close to his *familye*. And while I loved him, I couldn't imagine myself married to him unless he was Amish."

"What happened?" Noah asked. She and Noah knew what happened next from CJ's last letter, of course, but Ivy was as caught up in Cevilla's account as he seemed to be.

Cevilla sighed again. "I hurt him. When I got that last letter from him, I knew I had to tell him the truth. I was scared, but I also had courage. I wrote I was going back to Iowa, and why. As soon as he was home, he came to see me. I explained everything—how much I loved him, but that returning to the Amish was something I had to do. He begged me to stay, and I was tempted. But I knew I couldn't ignore God or *mei* heart.

"He was so angry with me. After that, I moved to Iowa and never saw him again. I heard through Glenda that he'd married and had *kinner*, and he'd also become a local judge and was very successful. And I was happy for him. He had moved on with his life, and I had moved on with mine."

Noah sat back in his chair, but he didn't say anything. Ivy looked at Cevilla, seeing her with a newfound respect. She had given up romantic love to follow God's lead, and it had been a difficult decision. "Do you have any regrets?" Ivy asked.

Cevilla paused. "*Mei* only regret is hurting him. I never met a *mann* I loved as much as CJ, but I loved God more than him. The Lord was and is enough for me." She picked up another napkin and dabbed at her eyes, and then she smiled. "And that's *mei* story. I've kept it inside for so long. I have to admit, it feels *gut* to talk about it after so many years."

"I put the letters back in the box last night," Noah said. "I can put it in *yer* room, if you'd like."

"*Danki.* I might . . . I might want to read them again someday."

"I just have one more question." Noah tilted his head as he looked at Cevilla. "Why did he call you Bunny?"

"Oh that." She chuckled. "When we first met in grade school, I had on a dress with a big bunny sewn on the front. I disliked it, but I wore it because Glenda's late mother had made it. I didn't want to hurt her feelings, so I never complained. Like I said, CJ was shy. He also couldn't remember *mei* name, so when he accidentally bumped into me on the playground he said, 'Sorry, uh, Bunny.' I couldn't help but laugh. He was so cute when he said it, and his face turned bright red with embarrassment." Cevilla smiled. "That was his private nickname for me after that." Her smile suddenly faded. She blew out a breath and looked at the table. "Oh dear, the food is cold now."

Noah picked up a pancake, put two slices of bacon in the middle, and then folded it in half. "I don't mind a cold breakfast," he said. Then he took a hearty bite.

"Me neither." Ivy put a pancake on her plate and poured syrup on it. She cut a small piece and took a bite. "It's still a little warm."

Cevilla looked at her, then at Noah, her lips trembling slightly. "*Danki*," she said in the softest tone Ivy had ever heard her use.

After breakfast, Cevilla insisted on cleaning the kitchen as usual. "I know you're eager to finish *yer* work in the attic."

"I wouldn't say eager," Noah said.

"Neither would I," Ivy added, not looking at him.

"I can't tell you how relieved I am that Glenda's things have been sorted through. I know she'd be happy that some of them have gone to *gut* use."

Ivy nodded. She still wasn't sure what to do with the magazines or the rest of the doilies they'd saved, but the thrift store was happy to receive the clothes, Abigail had plans for upcycling the doilies she'd taken, and they had found a lovely clock and a fancy watch.

She and Noah went upstairs and stood in the near-empty attic. Only five unopened boxes left. "We accomplished a lot in a week," Noah said.

"We did." She looked up at him. His expression was friendly, of course. She wondered if Noah Schlabach ever got angry. He seemed to have a nearly perpetual smile on his face. But she could see his eyes were troubled. She faced him. "That was quite a story Cevilla told us."

He nodded. "*Ya.*" He walked over to the bench and sat down. Ivy joined him. "I knew *mei grossvatter* left the Amish. I didn't realize grief had driven him away." He shook his head. "I can't imagine leaving *mei* faith. English people I've worked with have pointed out that *mei* business would be more successful, and *mei* job a lot easier, if I weren't Amish." He met Ivy's gaze. "But ease isn't a reason to abandon what you believe. Life is hard, for everyone. Why make it harder by leaving *yer* faith?"

Ivy didn't have an answer for that. "Do you think he might have returned if he hadn't met Glenda?"

"I don't know. But the story had a happy ending for everyone, even *mei aenti*. I knew she was a strong woman of faith, but until now I didn't realize how much strength she had." He slapped his hands on his knees. "We should finish things up here."

The rest of the morning went quickly and quietly. Both she and Noah were somber as they opened the last of the boxes. They were filled with clothing, mostly, this time a lot of jeans.

Ivy pulled out a pair with wide legs at the bottom. The fabric was also frayed at the hem.

"Bell bottoms," Noah said, opening another box. "They were popular in the seventies."

They also found a few T-shirts, a pair of rainbow suspenders, two long skirts in a calico fabric with white lace at the bottom, and of all things, a framed picture of a dark-haired man wearing a black leather jacket and giving a thumbs-up.

"Hey, that's the Fonz." Noah took the picture from her.

"Who?"

"A seventies television character. Who knew Glenda was a fan of *Happy Days*?" He set the picture on top of the clothing. "The thrift store might want this. It's a small piece of nostalgia."

"How do you remember all these things?"

"Steel trap." He pointed at his head. "I've got more useless information upstairs than I know what to do with. But it comes in handy at times like these."

When they reached the last box, Noah pushed it toward Ivy with the toe of his foot. "You have the honors."

Ivy knelt and ripped open the box, expecting more clothes. Instead, she found a rectangular black velvet box.

"Okay, this is different." Noah hunkered next to her.

She opened it. It held a sparkling necklace, and three round, bright jewels set on a thin gold chain winked at her.

"Let me see that." Noah took the box from her and examined the necklace. He took it out of the box and held it up to the light coming through the window. "Ivy, I think this is real."

"Real diamonds?"

He nodded, carefully placing the necklace back in its nesting place. "What else is in there?"

They pulled out more jewelry boxes. Some were similar to the velvet box. Two of them were wooden jewelry boxes with small drawers, and one was a girl's jewelry box that played a sweet, tinny tune when Ivy opened it. A tiny ballerina twirled to the music.

Noah spread the boxes out and inspected all the jewelry inside. He found necklaces, rings, bracelets, and earrings. Ivy watched, fascinated by all the gold and jewels, more than she'd ever seen before.

"Most of these are costume," he said, closing the girl's jewelry box. "They can be bought in a discount or department store. But these pieces"—he pointed to five small black boxes he had placed into one of the empty cardboard boxes—"I'm almost sure are real. The diamond necklace, a diamond tennis bracelet, and a topaz-and-diamond ring. The two pairs of earrings are definitely gold—I checked the stamp on them." He looked at Ivy and grinned. "If I'm right, we've got a tiny treasure here."

Ivy was a little awed. "I wonder if Glenda's *familye* realizes these were sent with the rest of the stuff."

"They packed up the boxes, so they must. *Mei* guess is they didn't realize some of the jewelry is valuable, just like Cevilla thinks the sapphire watch is a trinket." He closed the lid of the packing box, which held the rest of the jewelry and jewelry boxes Noah was sure weren't worth much. "These can go to the thrift store along with the clothes."

"And the Fonz," Ivy reminded him.

He chuckled. "Can't forget the Fonz."

She glanced at the boxes. "What about the jewelry you think is valuable?"

"I'll take those back with me to Iowa, along with the clocks and watches, and have them appraised. I need to tell Cevilla what we found, though."

"Of course."

He stood up and put his hands on his hips. "I guess that's it, then. The attic project is done."

Ivy looked around at the space, which seemed so much bigger now that it was nearly empty. All she saw was the bench beneath the window, a broom and dustpan in one corner along with her bucket of supplies, and a broken rocker in another. She walked over to the chair. "I wonder if this can be repaired." She looked at Noah. "Aden's *bruder*, Sol, is a carpenter. Maybe he can take a look at it."

"I'll come back up later and take it down." He picked up the box with the treasure. "Let's take these to Cevilla."

They found Cevilla sitting at the kitchen table, her expression pensive. "*Aenti*?" Noah said, going to the table. "We want to show you something." He set the small boxes on the table, and then opened each one.

"They're lovely," Cevilla said, looking up at him.

"They're also real gems and gold. At least, I'm pretty sure they are."

Her brow lifted. "Really? I had *nee* idea Glenda had anything as valuable as this." She tapped her fingers on the table. "I wonder if her *familye* knows about them."

"Let me get them appraised before you tell them anything. There's *nee* need to tell them until we're sure they're valuable."

As Noah closed the boxes, Ivy realized she had no reason to stay. "I guess I should *geh* home."

Noah paused and looked at her. "*Ya*," he said, his voice quiet. "I guess so."

She waited for Cevilla to come up with some excuse to keep her there. But all she said was, "*Danki* for *yer* help, Ivy."

"I'll get *yer* coat and things," Noah said. When he returned with them, he said, "I'll walk you home, too, and carry that bucket of supplies for you."

This time she didn't protest. And it had stopped snowing, so there was no reason not to walk.

The silence between them reminded her of the last time he'd walked her home, when he'd been so quiet because he'd had a headache. She looked up at him. If his head was hurting, he didn't show it. Maybe he had another reason not to be interested in a conversation.

A few moments later he said, "I can't get *mei* mind off CJ."

His admission surprised Ivy. "Why?"

"I understand where he was coming from. Not about the war, obviously." He put his hands in his coat pockets, the bucket's handle hanging from one wrist and gently bumping against his leg with each stride. "I keep thinking about how he must have felt when *mei aenti* broke it off with him."

"It was hard for her too."

"Oh, I know. I'm not saying it wasn't. It had to be hard to choose faith over love." He paused. "Sometimes it's hard to choose love, period."

"You sound like you have some experience with that."

He didn't reply.

She looked up at Noah's profile, surprised to see the muscle jerk in his jaw. "Someone hurt you," she said softly.

He took a few steps, and then blew out a breath. "I guess this is the day for confessions." He paused again. "I was in love once. When I was eighteen. Her name was Rebecca. Looking back on it now, I can't really blame her for dumping me. But at the time it was awful."

"What happened?"

"The short version is that she didn't want to be with someone who didn't have a secure future. Her father had always struggled to keep a job. I'm not going to gossip about him, but let's just say there were valid reasons why he couldn't. It wasn't a secret that her *familye* struggled to make ends meet. When we started dating, she said a few times how lucky I was to be part of a *familye* business. To not have to worry where the next meal came from or take handouts from the community."

Ivy nodded. She'd had firsthand experience with that. When her father's farm had fallen under hard times, meals had been meager and pennies were pinched. That changed once Emmanuel left, but Ivy would never forget those difficult years.

"When I was twenty and told her I was leaving *mei daed*'s business, she was upset. I explained that although it would take me a few years, I could make a *gut* living as an auctioneer. But she didn't believe me. She even said I didn't have enough potential to make it on *mei* own."

Ivy halted. "How could she say that to you?"

He stopped as well, turned, and looked at her, his mouth lifting in a half smile. "Ivy Yoder, are you getting indignant on *mei* behalf?"

"I . . ." She was, so there was no reason to be coy. "She shouldn't have said that."

He shrugged. "At the time she might have been right. No Amish *mann* made his living as an auctioneer, at least no one in our district or any districts nearby. But it was something I wanted to do. Something I had to do." He started walking again.

"Even so, I was willing to give it up for her. I was going to stay with the *familye* business and win her back." He let out a bitter laugh. "Two weeks later I heard she was dating another guy who owned a carpentry shop."

Ivy fell into step beside him. She had to move her shorter legs a little faster to keep up. "I'm so sorry."

"Don't be. She did me a favor. I was so angry about the breakup and her lack of faith in me, I was determined to prove her wrong."

"And you did. You have a successful business."

"One I love. And that I'm *gut* at." He glanced up at the sky before looking at her again. "I'm not sure why I even told you all that." He paused, and the pain on his face disappeared. "I appreciate *yer* reaction, by the way." He put his hand over his heart and grinned. "Gives me all warm fuzzies inside."

"Stop," she said, slapping him on the arm and laughing. She was amazed at how quickly he could return to his normal, happy self.

It wasn't long before they reached the end of her driveway. They stopped, and he faced her. "I've decided to leave tomorrow."

"Oh." She'd known he'd be leaving, but tomorrow seemed too soon.

"I want to get the jewelry to *mei* friend for appraisal. I'll also get the costume jewelry and the last of the clothes to that thrift store in Barton and make sure the rocker gets to Aden's *bruder* before I leave. You said his name is Sol, right?"

"*Ya.* Cevilla knows where he lives."

Noah nodded, his smile dimming. "It's been *gut* working with you, Ivy." He handed her the bucket and then put his hand out to her. "I mean that."

She looked at his hand, and this time she didn't hesitate to slip hers into his. It was warm. Safe, just like she remembered. Just like Noah himself.

He released her hand. "I'll see you in February, when I come back to set up the auction." He started backing away, his eyes still holding hers. "Take care, Ivy Yoder."

"You, too, Noah Schlabach."

"Don't miss me too much!" He grinned, waved, and then turned and walked away.

Snowflakes suddenly appeared, and she crossed her arms and continued to watch him until he disappeared down the road.

I'm missing you right now.

Chapter 14

The day after Noah left, Ivy started making plans for Christmas, which was only a few days away. After lunch, she made a list of gifts for her family—candles for the females, candy for the males, and some small toys for the little ones. She'd make a trip into Barton for the toys, and she could make the candles and candy herself.

She went outside, cut some fresh pine boughs, and brought them into the mudroom. She was trimming off a few dead twigs when Judah walked through the door. It had started to snow again, and snowflakes glinted on his navy-blue knitted cap.

"Found this on the front porch," he said, holding out a brown paper-wrapped gift with a red ribbon around it. "Has *yer* name on it." He handed it to her and dashed outside.

Ivy examined the package. Sure enough, her name was written on the tag. She took it and the pine boughs into the kitchen, where she laid them both on the table. She untied the ribbon on the package and carefully opened the paper. Inside was a new scarf, identical to her old one, except there wasn't a hole in it. Underneath it was a note.

Dear Ivy,

I noticed the hole in your scarf, and I thought you might need a new one. Merry Christmas.

Noah

Ivy grinned as she lifted the scarf to her chin. Then her smile faded. Why hadn't he given this to her himself? When had he dropped it off? It couldn't have been that long ago.

"*Mamm*," she said, calling to the living room as she wrapped the scarf around her neck. "I'm going to Cevilla's for a little while."

"I thought Noah left already."

"He did." Or maybe he hadn't left yet. "I'll be back soon."

She hurried over to Cevilla's and knocked five times on the front door, but before she could go in, Cevilla answered. "Ivy," she said, opening the door wider. "Come in here out of the cold."

She didn't want to tell Cevilla she wasn't that cold, considering she practically ran to the woman's house. Now that she was here, she wasn't sure what to say. "Uh, has Noah left yet?"

"*Ya.*" Cevilla sat down on her favorite chair. "About an hour or so ago." Then a sly grin crossed her face. "Why, may I ask?"

"I, um . . ." Without thinking, she touched the scarf. She wished she could have thanked him for it in person.

"New scarf? Or did you darn the hole?"

"It's new," she said, trying to think of an excuse for being here. She also ignored the crafty twinkle in Cevilla's eye. "I was going to talk to him about the upcoming auction," she said, grimacing. Not only a lie, but a terrible one.

"I'm sorry you missed him, then." Cevilla folded her hands across her slightly rounded middle. "He'll be back, soon enough."

"*Ya.*" She paused. "I'm sorry I bothered you."

"You're never a bother, Ivy. You can come visit me anytime you'd like."

Ivy looked around Cevilla's small house. Not a single sign of Christmas. "What do you usually do for Christmas?"

"When I was younger I used to *geh* back to Iowa. Now I just visit with the families here. I usually have three or four invitations to choose from."

Ivy moved to sit on the couch across from her. "If you're free, would you like to drop by Jalon and Phoebe's *haus* on Second Christmas? Our families are getting together at their place this year."

Cevilla's eyes misted. "I would love to."

Smiling, Ivy glanced around the room again. "This place needs some decorations."

"Indeed it does." She tapped her cane on the floor. "I have a small box of candles somewhere around here."

"We'll put them in the windows. How about we bake some Christmas cookies too?"

"That would be delightful. I'll get the candles." Cevilla started to leave, but then she stopped and looked at Ivy. "You're one special *maedel*, you know that?"

"So are you."

Later that afternoon, after she and Cevilla had decorated her house with candles and pine boughs and made a dozen sugar cookies, Ivy returned home to help her mother with supper. After the family had eaten and the kitchen was cleaned, she went upstairs to her room and pulled out the stationery she kept in her nightstand drawer. It was the same stationery she'd used to write to John. But she wasn't thinking about John anymore. She smiled and started to write.

Dear Noah,

Thank you for the scarf. I'd been meaning to darn that hole, but I kept putting it off. I don't really like to sew very much.

I hope you had a good trip back to Iowa. I went to see Cevilla today and we decorated her house for Christmas. She's also joining our family for Second Christmas. Phoebe will have a houseful this year, so Cevilla will have plenty of people to tell her stories to.

Merry Christmas to you too.

Ivy

She folded the letter. She couldn't send it alone, not after he'd given her such a nice gift. What could she give him in return? Tapping her fingers against her chin, she tried to think of a good option. Then it came to her. Noah hadn't worn gloves while he was visiting Birch Creek. Maybe he'd forgotten to pack them. At any rate, a man could use more than one pair of gloves. She added that to her list of items to get when she went to Barton tomorrow.

She looked at the scarf. Such a thoughtful gift. Then again, she wasn't surprised. Noah, among his many other wonderful qualities, was a thoughtful man.

On Second Christmas, the Chupp, Bontrager, and Yoder families, along with Cevilla, met at Phoebe and Jalon's house. Ivy wore her new scarf as she passed out the gifts she'd bought and made to her family. The women liked the scents of the candles, the men and boys were happy with the candy, and the little ones were thrilled with the toys. Jalon popped popcorn for everyone, Phoebe poured apple cider, and they all waited for *Daed* to read the Christmas story from the book of Luke, their family tradition.

"Cevilla," he said, holding out a well-worn Bible to her. "Would you mind?"

Cevilla took the book from his hands, adjusted her glasses, and looked up at him with misty eyes. "I'd be honored."

The children sat down on the floor at Cevilla's feet while the rest of the adults gathered in the room. As she listened to the story of Christ's birth, Ivy snuggled into her new scarf. Not much had changed in the past two weeks. She was still single with no prospects. She was still surrounded by couples and children and reminders that she was alone. Yet she didn't feel alone. She felt loved. Cevilla hadn't regretted choosing her faith over marriage, even though the decision had been difficult. Ivy wanted to live like that—content in her faith and circumstances even through hard times.

She thought about one other person. Noah. Was he enjoying Christmas as much as she was? She certainly hoped so.

Later in the evening, when everyone was getting ready to go. Ivy and *Mamm* decided to stay behind to help Phoebe with the cleanup. *Mamm* was already in the kitchen washing dishes when Cevilla walked up to Ivy, her coat buttoned up and her black bonnet in place.

"*Danki* again for inviting me over. I had a wonderful time." She touched Ivy on the shoulder. "You'll have to stop by soon and help me eat those delicious cookies we baked."

"I will. Do you want me to drive you home? I can take *yer* buggy back over tomorrow morning."

"*Nee.* I don't mind a brisk evening drive. The moon is out tonight, and I have plenty of light to drive by." She leaned forward. "I've been meaning to ask you. Have you given any more thought to the teaching position?"

Ivy stilled. She hadn't thought about teaching or school since the school board meeting. "*Nee*," she said, shaking her head, and feeling a little guilty she hadn't taken her father's request seriously enough to give it the attention and prayer it deserved. "I haven't."

"Hmm. Maybe you already know what you're going to decide, then." Cevilla patted her arm. "*Gute nacht*, and Merry Christmas."

"Merry Christmas."

After everything was cleaned up, Ivy was ready to go home. "I'll be there in a little while," *Mamm* said. She was rocking Phoebe's one-year-old daughter, Hannah, who was having trouble falling asleep. "She's overtired from all the excitement." *Mamm* touched the little girl's head, which was leaning against her shoulder. "It's nice to hold a little one again."

Ivy left to walk home alone. Cevilla was right. Plenty of moonlight illuminated the sky, enough that she didn't have to use her flashlight. A thin blanket of snow was on the ground, and instead of crossing the field to get to her house as she usually did, she walked along the side of the road. When she arrived home, her father was standing on the front porch. "Waiting up for us?" Ivy asked, climbing the steps.

"Maybe." Her father gave her a slight grin. "Where's *yer mamm*?"

Ivy explained about Hannah, and *Daed* nodded. "I'll *geh* over there in a bit and walk her home."

Ivy threaded her fingers together. "I need to talk to you about something first."

"All right. I'm listening."

"I'm not going to take the teaching job." As soon as she said the words, it was as if a burden had been lifted. "I don't want to be a teacher. I don't think I'd be *gut* at it, either. I know you wanted to hire someone from the district, and I know I'm the only viable candidate . . ." She glanced at the wood porch slats. "I'm sorry to disappoint you."

Her father went to her. "Ivy," he said, tilting up her chin to look at her. "I could never be disappointed in you. It's okay to say *nee* to something you don't feel suited to do. We all understand that." He sighed. "I've been thinking about it too. You didn't look happy at the board meeting when we brought up the subject. I should have nixed it right there. But you're a grown woman, and I didn't want to make that decision for you."

"Danki, Daed."

"Don't worry. We'll find the right teachers. We still have plenty of time for that. And some of the older *maed* in the school have been a big help with the younger ones, so Sarah isn't as overwhelmed as we thought."

"I'm glad to hear that."

"I guess I better head over to the Chupps' before *yer mamm* decides to spend the night there." Then he did something he hadn't done since Ivy was a young girl. He swooped her up in his arms and gave her a tight hug. "I love you, Ivy. Merry Christmas." He set her down and left for the Chupps'.

Tears formed in Ivy's eyes. Her father's understanding and his hug were like a little gift from God, reminding her that she would never be lonely. Not as long as she had her family, her friends . . . and him.

Chapter 15

Noah slipped on the gloves Ivy sent him and smiled. He hadn't expected the gift. He'd noticed a scarf identical to hers for sale at Schrock Grocery, and he'd stopped there before he left Birch Creek to get it for her. After leaving the package on her porch, he wished he had given it to her in person. But he was worried she wouldn't take it from him, or that she would see meaning in the gesture that wasn't there. It was a gift from a friend to a friend. That was all.

Just like these gloves. He couldn't stop smiling as he thought about Ivy purchasing them. Had she tried them on? Imagining these huge gloves on her small hands made him grin wider. They were nice and warm and of good quality.

He took them off, got out pen and paper, and started to write.

Dear Ivy,

Thank you so much for the gloves. They're a perfect fit. My pair was getting worn-out, so these will get a lot of use.

Did you have a nice Christmas? I spent mine with my parents and my older sisters and their husbands and kids. It was nice. My mother made fruitcake, which is a favorite of mine.

No one else in my family likes it. Actually, I don't know anyone who likes it, but I think it's delicious. The thicker and stickier the better.

I'm heading to Des Moines this week to visit my friend and show him Glenda's jewelry. He was on vacation right before Christmas. I'll let you know what he says about it.

Thanks for inviting Cevilla to spend Second Christmas with your family. It means a lot to me.

Noah

He reread the letter before putting it in an envelope. He'd mail it on the way to Ottumwa. He wasn't going there just to visit his friend, though. He'd called for a doctor's appointment as soon as he returned home, and fortunately the doctor had a last-minute cancellation. He had another dizzy spell on the bus ride home from Birch Creek, and the buzzing in his ears had been low, but persistent. He had to find out what was wrong. It was probably an ear infection he couldn't kick or something else a pill and more rest would take care of.

The doctor—a short, thin guy with receding red hair—gave him a thorough examination. "Do your ears feel full?" he asked after he'd looked in both of them with an instrument.

"Yes. The right one more than the other. It's like I've been up in the mountains. And then sometimes it goes away and I feel fine."

"Do you have any trouble hearing?"

He thought about the times he hadn't been able to hear

Cevilla and Ivy. He hadn't had another episode like it, but there were times when sounds around him were muffled, including when others were talking. "Yes," he said, dread forming in the pit of his stomach.

"Any nausea? Anxiety?"

"Just when I'm dizzy. And of course I'm anxious about this." He sounded sharper than he intended, but the doctor's stern expression was alarming him. "It's why I'm here. I want to know what's going on."

The doctor listened to his heart for a minute, and then he put the stethoscope around his neck and asked Noah to take the chair in the corner of the room. The doctor sat down on a stool and started to type notes into a small laptop.

Noah's foot tapped furiously against the floor.

After he finished typing, the doctor looked at him. "The good news, Mr. Schlabach, is your heart sounds perfect."

Noah steeled himself. "And the bad?"

"I'm almost positive you have Meniere's disease."

"What's that?"

"It's an inner ear disorder. We're not sure what causes it—some people think it's a virus, others think it's an autoimmune disease—but you have all the symptoms. Fullness in the ears, some hearing loss, tinnitus—"

"That's the buzzing and humming and ringing, right?"

"Right." The doctor pressed his lips together. "I can send you to a specialist in Des Moines, but I'm sure he'll tell you the same thing."

"All right." Noah nodded, absorbing the information. "What's the cure?"

The doctor paused. "There is no cure."

Noah froze. "What?"

He rolled closer to Noah. "We can only manage the symptoms. I can give you medicine for the dizziness and vertigo. That will help with the nausea. If anxiety becomes a problem, then I can give you something for that too. Are you having any pain?"

"Yes," he said quietly.

"I can help you with that also."

"What about the tinnitus? The fullness in my ears? Can you make it go away?"

He shook his head. "There's nothing I can do about that."

Noah gulped. "Will I lose my hearing?"

The doctor paused. "In all likelihood, yes."

Noah's foot stilled. He could barely grasp what the doctor was saying. Hearing loss? No cure? He'd have to spend the rest of his life on medication so he wouldn't pass out from vertigo? "Who's the specialist in Des Moines?"

"Do you want me to set up an appointment with him—"

"Yes!" Noah stood. "I want a second opinion."

The doctor nodded. "I don't blame you. Stop by the receptionist's desk on the way out and she'll make an appointment for you." He closed his laptop and stood. "I'll have a nurse bring you a prescription for the vertigo." He looked up at Noah. "I wish I had better news for you."

Noah fell back in the chair. This couldn't be happening. He couldn't lose his hearing. He couldn't do his job without it. Everything he'd worked for would come crashing down around him.

He took a deep breath and calmed himself. The doctor could be wrong. He could just have a weird ear infection. The specialist would make the right diagnosis. Until then, Noah wasn't going to panic. He couldn't afford to.

The nurse came in and gave him the prescription, and then he stopped by the receptionist's desk. "Do you have a phone?" she asked.

He nodded, adjusting his hat. "For business purposes only."

"Can I have the ENT call you with your appointment?"

This was definitely related to his business. "Yes. That's fine."

"It will probably take a few days. Holiday time is usually hectic and short-staffed."

He nodded and left, stopping by the pharmacy near Arbor Grove to get his prescription filled. While he was waiting in line to pay, the store started to spin. He took a step back and shook his head. The buzzing increased as his stomach churned.

"Sir?" a woman said behind him. "Are you all right?"

"Yes," he said, grinning at her, even though she was spinning with the rest of his surroundings. Her voice also sounded muffled. "I'm fine."

Then the spinning stopped, just like every other time. It came and left out of the blue, with no warning.

The doctor's words echoed in his mind. *Hearing loss . . . no cure.*

He had to pull it together. He took another breath and said a quick prayer. By the time he got to the register, he still had the buzzing, but at least he didn't feel like throwing up. As soon as he paid for the pills and left the store, he dry-swallowed one of them. Not the smartest thing to do, but he was desperate.

He also refused to accept what the doctor said. He wouldn't lose his hearing or everything he worked for. He wouldn't allow that to happen.

Dear Noah,

I'm glad you liked the gloves. I was worried they wouldn't fit. I tried them on and they were huge, so I guessed they might work for you.

I can't believe you like fruitcake. I could never stand to eat it. My mother made one once, but when my father called it a jawbreaker, she never made another one. My favorite Christmas treat is peppermint candy sticks. I know you can get them year-round, but there's something special about them at Christmastime.

Cevilla and I are planning to go to Noelle's yarn store next week for her grand opening. Who knows, one day I might learn how to crochet. If I do, I'll be sure to make you a few special doilies.

Ivy

Dear Ivy,

Please, no doilies. I don't think I ever want to see another one of those again.

Carl—my friend the jewelry appraiser—said it will take a little time for him to determine the value of the jewelry. He wants to research a few pieces before he gives me his appraisal. He's very thorough like that.

Otherwise, there's not much happening here.

Tell your mother if she ever wants to make fruitcake again, I'll eat it.

Noah

Dear Noah,

I'll tell my mother about the fruitcake. I'm sure she'll be happy to make you one.

I started working at the Schrocks' this week. I really like working there. Aden says business is slower now that it's January and the holiday rush is over, but I'm glad because it gives me a chance to learn everything there is to know about the store—even about all the tools they sell as well as groceries. I like interacting with the customers. It's a better job than packing shipments of books, although I'd never tell the Millers that.

I picked up the cuckoo clock from Leanna. It works beautifully. The tiny bird is so sweet, and the two couples spin around when the clock chimes. I asked Cevilla what she wanted to do with it, and she asked me to hang on to it while she decides. It's on my dresser in my bedroom, although I always thought it should be in a more public place, like the living room, so other people can enjoy it.

It's snowing hard right now. My father said he heard weather forecasters are calling for several feet, our biggest snowfall this winter. Have you had a lot of snow?

Ivy

Dear Ivy,

I'm glad the clock is working now. I couldn't guess what Cevilla might want to do with it. It's nice that you're getting some enjoyment out of it. That's another great thing about antiques and heirlooms—the happiness they bring. Not everyone gets that, and some people see them as junk. But regardless, they're pieces of history, and that clock is a piece of Cevilla's history. I hope she decides to keep it.

We haven't had too much snow this year, which is a surprise. But I did help my nieces and nephews build a snowman last Saturday. Reminded me of the ones I used to make as a kid.

I had to cancel one of my auctions because of unforeseen circumstances. I think this is the longest I've stayed in one place for years. Usually even in the winter I'm traveling around and networking. I admit it's kind of nice spending more time with my family.

Noah

Ivy hurried to the mailbox. It was the last Saturday in January, and since a winter thaw had left plenty of slushy snow on the ground, she had to watch her footing. She opened the mailbox and smiled. There it was. She and Noah had been writing to each other for the past month, and she had come to really anticipate his letters, which were short but interesting. She'd learned a few things about him over that time, and not just that he was a little bit *seltsam* for liking fruitcake. He carried lemon drops in his pocket because they reminded him of his grandfather, who always had the candy on him. He loved antiques because they were a connection to the past, and there was an interesting story behind every object. His favorite part of being an auctioneer was the tension of the bidding and watching something go for more than anticipated.

Ivy had told him about her job at the store, which she still enjoyed, and that Karen and Adam were going to Florida on vacation. She didn't mention anything about Leanna's pregnancy, even though several of the women knew about it now. She told him about skating with Judah and Malachi the other day and how she'd ended up landing on her behind in the middle of the pond. Noah had thought it was funny, and Ivy was a little indignant when she read those words. Then she read his next sentence.

I wish I'd been there to pick you up, dust you off, and skate with you around the pond. Then we could fall down together.

His words had made her laugh. They also made her heart flutter a little. Her heart was fluttering now as she opened his latest letter.

Dear Ivy,

Cevilla wrote and asked when I'm coming back to Birch Creek to get ready for the auction. But an auction this small in scale, even though it probably seems large to all of you, doesn't take much time to set up. Cevilla, of course, asked me why I couldn't come right now. She misses me, I think.

Noah

Ivy smiled and put the letter back in the envelope. Cevilla wasn't the only one who missed him.

She headed back to the house. This was her Saturday off from working at the Schrocks', and she was planning to go with Cevilla into Barton after lunch to visit Noelle's shop. A flyer in the mail the other day had announced the grand opening. When she walked into the kitchen, *Mamm* was there baking pies for tomorrow's service at Joanna and Andrew Beiler's. "Another letter?" she said, lifting a brow.

"*Ya.*" Ivy put it behind her back.

"From Noah?"

Ivy's face heated. "*Ya.*"

Mamm grinned, and then she went back to hand-beating egg whites for her meringue. True to her word, she hadn't said anything about Ivy's love life. But that didn't mean she was keeping her feelings hidden. Ivy went upstairs and opened the top drawer of her bureau, where she kept Noah's letters. She added this letter to the stack and shut the drawer.

She heard a car horn honking in the driveway and went back down to the kitchen. "I'll be back later this evening, *Mamm*. Do you need anything from Noelle's?"

"Not this time. I'll take a trip into town next week and check out her store myself. Have fun with Cevilla."

A short while later the taxi pulled up in front of Noelle's shop. "Wow," Cevilla said as she got out of the car. "This place has changed since the last time we were here."

A hand-painted sign above the store's large picture window said Noelle's Yarn and Notions. Cevilla and Ivy walked inside. The place had been transformed and filled with yarn, fabric, and sewing notions. A table with trays of cookies and a punch bowl were on one side. Several Amish and English women were perusing the goods on the shelves.

"Cevilla, Ivy" Noelle said, smiling as she walked over to them. "I'm so glad to see you again."

"What a lovely store," Cevilla said. "There's so much variety here."

"That's what I was aiming for." She went to the counter, picked up two flyers from a stack by the cash register, and handed them to Ivy and Cevilla. "Here's a list of our upcoming classes."

Ivy scanned the crochet, knitting, and quilting classes.

Then at the bottom of the page she spied something interesting. "You're having an upcycling class?"

Noelle nodded. "I try to be a good steward of the environment. I've heard of so many creative ways to take items people tend to throw away and remake them into something new and useful."

Ivy thought about the boxes in her bedroom, the ones she'd taken from Cevilla's attic. "I've got piles of old doilies and stacks of magazines," Ivy said. "Can you use any of those?"

Noelle's eyes lit up. "Of course. I'll take whatever you have. I hope to have some children's upcycling classes too. The magazines will definitely come in use with them."

"I'll make sure to get them to you."

The bell above the door jingled, and Ivy turned to see an English man walk in. He was broad-shouldered, and even though he wore a thick winter coat, Ivy could tell he was strong. He wore cracked leather gloves and a hat that said Dienner's Furniture.

"Can I help you?" Noelle asked.

"I've got a delivery for you. Some cabinet shelving."

Noelle nodded. "I didn't think you were bringing it until Tuesday."

"We got a head start on our deliveries this week." The man looked around the shop. "Where do you want it?"

"Over here." Noelle walked over to the other side of the store, near the window. "I plan to put our specialty yarns here, and I wanted a nice shelving unit to display them."

The delivery man turned and looked at the door. "I think this is wide enough that we can just bring it through here. Can I keep the door open?"

"Of course."

Ivy was losing interest in their conversation, so she went to a tall bin that said Scrap Yarn. Inside were small balls of yarn in a variety of colors. Each one was sealed in a plastic bag.

"I helped her with those," Cevilla said, using her cane to point at one of the balls.

Ivy turned to tell her that was nice, only to freeze as two men brought the cabinet through the door. *Nee* . . . She looked at the man who had entered the store first. He was stocky and broad-shouldered like the first man, but unlike the first man he was Amish. And she would have recognized him anywhere.

The men brought the cabinet inside and placed it against the wall. Ivy's gaze darted around the store. She saw plenty of places to hide, but her feet wouldn't move.

The Amish man brushed off his hands and turned around. "Does that look all right to you, ma'am?" he asked Noelle.

"Perfect." Noelle was looking at the cabinet, a pleased expression on her face.

Ivy finally could move, but the paths to those hiding places were now blocked by customers. "Excuse me," she whispered, trying to slip past the men. But several new women walked into the store, and she was trapped. She felt someone touch her arm. Her stomach suddenly turned upside down. "Wait," a familiar voice said.

When she turned around, she found herself face-to-face with John King.

Chapter 16

John couldn't believe his eyes. What were the chances of running into Ivy here, of all places? He hadn't paid much attention to the GPS while Craig was driving, and he'd fallen asleep on the last leg of the trip. Which had to be the reason he didn't realize they were anywhere near Birch Creek.

Craig clapped him on the back. "Time for the next delivery."

But John felt frozen in place. It had been over a year since he'd seen Ivy. He'd always thought she was cute, from the moment he first laid eyes on her. But he hadn't remembered her being this attractive. The pretty blue eyes, the lightly freckled skin, the sweet rosy cheeks—

"John, we've got to go."

His heart melted when Ivy looked at him, much the way it had when they were together. How had he forgotten this wonderful feeling? Why had he thrown it away?

"John!" Craig barked.

He turned from Ivy and said, "I'm coming." When he turned back around, Ivy was gone, and an old woman with silver glasses was glaring at him. He scanned the store for Ivy, but he didn't see her anywhere. He couldn't keep Craig waiting any longer.

When John climbed into the cab of the delivery truck, Craig said, "What was all that about? You suddenly lose your hearing or something?"

John shook his head, staring at the yarn shop as Craig drove off. He leaned back in the cab, his thoughts filled with Ivy Yoder.

"Ivy? Are you all right?"

Ivy looked at Cevilla, who had insisted on sitting next to her in the backseat on the cab ride home. She nodded. "I'm fine."

"You don't look fine. You've been looking a little green around the gills ever since those delivery men came into Noelle's."

John. She still couldn't believe she'd seen him again. He looked the same—blond, dark-brown eyes, fair skin, silver glasses. Unlike Noah, he was on the short side—probably about five feet seven or eight—which was still tall to Ivy. And unlike Noah, he was broad and muscular. Her feelings were a jumbled mix right now. Hurt, anger, resentment. But what struck her the most was what she wasn't feeling. No attraction. No longing. Her heart hadn't flipped the way it had when they were together.

She turned to Cevilla. "I'm fine. I was just surprised. The Amish *mann* reminded me of someone I once knew." It wasn't as though Cevilla would ever see John again. Neither would Ivy. Fudging the truth a bit would keep Cevilla from questioning her. John was in the past, and she didn't want to talk about him.

Ivy settled against the seat and smiled to herself. She really was over him. She'd seen him again and felt nothing for him.

"If you say so. Although that doesn't explain . . ." Cevilla turned and faced the front. She didn't speak for a moment. Then she said, "Have you heard from Noah recently?" When Ivy hesitated, she added, "I know you two have been writing to each other."

"You do? How? Did Noah tell you?"

"No, not Noah. I may have overheard a little something *yer* mother said to Phoebe's mother about it. And *nee*, I wasn't eavesdropping. They were talking overly loud."

Ivy sighed. She should have known her mother wouldn't stay quiet about it. Since she couldn't bring up the topic with Ivy, she had to tell someone. But Ivy couldn't get upset with her. "Noah's a friend," Ivy said. "We're just pen pals."

"I see." Cevilla shifted her purse in her lap. "Pen pals only. Got it." She turned and looked at Ivy. "Just remember that the Lord knows when you're lying."

Brother. Bad enough that she was feeling guilty over not telling Cevilla the truth about John, but now Cevilla was driving the stake home by pointing out she wasn't being honest about her relationship with Noah. At least not completely. They were pen pals and they were friends . . . but she wanted more.

"He doesn't know how I feel," she said.

"Why not?"

"Because I haven't—and I won't—tell him. It's not his fault that I . . ."

"You what?"

"That I have feelings for him." There, she said it out loud.

"Why should you deny those? Or keep them a secret from him?"

"Because he doesn't feel the same way." Ivy looked out the car window. "He was very clear that he isn't interested in me romantically."

"Maybe his feelings have changed."

"Over a few letters?" Ivy scoffed. Noah had never written anything romantic to her. Definitely nothing like what CJ had written to Cevilla.

And it wasn't over just a few letters for her. If she was honest with herself, she'd have to admit she'd started falling for Noah when he was in Birch Creek. And giving her the scarf because he'd noticed a tiny hole in the other one was the tipping point for her. She realized that. He was kind, funny, a little quirky, and yes, handsome. How could she not fall for him?

"You underestimate *yerself*," Cevilla said. Did she know something Ivy didn't?

Ivy turned toward Cevilla and then stared at her. The woman was looking at—and talking to—the ceiling of the car. "I know. I know. I promised I wouldn't interfere, Lord. And I'll keep that promise." She turned to Ivy. "All I'm going to say is don't close the door on any possibilities." She made a zipping gesture across her lips.

Since she didn't know how to respond to that, Ivy turned her stare straight ahead at the driver's seat in front of her. Was there really a possibility she and Noah could be more than friends?

The taxi pulled into Cevilla's driveway. "After you drop me off, take her home, please," she told the driver. When he stopped in front of her home, she handed him payment and then turned to Ivy. "Why don't you come over sometime soon? I'll give you some crocheting lessons."

Ivy wasn't all that interested, but since thoughts of Noah were distracting her at the moment, she nodded. "Sure."

"Remember—*nee* closed doors." Cevilla got out of the car.

As Ivy rode home, she thought about Cevilla's caution. Even

if she didn't give up on the notion of something more between her and Noah, she didn't know how to make it happen. Should she do what CJ did and admit her feelings in a letter? That seemed too impersonal—not to mention risky. And she'd already done that with John.

John. She'd fallen for him just as fast as she had for Noah. What if she were making the same mistake? What if she trusted her heart to Noah and he broke it? How could she bounce back from two rejections?

"We're here."

She looked up to see the taxi was parked in front of her house. "Thanks," she said, getting out of the car in a daze. Her emotions were in turmoil, and she wasn't sure what to do. She knew what she wanted—Noah. But she also wanted to protect her heart.

The only way she could do that was to push Noah from both her mind *and* her heart, regardless of what Cevilla said.

Two weeks later Ivy took Cevilla up on her offer to learn how to crochet. She stopped by after work on Tuesday evening, and after a quick bite, the two of them began the lesson in Cevilla's living room. Cevilla hadn't mentioned Noah since the taxi ride on the way home from Barton, and Ivy had focused on keeping thoughts of Noah—and Noah himself—at bay.

She hadn't written to him again, even though she had a letter to answer. Better to cut things off now. He would be back in Birch Creek soon, and she would avoid him as much as possible. It would be fairly simple to do—she had her job and he'd be focused on the auction. Once that was over he would return to Iowa, and her life would go back to normal. That was her plan, and it was a good one.

But as she mentally went through her fantastic strategy for the dozenth time, she fought with the yarn wrapped around her hook. No matter how many times she tried not to think about Noah, he popped into her mind. She missed writing to him. She missed his friendship. She missed the way he would invade her personal space and how he smelled like lemon drops and some scent purely him. When she closed her eyes at night, she envisioned his face and heard his laughter. It had never been that way with John.

She had pined for him.

She ached for Noah.

"I'm hopeless." She tossed the yarn into the basket of yarn and hooks on the floor near Cevilla's chair. "I don't know why I thought I could do this."

"You seem distracted." Cevilla bent over and picked up the discarded yarn. Then she gestured to the coffee table. "Have a cookie."

Ivy got up and took one of the cookies. "Oatmeal raisin."

"Noah's favorite." She tapped her mouth with her fingers. "Silly me. I guess that slipped right out."

Ivy had just given her a look of warning when they heard a knock on the door. "Do you want me to get that?"

"Would you mind, sweetie?"

She set down the cookie before she walked to the door. She opened it . . . and saw Noah. He didn't move, just looked at her with those mesmerizing eyes. Now butterflies were dancing to the rapid beat of her heart, which gave her a spark of hope. Was there something between them after all?

He suddenly grinned. "Hi, Ivy." He reached out and awkwardly patted her shoulder. "Didn't expect to see you here."

That brought her crashing back to reality. Here was the same Noah and the same friendly smile he gave everyone, touching her the same way he would touch a friend. *Or a pet.* She stopped herself from frowning before she turned and looked at Cevilla, who started humming while still working on her crochet. No wonder the woman insisted Ivy come over tonight instead of Wednesday, the day Ivy had suggested. *She's still sneaky.* But clearly her sneakiness was pointless.

Ivy lifted her chin, reminding herself that she wasn't supposed to be affected by Noah. *Friends, remember?* "I didn't know you were coming back to Birch Creek tonight."

"Oh? Cevilla didn't tell you?" He peered around Ivy to look at his aunt. "What a surprise."

"Don't just stand outside," Cevilla said, calling from her chair. "Get in the *haus* before we all freeze."

Ivy moved aside as Noah came in. He shut the door behind him and then set a small suitcase on the floor. He pulled off his gloves—the gloves she'd sent him, Ivy noticed—and tucked them into the pocket of his coat. "I decided to get a head start on the auction," he said, slipping off his coat and boots. He hung the coat on the peg rack by the door, along with his hat.

Ivy took a closer look at him. His hair was longer, and the waves were a little more unruly. The flutter kicked into high gear. Before she knew what she was doing, she put her hands over her heart, only to snatch them away and put them behind her back.

"It's *gut* to see you, Noah." Cevilla set down her crochet and stood.

"Glad to see you too." He crossed the room and kissed Cevilla on the cheek. Then he turned and looked at Ivy again. "Am I interrupting something here?"

"Heavens no." Cevilla reached for her cane. "I was teaching Ivy how to crochet." She leaned over and whispered loudly, "Don't tell her this, but she's not a very *gut* student."

Ivy chuckled, glad for the comic relief. "It's *mei* first lesson. I'll get better."

"I know you will."

"I'm glad both of you are here," Noah said. "I can give you the *gut* news at the same time."

"What news?" both Ivy and Cevilla said simultaneously.

"I finally got the jewelry appraisal from my friend. It's worth . . ." He paused for dramatic effect. "Ten thousand dollars."

Ivy's mouth fell open. Had she heard him correctly? "Ten thousand dollars?"

"*Ya.*" He looked at Cevilla. "Isn't that great news?"

But Cevilla wasn't smiling. Her expression sharp, she said, "Did you contact Glenda's family?"

"*Nee.* I wanted to tell you first."

"Sell the jewelry and send them the money." Cevilla gripped the handle of her cane.

"Of course I can do that," Noah said. "But you should give it some more thought. You're entitled to a portion of the proceeds, if not all, since the jewelry was in your possession."

"I don't want the money. I also don't want to mention this again." She rose from her chair and gave an exaggerated yawn. "Now that's settled, and I'm turning in for the night."

Noah frowned. "Don't do that on *mei* account. I'll get settled in *mei* room while you and Ivy continue with your lesson."

She shook her head. "It's past *mei* bedtime."

"It's only seven thirty."

"Oh. Well, I'm ready to lie down anyway. I feel a touch of a headache coming on. Help *yerself* to cookies and tea, Noah. *Gute nacht*, Ivy." She gave her a quick wink before leaving the room.

"She's still the same, I see." Noah turned to Ivy and smiled again. "Can't say I'm surprised at her decision about the money."

"Me either." It was a staggering amount of money to Ivy, but she hoped that if she was in Cevilla's position, she would have made the same decision. Ivy didn't need to be rich. She had everything she needed here in Birch Creek . . . except one thing.

She looked down at her toes and curled them under, suddenly feeling a bit dejected.

"Are you okay?" He moved two steps toward her, his voice low, concerned, and very attractive.

She lifted her gaze to his. No, she wasn't okay. Now that he was here, it was impossible to ignore how drawn she was to him. "*Ya*," she said brightly. "I'm fine."

"That's a relief." He kept his eyes on her. "I was a little worried when I didn't hear back from you after *mei* last letter."

"Oh." She felt a bit guilty. "I didn't mean to worry you."

"It's all right. I figured if there was a big problem Cevilla would have contacted me. Are you busy at work?"

"A little." The store wasn't that busy, but she wasn't going to admit that. Food. That would be a good distraction. "Are you hungry?"

"Ivy, you know I'm always hungry." He gave her a lopsided grin.

There went the speed of her heartbeat rising another notch. "I can make you a sandwich. Or two."

"Two sounds *gut*." He swept his hand toward the kitchen. "Lead the way. While we're eating, we can discuss auction plans."

She nodded and blew out a breath as she went to the kitchen, aware that Noah was following close behind. At least the mention of food had broken the awkwardness between them. That didn't keep the slight feeling of heat from her cheeks, or the glad feeling she felt because he was back. Her palms felt slightly damp. *Oh Lord . . . I think I'm in trouble here.*

Cevilla watched from the hallway as Noah and Ivy went to the kitchen. She smiled. As soon as she heard from Mary that Ivy and Noah were writing to each other, she knew there was something more than friendship between them. Obviously, Ivy was aware of that, but Cevilla had to wonder if Noah knew his own feelings. He could be quite oblivious when it came to matters of the heart. But Cevilla was sure he wouldn't bother writing letters to a woman if he didn't feel something toward her, even if he couldn't explain it himself.

She retreated to her bedroom. She didn't have a headache, of course, but her excuse was easily believed. Pretending ailments and to want to take sleep was easy for someone of her delicate age.

She was tempted to go back into the kitchen and tell Noah to propose to Ivy already. But she had told the Lord she would stay out of it, and so far, she had. At least for the most part. God was handling the growing relationship between her nephew and Ivy Yoder. "As it should be," she said, sitting down on the edge of her bed.

Cevilla looked at the wooden box Noah had put in her room.

CJ's letters. She hadn't read them when Noah brought the box back to her. Those early memories and the love she had for CJ had been long buried . . . until she saw that box in the attic, and then when Noah and Ivy found the letters. No, she'd uncovered those memories and that love even before that, four years ago when . . .

She wouldn't think about that now. But one letter was missing from the bundle. One she had kept close to her heart for many years.

She reached for the bedside table, only to pull back her hand. Telling Ivy and Noah about her past in Pennsylvania had opened a floodgate of emotions, some she'd thought she'd set aside long ago. But even now she could remember her break up with CJ as if it had happened an hour ago, not decades in the past.

You said you loved me." CJ paced on Glenda's front porch. "You said you wanted to get married."

"I know." A lump formed in Cevilla's throat. "And I do love you."

"Then why are you doing this?"

He was wearing his army uniform. He was on the thin side, and she knew underneath it he still wore bandages over his bullet wounds. And here she was, delivering another wound, straight to his heart. Lord, help me. If this is what you want me to do, give me the strength to do it. "Because . . ." Tears dripped from her eyes. "I have to."

"You have to become Amish? You have to throw away everything we have, our future, for crying out loud, to drive around in a buggy and live off the land?"

"You don't understand—"

"You're right. I don't." He shoved his hand through his short, light-red hair. "I don't understand any of this. All I thought about while I was in Korea was you. Seeing you, kissing you, marrying you. I could even see our children and grandchildren. We'd grow old together, holding hands while sitting in our rocking chairs, reminiscing about the good times and bad." He closed the gap between them. "That's what got me through the war. That's what got me through that hell." He brushed the back of his knuckles over her cheek.

She shivered, her heart swelling with love for him. She could envision his dreams too. In fact, she had. She'd also worried for him, prayed for him, wished for him to come home. And now he was here, and all she had to do was fall into his arms and agree to be his wife. They would have everything they both dreamed of.

But it wouldn't be enough. It wouldn't fill the soul-longing she had, the longing that had started to fill when she was back with the Amish. CJ, as much as she loved him, wasn't enough. Not for her. God was.

She put her hand over his, and then she kissed his palm before letting him go. "I'm sorry," she whispered, her voice thick.

"Bunny—"

"Don't call me that!" She swallowed the boulder-size lump in her throat. "I'm Cevilla now. Bunny no longer exists." Then she turned around and went inside.

It was the last time she saw him.

Cevilla brought her hand to one cheek, feeling the tears. Strange how the pain still felt so real and fresh, even though she knew she'd made the right decision. Just like she'd made the right one by moving to Birch Creek nearly twenty years ago. God had called her here too. She still wasn't sure what the reason was, especially since she could tell right away that Emmanuel Troyer wasn't a man after God's heart, at least not based on how he behaved. But she had kept her peace and her silence over the years. The community was her second family now. She couldn't imagine living anywhere else. And while she'd probably never know why God had put it on her heart to move from Iowa to Ohio, it didn't matter. She trusted his plan.

She had to trust him now, with her nephew. Something was still going on with Noah. He'd been smiling and friendly as usual, but even in the low light of the living room oil lamps, she could tell he was troubled. It was in his eyes, barely a flicker, but she knew him well. She doubted even Ivy could sense it. "I leave it all in *yer* hands, Lord."

And she would save the letter in her nightstand for later. She wasn't ready. Not today.

Chapter 17

Noah couldn't stop looking at Ivy as she wrote down what they needed to do for the auction. It wasn't that she'd changed since the last time he saw her. She hadn't changed at all. And that was the point. He'd always thought she was cute. Now he was so attracted to her he could barely breathe. Being with her again, sitting close to her, had driven that point home. He'd never had trouble being in close physical proximity to people, but right now he was sure she could hear his heart thumping as though it could jump right out of his chest.

And that was a problem. A huge problem.

The ringing in his ears was nearly constant now. Even as he was trying to focus on her, he could barely hear what she was saying. Same with Cevilla. He'd gone to Des Moines last month for his second opinion. Which had been the same as the first one—he had Meniere's disease. Or at least that's what the doctors tried to tell him. He didn't believe it. He'd even done some research himself on the Internet. Yes, it was breaking his vow to use the computer only for work-related purposes, but in his mind this was work-related. He couldn't do his job without his hearing. And while everything he read pointed to Meniere's, that didn't mean he had it. Or that God wouldn't heal his ears. He had to believe that.

Yet in those moments when he doubted, when fear had taken hold of him like a noose around his neck, he'd thought of Ivy. He'd even reread her letters. They didn't contain anything too revealing—definitely not anything romantic. But they made him feel closer to her. And now he was physically close to her. He had to focus on the auction planning as much as he could, but that was difficult when he was with Ivy. There was nothing wrong with his eyesight or his ability to have feelings for her. Yet he couldn't act on his feelings, even though he wanted to more than anything.

"I think that's enough for one night." He feigned a yawn. He wasn't tired, even though the tinnitus kept him from sleeping properly. "I'll get with *yer daed* and the rest of the planning committee within the next few days and finalize the details."

"That sounds *gut*." She leaned her chin on her hand and smiled at him. "*Danki* for doing this. I know the school auction will be a success because of you."

She was giving him too much credit, but he smiled anyway. "Speaking of school, you didn't tell me what you decided to do about the teaching job."

"I turned it down." She explained what she'd told her father, and how he had accepted her decision. "I'm enjoying working in the store too much, and I don't believe God's leading me to be a teacher. It's better for the students if they hire someone who really wants to teach."

And this was one of the many reasons he'd fallen for Ivy Yoder. She was always thinking about others above herself. He knew it was a hard decision for her to make since the committee made it clear they wanted to hire from within the district, but she was right—the students deserved a teacher who wanted to be there.

He held her gaze. He could look into her blue eyes all night. They were clear, like a bright summer sky, drawing him to her. The ringing in his ears diminished a bit as he allowed himself a few seconds to take her in. He also allowed his imagination free rein, because he thought he felt a spark of attraction between them.

Which was enough to bring him back to earth. That, and the sudden sharp pain in his left ear. He'd been experiencing those recently, too, a stark reminder that his future hung in the balance until he could find a way to fix this. He hadn't mentioned his hearing problems to Ivy in any of his letters. He wasn't going to tell her about it now, either. It was his secret—and his burden—to bear.

Cevilla entered the room. "Just getting a drink of water," she said. "Don't mind me."

Noah frowned. His aunt's voice sounded funny, and her eyes were red-rimmed. He glanced at Ivy. From the concerned expression on her face, he could see she had noticed too. "*Aenti*," he said, getting up from the table, "are you all right?"

"Me?" She let out a tinny laugh. "Of course. I'm always all right." She filled a cup with water and took a sip. "Have you two had enough time to catch up?"

There would never be enough time where Ivy was concerned, but Noah nodded. "I should *geh* unpack," he said. He hadn't brought much with him, but it was an excuse to get Ivy to leave. If she didn't, he might end up telling her the truth after all, and he would regret doing that.

"Oh." She looked crestfallen. "I should be going, then."

"There's plenty of time for unpacking," Cevilla said. "*Nee* need to rush off."

"I'm sure Ivy has other things to do." Noah looked at her, making sure his expression was impassive. "Don't you?"

"*Ya.*" Her voice was small as she got up.

Noah gripped the back of his chair. He'd hurt her. It was plain on her face. But he couldn't take the words back, even though he wanted to.

"It was *gut* to see you, Noah," she said, looking up at him. "I'll see myself out."

He remained in place as she left the room, but everything in him was tempted to swoop her up in his arms and apologize. He flinched as he heard the front door shut. Then he felt a swat on his arm.

"Noah Schlabach," Cevilla said. "What did you do that for?"

"Do what?" he said, rubbing the place she'd whacked. "That kind of hurt, by the way."

"I meant it to." She sat down at the table. "You couldn't have made it clearer that you wanted Ivy to leave. The question is why."

"We were finished discussing the auction. There was *nee* other reason for her to stay."

"*Nee* other reason?"

Noah withered under her gaze. "*Nee*," he lied, and then swallowed. "*Nee* other reason."

"How about the fact that you love her?"

He blinked. "How did you—"

"For goodness' sake, you and Ivy are going to put me in an early grave. I've always known you two would fall in love.

Granted, I might have been a little pushy about that in the beginning."

"A little pushy?"

"But God showed me the error of *mei* ways, and he's taken over quite nicely." She frowned. "And there you *geh* mucking up the works."

"I'm not mucking up anything." He sat down across from her. "You don't understand," he mumbled.

"Then explain it to me."

He lifted his head. "I can't."

She closed her eyes for a moment. "You can't imagine how hard it is for me to mind *mei* own business." She opened her eyes. "But a promise is a promise." She rose from her chair. "I just have one thing to say to you."

"What?"

"Don't do something stupid like let Ivy Yoder get away. She's one of a kind." Cevilla sniffed and left the kitchen.

Noah let his head fall into his hands. The ringing was loud, and his head hurt. The kitchen suddenly felt stuffy, and he pushed away from the table and marched outside. The crisp, cold night air slammed into him, but he didn't care. It was easy for Cevilla to tell him not to let Ivy get away. She didn't know the reality of the situation.

But it wasn't those words that had stuck with him. *I've always known you two would fall in love*, she'd said. Love? Did that mean . . . Did Ivy care for him?

Despite the pain in his head, he smiled. Cevilla wouldn't have said that with such certainty if she didn't think it was true. His aunt might be pushy, manipulating, headstrong, and a bit more forthright than was appropriate, but she wasn't dishonest.

This might change things. If Ivy had feelings for him . . .

He started to walk around the backyard. He'd been prepared to keep his feelings for Ivy to himself. And he should still do that. Nothing about his situation had changed. The only change was learning Ivy might have feelings toward him.

He stopped walking. What if he did tell her everything? How he felt, what his diagnosis was, how unsure he was about his future? What if he took a risk and revealed the truth? As an auctioneer and antiques appraiser, he took risks all the time. Going into his profession and walking away from his father's business was a risk that had paid off. Could telling Ivy the truth also pay off? Besides, he believed there was a chance he'd be cured. Doctors didn't know everything. Tomorrow he could wake up with his hearing problems gone.

Tell her. He closed his eyes, hearing the words as plain as if they'd been said out loud in his ear. *Tell her.*

He couldn't ignore those words if he tried.

The next morning Ivy was manning the grocery store by herself for a few hours. Wednesdays were sometimes slow in the morning, with business picking up in the afternoon. Aden often spent those mornings back in the office doing paperwork, but today he and Sadie had an appointment in Barton. "We'll be back by one," Aden had said.

She spent the first hour of the day straightening stock on the shelves and sweeping the floor. She also spent that time trying to forget about last night. She'd been happy and at ease with Noah while they talked about the auction. They were back to the way they were . . . Except, as he sat close to her, she felt something strong she couldn't ignore, especially when she found herself looking into his eyes. Her heart had pounded and danced at the same time. She also wondered how he'd been doing with whatever "unforeseen circumstances" had caused him to cancel one of his auctions. He seemed to have lost a little weight, which concerned her.

And then Cevilla walked in. Ivy could tell there was something off about her. But she had reverted to her usual self in trying to convince Ivy to stay longer. Then Noah had slammed that door shut. He couldn't have been clearer about wanting her to leave.

She leaned her forehead against the shelf of baking ingredients. She was so confused. How could she keep thinking there was something between her and Noah? Was she that naïve? Or worse, that desperate?

Ivy lifted her head. She wasn't desperate. She was inexperienced, though, and that had to be the reason she was so confused.

Trying to put him out of her mind again, she continued to straighten items on the shelves. Half an hour later she heard the bell above the door ring. Finally, a customer. She moved out from behind the display of the last of the woven rugs Abigail had made for the past couple of years. Abigail had decided not to make and sell any more of them since she was busy with her children at home.

"Hi," she said, smoothing her dress as she slipped behind the counter. She looked up as she added, "Can I help you—" She froze, her insides shaking. *Not again*. "John." She could barely get out his name.

He took off his hat and held it in his hands, pressing the brim until she thought he would crease it in half. "Hello, Ivy."

She looked at him for a long moment, waiting for him to explain himself. She also waited for the attraction she'd had for him to appear. *No . . . still nothing.* She truly was over him, and this was more proof. "Why are you here?" she asked in her most business-like tone when he remained silent. "Do you have a delivery nearby?"

He shook his head and pushed the bridge of his glasses. "*Nee* deliveries. I took some time off work." He inhaled a deep breath. "To come see you."

The knot of dread in her stomach tightened. "Why?"

He took a small step toward her. "When I saw you in that yarn shop a couple of weeks ago . . ." He swallowed, hard enough that she could see his Adam's apple move up and down. "I can't get you off *mei* mind, Ivy." He moved closer to her. "I know I made a mistake. A big one. And I want a chance to explain."

But she didn't want to hear his explanation. She had moved on from the past, and now it was slamming her in the face. Her fingers gripped the edge of the counter. "You shouldn't have come."

"I know that too. But I couldn't stay away." His voice lowered, his dark-brown eyes holding the appealing gleam that had attracted her to him in the first place. They also held a touch of desperation. "I have to talk to you, Ivy. I have to tell you how I feel."

Pain shot through her fingers. She glanced down and saw that her knuckles were white. She released her death grip on the counter's edge. "You don't have to explain anything."

"*Nee*, you don't—"

The bell above the door rang again. Ivy turned to see Noah and cringed. Talk about rotten timing. Now these two men—one for whom she'd had feelings in the past and one for whom she had feelings now—were face-to-face.

Noah paused and looked at her, and then at John. A dark cloud passed over his face, one she'd never seen before. "Everything okay, Ivy?" he said, turning to her, his normally cheerful tone sharply edged.

"Everything is fine," John interjected. "We were just talking."

Noah moved closer to him. Too close, and Ivy wondered if he was doing it on purpose. She could never tell with Noah. John took a step back, but he didn't turn away. He kept his gaze squared on Noah, despite their height discrepancy.

Lord . . . What should I do? She didn't want John here, and she didn't like the way Noah was looking at him. He seemed angry. Even jealous? But after he'd practically pushed her out the door last night, she had to be reading that emotion wrong. Noah couldn't be jealous of John, could he?

She sighed. What was it with her and men? Neither Noah nor John was interested in a romantic relationship with her, yet they were both acting as though they were guarding their territory. Instead of surprised or confused, she was now annoyed. "Excuse me," she said, moving around the counter to stand between them. "This is a place of business, and I'm working right now. If either one of you needs help with purchasing groceries, let me know. If not, then you'll need to leave."

Both John and Noah stared at her, obviously shocked. "Ivy," John said, "like I told you, we need to talk."

"I'm not going to talk to you here." She folded her arms, pleased that she was standing her ground. "You can't come in here and expect me to drop everything because you want to have a conversation."

He paused, his eyes still filled with surprise. "All right," he said, moving away from her. "I'll *geh*." He gave Noah one last long look before walking out the door.

When he was gone Ivy leaned back against the counter, relieved. Hopefully she'd convinced him there was nothing to discuss and he'd head back to Michigan as soon as possible.

"Who was that?" Noah asked in a cutting tone.

Ivy looked up at him, her relief short-lived. His thick dark eyebrows were raised over his eyes, which were sparking with anger. "*Nee* one important." She turned from him and walked back behind the counter, needing a barrier between the two of them.

"He seemed to think he was important to you."

At one time he was. She shook her head. Only one man was important to her now, and he was standing in front of her, now looking upset. But John's arrival had her shaken, and she was fighting for her bearings. She rubbed her temple with her fingertip.

"Ivy, I need to talk to you."

Of course you do. She closed her eyes at the irony of them both seeking her out at work, at the same time, for the same reason—to talk. Now she really was getting a headache. She didn't want to talk. "I'm busy." She straightened the cup of pencils near the cash register.

"Ivy, I . . ."

She ignored him and walked over to a shelf of canned goods. She started straightening cans of navy beans, not looking at him. Finally, he left.

Her head drooped as guilt washed over her. He hadn't really done anything to deserve her rudeness. She'd have to apologize the next time she saw him. But that didn't mean she was going to seek him out. And after his curtness last night, she wasn't all that interested in hearing what he had to say.

The more she stewed, the more she decided she was done with men. Period. They played with her emotions, making her fall for them, only to pull back and break her heart. No more. She was finished.

Chapter 18

At the end of her workday, Ivy left Schrock Grocery to walk home, exhausted. Fortunately, she'd had a steady stream of customers all afternoon, which helped keep Noah and John on the back burner of her mind. She wished she could forget about them completely, but they filled her thoughts as she made her way home, something that annoyed her even more than she already was. How could she be done with men when she couldn't stop thinking about these two?

One thing she knew for sure—she wasn't interested in hearing John's side of the story. He'd had his chance to explain his behavior months ago. He could have responded to at least one of her letters, but he never did. Now he showed up out of the blue and expected her to listen to him? He had a lot of nerve.

Then there was Noah, and even though she was still irritated with him, she was also curious to know what he wanted to talk about. Probably about the auction, although she couldn't imagine what was so important that he had to make a special trip to her workplace.

Unless he had something else to tell her . . . something more personal . . .

"Stop it," she said as she walked into her house. She went upstairs and dropped facedown onto her bed, Noah's image still in her head. Then she rolled over on her back and squeezed her eyes shut. *Lord, why am I so hopeless?*

"Ivy?"

Seth's knock on her bedroom door startled her. She sighed. Ivy knew her parents and other brothers were out for the evening having supper with friends. Seth had declined to join them, saying he had some things to do around the house.

"Ivy?" He knocked again, more forcefully this time.

What did he want? Probably some supper if *Mamm* hadn't left him something already prepared. She got up from her bed and opened the door. "*Ya*?" she said, annoyed.

"You have a visitor." Seth frowned. "Some guy. I've never seen him before."

She crossed her arms over her chest. "Blond hair? Glasses?" At Seth's nod, her fingers turned cold. John hadn't gotten the message after all.

"Who is he?" Seth asked.

"Someone I used to know." She ground her teeth and pushed past Seth, muttering, "I'm going to set him straight once and for all."

John stood in the living room, bending his hat back and forth again. When Ivy reached the bottom of the stairs, he started toward her. She held up her hand. "Don't come any closer. I haven't changed *mei* mind. I don't want to talk to you."

He scraped back his hair, almost tugging on it at the ends. "You're not being fair, Ivy."

"Not fair?" Pounding started in her ears. "I don't hear from you in over a year and you have the nerve to say I'm being unfair?"

He backed away, his eyes widening. "Sorry." He clenched his hat. "You're right, of course. I shouldn't have said that. I just wanted a chance to tell you why I didn't write."

"I don't care why." But her anger was already cooling off. She'd never exploded like that before in her life. It didn't feel good. Actually, she felt terrible. And John must be spending a fortune on taxis without a horse and buggy at his disposal. Either that or wearing out a pair of boots.

His eyes pleaded with her. "Please, Ivy. I rode a bus all the way from Michigan to see you."

She paused. As much as she wanted to send him away, her conscience wouldn't let her. "Fine."

A spark of hope flashed in his eyes, and without waiting for her to invite him to sit, he went to the couch and plopped down. He patted the empty spot beside him.

She shook her head and sat down in the chair opposite him.

The spark dimmed but didn't disappear completely. "Who was that tall guy at the store?" John placed his hat beside him.

She crossed her legs and tapped her foot. Since her legs were so short she was batting at air, but she didn't care. "He's a . . . friend."

His eyebrow arched. "What *kind* of friend?"

Her foot moved faster. "You don't have the right to question anything about *mei* friends."

John eyed her for a moment. "You've changed, Ivy. You never used to be this—"

"Confident?" As soon as she said the word, she realized she was. Now that she was absolutely sure she had no residual feelings for John, she had the courage to tell him the truth. Even now with him here, she wondered why she'd found him so attractive in the first place. Yes, he was a decent-looking man, but he'd proven himself not a decent man.

Her foot stilled and she relaxed in the chair. "What did you do with all the letters I sent you? Did you even open them?"

He shifted in his seat a bit. "I . . . See, that's the part I wanted to explain." He ran his palms over his legs. "I was protecting you."

"Protecting me? From what?"

"Shortly after you left, I met someone else."

Her jaw dropped. She hadn't expected that answer. "How shortly?"

"Two days." He at least had the grace to look a bit ashamed. "I wasn't expecting it, Ivy. I promise. But she was the *schwester* of one of *mei* friends, and she had been living in another state. When she came back to Michigan, Judith was different. She wasn't the little *maedel* I'd known all those years ago, and I . . ." He looked down at his lap. "I'm sorry."

Ivy stilled. No, she didn't have romantic feelings for him now. But realizing that he was with someone else while she had poured her heart out to him in her letters . . . while she had expected him to return the same feelings . . . The anger started to burn again. "Does she know you're here?"

He shook his head. "It's not any of her business. We're not engaged anymore."

"Engaged?" Ivy ground out. "You were *engaged*?"

"Now, don't get mad again." He held up his hands. "Not before I give you the rest of the story."

She bit the inside of her cheek. "*Geh* on. Tell me *all* about *yer* fiancée."

"We're not together anymore." He leaned forward. "I didn't come here to talk about her. I want to talk about us."

"There is *nee* us."

"But I want there to be. When I saw you again, I realized how much I missed you. How much I want us to be together. I made a mistake."

"What mistake was that? About me? Or about Judith?"

His mouth opened, but then clamped shut. He averted his gaze and rubbed his pant legs until she thought the fabric would rip open.

"How long were you engaged?" she asked.

His brow shot up. "What?"

"How long were you and Judith engaged?"

"Um . . ." He looked at his lap again. "Up until a month ago."

Almost a year. He had been in love with another woman for almost a year, and now he was telling her he cared about her? Did he even know his own mind, much less his heart?

John got up and kneeled in front of her. "Ivy, I'm so sorry. For everything. Judith isn't the woman for me. You are."

"Why?"

His glasses slipped down his nose a little bit. "What?"

"Why am I the woman for you?"

"Because you're nice." A pause and a frown. "You're pretty. And you're, uh, nice."

"Anything else?"

He smiled, but she could tell it was forced. "Of course there is. And we can talk all about that, and our future." His face relaxed and his smile widened. "*Danki* for giving me a second chance."

She huffed. "I never said I would."

His smile disappeared. "Ivy, come on. I'll make everything up to you. I promise."

"You've made promises to me before."

"I know." He looked up at her. "But this time I mean it."

She stilled. "This time? So you didn't mean what you said before?"

"*Nee*, that's not what I'm saying. Why are you mixing everything up?"

Ivy slapped her hands on the arms of the chair and shoved up to a standing position. He stood and stepped backward, almost stumbling over his feet. He was nowhere near as tall as Noah, but she still had to look up to meet his eyes. "You can't even make up *yer* mind, John. The only reason you're here is because you're on the rebound."

"That's not true. I want you, Ivy. We belong together." A muscle jerked in his cheek. "I'm willing to prove it to you."

She shook her head. "I don't want that."

He moved closer to her. "You did at one time."

Ivy looked at him, and for a split second she remembered how she felt when they were together. He wasn't anything like Noah. John was serious and intense. But he was also kind—except for what he'd done to her in the end. And even in her anger she could see he was acting more out of confusion than anything else. During their time together in Michigan, he'd been attentive and a good listener. John King wasn't a bad man, but when it came to relationships, he didn't seem to understand how much he hurt her or how confused he was. He didn't seem to understand anything.

Despite her sympathy for him, she had to protect herself. "I did feel something for you at one time. But that was in the past. I've moved on."

His eyes narrowed to sharp points. "With *yer* tall, skinny friend?"

Her heart pinched at the irony that he would be jealous of her relationship with Noah. *If he only knew.* She wasn't moving on with Noah, but she was moving on from John. "That's none of *yer* business. You lost the right to make assumptions about *mei* life."

Loud, heavy footsteps sounded on the stairs. "What's going on here?" Seth said, his feet hitting the floor with a thud. He went to John and put himself between him and Ivy. "Who are you and why are you bothering *mei schwester*?"

Seth was taller and a bit broader than John, and the hard look her brother gave him even took Ivy by surprise.

"I'm a friend of Ivy's," John said.

"That's not what it looks like to me." Seth took a step toward him. "You should leave. Now."

"Ivy," John said, ignoring Seth and turning to her. "Please . . ."

For once she was glad Seth was in her corner. "You heard what *mei bruder* said." She crossed her arms again.

He didn't say anything, just gave her a long look. Seth opened the door and a rush of cold air blew inside. John turned and left. She could see a taxi waiting for him in their driveway.

Seth scowled as he shut the door behind him. "Is that the guy from Michigan?"

"How did you know?"

"It's not hard to figure out." He tilted his head and gave her an odd look, the hard expression on his face since he'd come downstairs abating. Then he shrugged. "I had *nee* idea you had such a complicated love life." He started up the stairs. "I like Noah better," he called out as he took the steps two at a time.

Ivy plopped onto the couch, her hands shaking. Despite her confidence, despite standing her ground, despite hoping—no, praying—that John had finally heard her and would give up on trying to win her back, she was drained. She leaned forward, her head falling into her hands.

Another knock sounded on the front door, causing her to jump. Oh no. John was back? She looked at the staircase. Should she get Seth? No. She had to handle this herself. She stood and straightened to her full height. She didn't need her little brother to fight her battles. Determined to send him away fifty times if she had to, she went to the door. As she opened it, she said, "John, there's *nee* point in talking anymore—" She froze when she saw Noah.

His eyes pierced her. "Who's John?"

Noah had fought with himself about going to Ivy's, but after seeing her upset with him in the store that morning, after seeing her with that guy who had clearly upset her too—he needed to find out what was going on. Cevilla had gone to bed right after they'd had an early supper, so he didn't have to explain himself to her. Which was good. He wasn't in the mood for a Cevilla lecture, or an *I told you so.*

But he forgot about all that as he took in Ivy's expression. She was still upset. "What happened?" he asked.

"*Nix.*" She looked away, still holding on to the side of the door.

"Ivy," Noah said, not bothering to wait for an invitation inside. He took her hand and freed it from her grip on the door, and then shut it and led her to the couch. He joined her there as soon as he shucked his boots, hat, and coat. "Now talk to me."

"It's *nix* I can't handle. And it's *mei* problem."

The buzzing in his ears had been at a dull roar during the walk to Ivy's, but now it was so loud he had to concentrate to hear her. "I want to help."

"You can't."

"Then I'll just listen." Which was ironic since he was having trouble hearing. But this wasn't about him. It was about Ivy, and she was clearly distressed.

She let out a deep breath. "The man you saw talking to me at the store this morning was just here. His name is John. Last year I visited *mei* cousin in Michigan. She was pregnant and on bedrest, and I went to help her. I met him there, and . . ." She glanced away. "I liked him. A lot. He liked me back, or so I thought."

Noah listened as she explained how this John had promised to write but never did, and how she had finally given up on him. "That was when you came here to help Cevilla . . . and I started having feelings for someone else."

He met her gaze, and something stirred within him. She wasn't coming right out and saying it, but her meaning was clear. That someone else was him.

A stabbing pain shot through his head, and it took everything he could not to let Ivy see how it affected him. He couldn't even bask in the joy of knowing she cared about him. His plans to tell her his feelings disintegrated as the pain increased. He'd have to take one of his pills when he went back to Cevilla's. The fact that he was dependent on medicine drove the point home. How could he tell her how much he cared about her when he was so ill?

"I don't know what to do," she said. "He said he was sorry, but that doesn't make up for what he did."

He looked at her, not really comprehending what she'd just said. Instead, he was focused on what she wasn't saying. She'd practically admitted that she had some feelings for him, which made Cevilla right, as usual. But she'd also cared for someone else in the past, and that person was back in her life. The fact that she was distraught showed she wasn't completely over him. At least he thought so. It was hard to think straight with his head pounding like a jackhammer.

"Maybe you should give him another chance," he blurted. Wait. What was he saying?

"What?"

Another stabbing pain hit him, this one directly in his ear. If she cared for John at one time, then she could care for him again. And she deserved to have someone to care for her. Someone who didn't have an incurable disease. "He said he was sorry."

"He hurt me, Noah. Didn't you hear anything I said?"

"*Ya.* I heard you." He tried to smile, but he managed only a half one. It was killing him to say these things to her, but he was doing the right thing. Knowing that strengthened his resolve. "He made a mistake, but maybe you should give him a break."

"You're telling me you want me to get back together with him?"

Noah nodded. He had to get out of here. He had to *geh* back to Cevilla's and down one of his pain pills. Possibly two, although that would knock him out for the night. Not that it mattered. Anything to get rid of the misery. "That's . . ." He gulped down a cry of pain. "That's exactly what I'm saying."

She stared at him for a long moment, her beautiful face twisting in confusion. "And is that how you really feel?"

No, it wasn't how he felt. He felt like dying inside. Not just in his head, but in his heart. But now was the time to cut Ivy loose, for her own good. "*Ya.* It's how I feel."

Ivy stiffened. She got up from the couch. "Then," she said, her hands clasped tightly together in front of her, "we have *nix* left to talk about."

He stood, ready to bolt out the door. The room was starting to spin. Nee, *God. Not now.* "Guess not."

"Good-bye, Noah." She turned and went up the stairs.

He jammed his feet into his boots and threw on his coat and hat, realizing his coat was half off his body only after he let himself out and shut the door. He rushed down the porch steps and into the darkness. He fumbled inside the pocket of his pants and reached for his vertigo medicine. Thank God he'd at least brought that with him. After the episode in the pharmacy he was never without it. He dry-swallowed one of the pills, and then he managed to make his way down the street before he leaned against a tree and shut his eyes. He didn't know how long he stood there waiting for the medicine to take effect, praying that he would remain upright. Finally, it did, and the world settled into stillness.

He turned around, his shoulders slumping, his head still pounding, his heart thrumming in his chest. He squinted, able to see Ivy's house from here. She must have come back downstairs since the lights in the living room were now off. Everything felt final now. Her good-bye wasn't just for this evening. It was forever. And he had only himself to blame.

For the next few days, Ivy's mind and heart were in a haze. She couldn't believe Noah had not only rejected her feelings but pushed her toward John. When she admitted to him that her feelings had changed after they met, she wasn't sure how he was going to react. The last thing she thought was that he would want her to get back together with John. She couldn't figure out which hurt more—his rejection or that he felt so little for her that he'd want her to be with another man.

Speaking of John, at least she didn't have to deal with him. She hadn't seen him since he left her house Wednesday night. She also hadn't seen Noah. And by the time the weekend rolled around, her shock had turned to anger. He didn't want her? Fine. He didn't deserve her anyway. She got over John. She would get over Noah.

Yet telling herself that didn't soothe the pain in her heart.

The night before the auction, when everyone was setting up the chairs and the stage and bringing in items to be auctioned, she couldn't avoid seeing him. Noah had secured a large meeting hall in Barton, and he had advertised the auction well, so a good turnout was expected. As she saw him talking to her brother Seth, Asa Bontrager, and Andrew Beiler, she tried not to stare at him. But she couldn't help it. She couldn't turn off the feelings she had for him, no matter how hard she tried.

The turnout was even better than expected. Noah ran the auction with ease, and Ivy stayed busy helping with the donut and cider stand Phoebe was manning. Fortunately, her mother hadn't made any of the donuts. It wasn't long before they sold out.

As the evening wore on, Ivy wandered the floor and visited with friends and neighbors, English and Amish alike. After years of being so isolated under Emmanuel Troyer's overseeing of the community as bishop, it was nice to feel free to be friendly with everyone, even making new friends. Birch Creek was an open community now, in that respect. Everyone was buzzing about the items that had been auctioned off—quilts, hauls of firewood, furniture, appliances, even services like Andrew Beiler's farrier service and Sol Troyer's carpentry skills. Each item had brought a good price, and while Ivy didn't know the total collected so far, she sensed the auction had been a success.

But although she was trying to enjoy herself, she was aching inside. Noah's resonant auction cadence, his friendly bantering with the crowd, his jokes—some clever, some corny—were a continual reminder of his presence. He was so close, yet he couldn't be further away.

"The last item is up for bids," Noah said.

Good, the auction was almost over, apparently wrapping up with the item she most wanted to see bring a good price. She went to the opposite side of the room so she could help with the cleanup, but she couldn't stop herself from turning around and watching Noah instead. It might be the last time she ever saw him.

"But first I want to thank everyone for contributing to the success of tonight's auction. It's for a good cause, and the children and families of Birch Creek appreciate your support." He took a piece of paper from Timothy Glick, who was assisting him. "The last item is . . ." He peered at the paper and frowned. He blinked again, and then brought the paper closer to his face.

"Hi, Ivy."

She blanched at the familiar voice. Could the night get any worse? She turned and looked at John. "I thought you went back to Michigan."

"I started to, but I decided to stay." His expression was intense. "I don't give up that easily."

For crying out loud, he was hopeless. Ivy decided to ignore him and turned back to the stage.

"The last item is a cuckoo clock." Noah went to the clock and looked at it for a minute. "The donor has remained anonymous."

Ivy smiled. This was her and Cevilla's contribution to the auction, which Ivy had thought of just before coming tonight. She'd given it to Timothy to put with the other items as soon as Cevilla had approved of the idea. Ivy really liked the clock, but it would serve a greater purpose in the auction.

Noah looked around the room until their eyes met. His brow was furrowed as he held her gaze. She looked away. She didn't owe him any explanations.

The sound of Cevilla's cane thumping on the cement floor made Ivy turn around. "Are you sure about this?" the older woman asked. "I can have Noah stop the bidding. I know you're partial to that clock."

"I'm sure." She took Cevilla's hand and gave it a squeeze. "It's beautiful, and I know it will find a *gut* home."

Cevilla nodded and then peered around Ivy at John. "Who are you?" she said, pointing the end of her cane at him.

"Opening bid is fifty dollars." Noah started his auctioneer chant.

"I'm a *gut* friend of Ivy's." He held out his hand. "John King."

"Humph." She looked at his hand before accepting it. "She's never mentioned you."

"One hundred!" An English man Ivy didn't know matched the bid.

"One hundred fifty!" John shouted.

Ivy gaped at him. "Why did you do that?"

"You like the clock," he said, grinning as if he'd solved the quest for world peace. "I'm going to make sure you get it."

"John, *nee*." This couldn't be happening.

"You need to mind *yer* own business, *yung mann*," Cevilla added.

"Two fifty," the English man said.

"Three hundred," John yelled.

"I have half a mind to knock some sense into him," Cevilla mumbled, shaking her cane.

The other bidder shook his head.

Ivy was furious. She wasn't going to be in John's debt. "Four hundred!" she blurted.

"What?" Noah said, stopping his cadence. He looked at Ivy and rubbed his forehead. "Four hundred?"

The color drained from her face. Where was she going to get four hundred dollars? She hadn't earned that much working for the Schrocks. "That's what I said."

He looked at the cuckoo clock, then at her again. "That bid is invalid."

The crowd started to murmur.

"Why?" Now Noah wasn't going to let her spend her own money?

"Because . . ." Noah suddenly took a step back, his face turning sickly pale. "Because . . ."

"Something's wrong." Cevilla started toward the stage, moving faster than Ivy had ever seen her do.

Ivy watched in horror as Noah collapsed onto the floor of the stage.

Chapter 19

Noah opened his eyes to see Timothy Glick standing over him. One minute he'd been highly aggravated with John, who was clearly trying to use the auction for his own gain—to get Ivy back. Noah could run an auction in his sleep, so he realized right away what was going on when John started bidding. He wasn't going to let Ivy spend four hundred dollars because John was being manipulative. Never mind that he was the one pushing the two of them together. It didn't matter, because all he could see when he looked at the man was red.

The next minute the room had spun like never before. Then nothing, until now.

He looked up at Timothy, who was mouthing something, but Noah couldn't hear him. He couldn't hear anything but the roaring in his ears. He fumbled to his feet and saw Ivy looking at him, her face drained of color. Cevilla stood at the edge of the stage, looking the same. The roaring continued, but he managed to grab the mic. How he did it with the mic moving around in his vision he had no idea. "Sorry, folks," he said, trying to laugh off his fall. He took his gavel and slammed it down on the table. "The clock is sold to Ivy Yoder for one hundred dollars."

"She bid four hundred," someone from the crowd called out.

Noah's stomach started rolling like a tumbleweed across the desert. He turned to Timothy. "Could you take over for a minute?" he said, trying to keep the man in focus.

"*Ya*. You okay?"

"Must have been something I ate," Noah said. "I'll be back."

He managed to get down from the stage and start for the back door of the meeting hall, but then John King stepped in front of him.

"Don't think I don't know what you did back there," John said.

Anger punched through the vertigo. "And don't think I don't know what you were doing. You can't buy Ivy. She won't allow it."

"You seem to know her pretty well," John said, moving closer to him.

Noah felt his stomach lurch. "I don't have time for this." He shoved past John and hurried outside—and promptly threw up in the grass before hitting the ground again. This time he didn't pass out, but he couldn't move. The spinning, the roaring . . . It was too much.

He felt a soft hand on his forehead. Small fingers grasping his hand. A soft touch stroking his hair. He opened his eyes, and in the light of a streetlamp he could see Ivy kneeling over him. She was talking, but he couldn't hear her. Then his world started spinning again, and he closed his eyes.

"Noah?"

Ivy's sweet voice finally penetrated through the haze and noise. He reached up and touched her cheek. He couldn't help himself. She was so pretty, so kind, so everything he'd ever wanted in a woman—and he hadn't known he even wanted it. He pushed up on his elbows and felt dizzy again. At least it wasn't vertigo. It also brought him to his senses.

"I'm okay." He got to a sitting position.

"*Nee*, you're not." She put the back of her hand against his forehead. "You don't feel like you have a fever, but you must have some kind of flu bug."

"*Ya*," he said. "That's it." When he thought he was stable, he got to his feet. He was still dizzy and the tinnitus felt like it was piercing his eardrums, but he didn't have the tunnel vision. "I've got to get to Cevilla's."

"I'm coming with you."

"*Nee*, I'm . . ." He was wobbly on his feet. "I'm fine."

Ivy took his arm and draped it over her shoulders. If he hadn't been in such bad shape he would have laughed. Their height difference prevented her from giving him any real physical support. But he didn't move his arm. Anything to keep her close, even though he was pushing her away in his heart.

Cevilla came out the door. "Noah," she said, hurrying toward him with surprising speed, considering her age and need for a cane. "What happened to you, *bu*?"

"Stomach bug," he said.

"Stomach bug *mei* aunt Fanny."

Noah wasn't aware she had an Aunt Fanny. His stomach lurched again. Who cared about Aunt Fanny?

"Ivy, take him back to *mei haus*," Cevilla ordered.

"I can *geh* on *mei* own," he said.

"*Nee*," the women said at the same time. "You can't."

He pulled away from Ivy and looked at them both. "I appreciate the worry, but it's just an upset stomach. I'll be fine." He wouldn't be, but they didn't have to know that. "Ivy, let Timothy know I'll settle up with him later. *Aenti*, I'm sure you can find another ride home." He sounded harsh, but he couldn't help it, and he knew anyone in Birch Creek would be happy to take her home. He continued to back away toward where the buggies were parked.

Somehow, he managed to hitch Cevilla's horse and climb into the buggy. He let the mare lead him home, closing his eyes against another bout of vertigo. Milder this time, but enough to raise his anxiety again. He moved to the center of the buggy seat in case he passed out—he didn't want to fall out of the buggy and onto the road. Finally, he made it home, put up the horse, went inside, and collapsed on the couch.

"What in the world is wrong with that *bu*?" Cevilla looked at Ivy.

Ivy clasped her hands together. "I don't know, but I think he's really sick." She stared in the direction he'd left, feeling helpless.

"Ivy," Cevilla said, putting her hand on her shoulder. "*Geh* check on him, please."

"What about you?"

"I'll find a ride home. Noah needs you right now. Not me."

Ivy nodded, hurried to her buggy, and drove as fast as she dared to Cevilla's. The front door was partway open, as if he'd been too weak and out of it to close it. She rushed inside and shut the door behind her. Noah was sprawled on the couch. She went to his side and touched his forehead. It was still cool.

He stirred and opened his eyes. "What are you doing here?" He sounded weak.

"Checking on you."

He faced away. "You don't have to."

"Now look who's being stubborn." She put her hands on her hips. "You're pushing me away, and I don't understand why. You're sick, so why won't you let me help you?"

He moved to sit up. "I'm fine." He slumped against the back of the couch.

Ivy looked at Noah more closely as she slipped off her coat. His eyes, usually so full of life, looked dull and bleary. His skin was pale, and now she knew why he looked thinner when he arrived in Birch Creek a few days ago. "You are not fine."

He got up from the couch, took a couple of steps forward, and started to wobble.

Ivy moved next to him and put his arm around her shoulder again. It was almost laughable. It wasn't as if she could support him if he went down. But she wanted him to know she was there. That she would always be there, right by his side, no matter what. "Noah, *geh* lie back down."

"Or what?" This was the first time she'd ever heard him sound snide. "You'll put me there *yerself*?"

"If that's what it takes. I may be small, but I'm mighty."

He glared down at her, but then his eyes softened. "*Ya*," he said quietly. "You are mighty." He removed his arm from her shoulder and went back to the couch. But he didn't lie down. He sat with his head hanging, his large hands dangling over his knees. "I know what's wrong," he finally said.

She sat down next to him. She wanted to ask him a million questions, but she didn't. She waited for him to speak.

After what seemed like hours, he did. "I have Meniere's disease." He finally looked at her, his gorgeous eyes filled with fear. "Cevilla doesn't know, and I don't want her to. The disease ringing and buzzing in *mei* ears to the point I can't hear. I have vertigo and nausea and headaches . . . and then there's the anxiety on top of all that."

Her hand went to her chest. She'd never heard of Meniere's disease. "You've been to a doctor, then?"

He nodded.

"How long until you're cured?"

He licked his lips, and then leaned back against the couch and closed his eyes. "There's *nee* cure."

She ignored the terror striking her heart. "God can do anything," she said, reaching for his hand.

He pulled away. "*Ya*. He gave me this. He ended *mei* career."

"Noah, this isn't the end—"

"Will you stop?" He moved away from her, his eyes squinting with pain. "You don't think I know what the future holds for me now? Hearing aids that may or may not make a difference, medication that may or may not work . . ." His Adam's apple bobbed. "I could have total hearing loss. How can I conduct auctions if I'm deaf? If I have to worry about whether I'll throw up or pass out in front of a crowd?"

Ivy didn't know what to say. She clenched her hands in her lap. Her failed attempts at comforting him had only made him more upset. How could she stand by his side when she couldn't help him?

But she couldn't—she wouldn't—leave him. "We'll figure this out together. Noah . . . I love you."

He stared at her for a long moment, and then he slowly got up. He hesitated before taking a step. Then another one. When he was across the room he turned and faced her. "I'm leaving, Ivy. First thing in the morning, I'm going back to Iowa."

"I'll come with you." She stood and started toward him, forgetting about how she didn't like to travel, how she'd always wanted to stay in Birch Creek. She would go anywhere he went. She loved him, and she wasn't going to let him go.

He backed away until he was against a wall. "I don't want you to," he said, his voice cracking. Then he opened his eyes fully and pinned her with his intense gaze. "I don't want *you*."

It was as if he had shot an arrow straight through her heart. She stumbled back from the blow. She'd said she loved him, and now he was throwing her away. Deep down she knew he was in pain and afraid, and that's why he was being so cruel, but that didn't alleviate the hurt.

"You're not willing to let me help you?" she said, tears streaming down her cheeks. "You're not willing to fight?"

He didn't say anything for a long moment. His eyes only held hers, his face unreadable except for the slight tremble of his chin. "There's *nix* to fight for." He turned and slowly climbed the stairs.

She waited for him to come back. Long, agonizing minutes. When she realized he wasn't going to, she wiped her eyes, grabbed her coat, and left. There was nothing else she could do.

Noah nearly collapsed when he heard Ivy leave. He leaned his forehead against the doorjamb of his bedroom. He'd had to escape her. The roaring and pain in his ears was deafening, but it was nothing compared to the agony in his heart.

He was losing everything—his hearing, his business . . . his Ivy. But she wasn't his. She never had been.

You're not willing to fight? Her words and her tears struck him as he turned and fell onto his bed. He couldn't fight an incurable disease. He had no idea if God would cure it. He didn't know about anything, other than he would never have Ivy. Even remembering that she told him she loved him didn't change his resolve. It couldn't.

He loved her enough to let her go. Hopefully, one day she would realize that.

John stood outside the house where Noah should be. Having dismissed his taxi, he'd walk back to the bed and breakfast where he was staying. He was sure he'd need the time to clear his head.

Avoiding the woman with the cane, he'd asked a few subtle questions about where Noah could be going after he and Ivy left the auction building. Then he had the driver follow the directions he'd been given to this home.

He'd seen Noah vomit and collapse outside. He had also seen how Ivy reacted. The way she rushed to Noah's side. The initial panic in her voice, the ashen color of her face as she ignored the vomit nearby and knelt next to him. The subsequent tenderness in her tone and touch as she comforted him.

All that had brought him to his senses. But was this Noah good enough for her? Was he here to determine if he was for himself? He wasn't sure.

The air was cold, but not as frigid as it had been in Michigan this past winter. He thrust his hands into the pockets of his coat and felt like a fool. Ivy would never love him. He knew that now.

She was in love with someone else. His last-ditch attempt to win her over by trying to buy the cuckoo clock she liked had backfired in a big way. But he wasn't mad at her. He wasn't even mad at Noah. He was angry with himself.

He should have returned to Michigan after Seth and Ivy booted him out of their house. But he couldn't get one thing out of his mind—Ivy had listened to him. She'd been angry and had every right to be. He had hurt her, and only now did he realize how much. But she'd also let him apologize. And even though she said she wouldn't give him a chance, he was certain she would have finally relented if her brother hadn't interfered.

He couldn't have been more wrong.

Tilting his head back and staring at the almost-full moon gleaming in the night sky, he said, "Lord, what am I doing?" How could he have lost his wits like this? When Judith ended their engagement, he'd been devastated. He also resented her for it. Seeing Ivy again had given him hope for the future when he'd felt as though there wasn't any. And now he was standing in front of the house of the man she loved, wondering why he'd bothered to come here. Noah wouldn't want anything to do with him, and he'd obviously been sick.

The sound of horse's hooves and buggy wheels rolling on gravel made him turn his head in the direction of the road. A buggy moving at a quick clip approached. John started to head down the road in the opposite direction, tucking his chin into his coat as he pulled his hat low on his head. He stopped when the buggy pulled up beside him.

"You can let me out here, Andrew."

John glanced at the buggy and saw the old woman with the cane.

"Are you sure, Cevilla?" the buggy driver said.

"One hundred percent."

"But *yer haus* is only a few feet away—"

"Andrew Beiler, you know better than to argue with *yer* elders!"

John hurried away, not interested in listening to probably the bossiest woman he'd ever encountered. He hadn't gone very far when he heard her call his name.

"Mr. King!"

Her voice, strong for her age, stopped him in his tracks. He turned around to see her standing on the side of the road as the buggy pulled away. Her cane was in front of her, and she leaned on it with both hands.

"I want to have a few words with you," she said. She thumped the cane on the road. "Now, if you please."

He walked toward her, knowing he couldn't say no. She'd probably toss her cane at his head if he did, and with his luck lately, it would knock him out cold. "Yes, ma'am?" he said, stopping in front of her, but keeping a decent distance.

"I have some questions for you. First, what are you doing in front of *mei haus*?"

"I, uh . . ." He wasn't sure how to answer that, since he wasn't sure why he'd come here.

"And second, what is *yer* relationship with Ivy?"

That question was easy to answer. "I don't have a relationship with her."

Cevilla straightened, lifting her chin. "Glad you're finally realizing that. I don't appreciate the stunt you pulled at the auction."

"I'm sorry." This woman had a way of making him feel like

he was five years old and in trouble with his mother. "I'm heading back home."

"And where is that?"

"Michigan."

"I see." She moved toward him. She was on the short side, but her presence overwhelmed him. In the silvery light of the moon, he could see the deep-set creases in her face. He could also see something else. Sympathy. He hadn't expected that.

"Are you really going home?" she asked, her tone softer this time.

He nodded. "*Ya.* I shouldn't have come to Ohio in the first place. I was trying to fix something I broke. But I can see I'm too late."

"The fact that you're acknowledging it is a *gut* sign. Were you here to talk to *mei* nephew?"

So Noah was her nephew. No wonder she had a stake in what was going on with him and Ivy. "Maybe. Guess I lost *mei* nerve."

"Then do you have a message I can give to him?"

John thought for a minute. "*Ya*," he said. "Tell him to take care of her. She's something special." Saying the words and officially letting Ivy go gave him some semblance of peace. Another surprise. She'd been right; he didn't know his own mind. He should have listened to her when she sent him away.

He turned to walk on, only to look over his shoulder and add, "Don't worry. I won't be coming back to Birch Creek." Then he started the long trek to his bed and breakfast. An even longer journey lay ahead. He had to get his life back on track. He just wasn't sure how to do that.

Dear Noah,

You left yesterday without saying good-bye. I guess you thought sending me away was your good-bye. I refuse to accept that. You might not be willing to fight right now, but I am. I will fight enough for both of us.

I read about Meniere's disease. Noah, please don't lose hope. You have options. Surgery. Hearing aids. New medications you can try. Like I said, we'll figure this out together. I don't want you to suffer alone.

Even if you don't want me to, I'm going to write to you. I'm going to tell you about my prayers for you, my dreams of a future with you, my love for you. And when you're ready, I'll come to you. I'll leave Birch Creek behind. Where you are is where my heart is. Please understand that. Please know that I love you, no matter what.

Love,
Ivy

Dear Noah,

The school board has made plans to break ground for the new addition to our school building. They also hired a new schoolteacher. His name is Christian, although he prefers to be called Chris. He and his sister are moving here from New York this summer. We've never had a male teacher before, and many people were surprised about it. But my father thinks he's a good fit for our community.

I didn't get a reply to my last letter to you. But that's okay. Nothing has changed, especially my feelings for you. I love you, Noah. I'm here for you. I'm not giving up on us, even if you have. Not until you tell me to my face that it's over. Not until I can see it in your eyes that there's no future for us. Until then, I'll keep hoping. I'll keep praying for you and that a cure for your disease is found. You are in my heart, Noah. In my soul. Don't ever forget that.

Love,

Ivy

Noah walked down a dirt road. At home, he fought to hear the birds chirping, the sounds of cows lowing in the pasture next door, the kids across the street yelling as they chased each other around the yard. All he heard was buzzing. All he felt was pain.

The medications the doctor initially gave him weren't working. Even the vertigo medicine hadn't kept two more spells away. He'd gone back to his doctor, who'd written more prescriptions. Noah filled them, but he didn't hold out much hope that they would work any better than the other ones.

His secret was out too. He couldn't keep it to himself, especially when he shut down his business. He didn't go into details, just let people know a health challenge was keeping him from traveling and he needed some time to regroup. He did admit the full truth to his family. He couldn't keep them in the dark. Of course, his mother was filled with worry and his father with pity, the exact opposite of what Noah wanted. His sisters pledged their support, but what could they do?

As was his habit lately, like today, he roamed around the back roads of his district. A few times he'd almost been hit by a car because he couldn't hear its approach. He made sure now that he walked facing traffic and kept his head up. He'd walk for hours, skipping meals, the buzzing filling his ears, despair filling his soul. The livelihood he'd successfully created had been snatched out from under him, along with the woman he loved. He couldn't go on like this, but he felt helpless to break the cycle.

He also felt helpless trying to forget about Ivy. She'd written him two letters in the two months since he left Birch Creek, and he'd responded to neither of them. He wondered if he'd hear from her again. A part of him hoped he wouldn't since he didn't want to keep hurting her.

But a part of him ached for her. He didn't know if he was ever going to be able to let her go.

It was almost dusk by the time he returned home, and he'd accomplished nothing. He was no closer to getting out of his funk than he'd been that morning. Yet what would pull him out? What kind of job could he have now? What kind of life? He opened the front door and walked inside. A light immediately turned on, and he jumped. Cevilla was sitting in his living room. "How did you get inside?" he asked, his hand over his chest.

"*Yer mamm* gave me a key." She held it up. "*Danki* for moving closer to *yer* parents. It wasn't that far of a walk from their place to here." She was perched on the edge of the couch, holding her cane and looking more stern than he'd ever seen her. Noah sighed and sat down on the chair across from her, but he didn't say anything. He tried to hold eye contact, but the disapproval she was throwing his way made him avert his eyes.

"I'd say you look *gut*," Cevilla said loudly and without preamble, "but you look worse than what the cat dragged in."

Although Noah could make out what she was saying, though

barely, he folded his arms across his chest and pretended not to hear her.

"Ivy finally filled me in on *yer* condition." Cevilla's mouth twisted. "How could you not tell me about this? I should have realized you were sick. You were preoccupied, and I could tell you'd lost weight when you came back for the auction. Honestly, I had started to think you were still pining away for that Rebecca woman."

His head shot up. "You knew about Rebecca?"

"Ah, so you can hear me." She smiled. "The thing about being a woman of delicate age is that people tend to overlook you. Also, you're terrible at hiding *yer* feelings. I visited here right after that dumb *maedel* dumped you, and you couldn't keep *yer* heart out of *yer* eyes when you looked at her."

Noah remembered how painful it had been in the months—no, years—after his relationship with Rebecca ended. That was one reason he started branching his business away from the area. Rebecca had found someone else almost immediately, and he couldn't stand to see them together. Eventually he was gone enough that the pain dulled. That didn't mean he was willing to open his heart to anyone like that again.

Except for Ivy. And she had no idea how he really felt. Not unless Cevilla had told her. He was about to ask her if she had when she continued.

"I'm not here to talk about the past, Noah." She brushed her finger under her nose. "I'm here to give you a *gut* scolding."

"I'm not surprised," he muttered, looking away from her again.

"How can you let the best thing to ever happen to you slip away?" Cevilla shook her head. "For a smart *mann*, you sure are acting like a *dummkopf*."

"You don't understand—"

She slammed the end of her cane on the floor. "*Nee. You* don't understand. Something terrible has happened to you. I'm not denying that. I also know you're angry and afraid. You have the right to be. But God has given you a special woman to help you. She's done everything she can think of short of coming here and knocking you upside the head. And since she's not here to do that"—Cevilla poked him in the foot with her cane—"I will."

"Stay out of this, *Aenti*."

"I tried. I even told God I would. And I didn't tell Ivy you admitted to me that you love her. But now I believe the Lord would have me confront you on this, Noah." Cevilla glared at him for a long moment, but then she softened. "Do you know why you're *mei* favorite nephew?"

He felt a lump growing in his throat as he shook his head.

"Because you remind me of myself. A free spirit. You don't let people tell you what to do. You follow *yer* heart. You made a career out of work that's usually a hobby for an Amish *mann*. You didn't let a woman's rejection stop you. In fact, you made it into a challenge."

He looked up at Cevilla. Her eyes were filled with tears, not with anger. And she was right. He had taken Rebecca's rejection as a challenge to prove her wrong. And he'd done that. He'd also healed.

"Why are you backing down now?" His aunt leaned forward. "Why, when the stakes are higher than ever before, are you throwing in the towel?"

"I don't have a choice." His voice quavered, and he hated showing so much weakness. But this was Cevilla. He could be honest with her. "I . . . don't know what to do."

"You make a decision." Cevilla set her cane to the side. "You can stay on this path, wallow in pity, wall *yerself* from God and everyone else, and do *nix*. Or you can follow *yer* heart to Birch Creek . . . and to healing."

"It's not that easy." He cleared his throat. "Ivy deserves better than me."

"She wants you. Why are you making the choice for her?"

He turned away and didn't say anything. A few moments later he felt Cevilla tap him on the shoulder.

"She wanted me to give you this." She handed him an envelope. "I better get back to *yer* parents' *haus*. I always promise myself I'll visit more often, but time has a way of slipping through our fingers." She reached down and tilted his chin up, like she used to do when he was a young boy. "We shouldn't allow that to happen."

After she left, he clenched his fists. How dare she tell him what to do? How to live his life? She was a meddling old biddy. That's what she was. Never could she mind her own business, and this was the one time he should have set her straight.

Ivy's letter was balled up in his hand. When he smoothed it out, he saw her small, neat handwriting. Thought about her sitting at the kitchen table, writing yet again, knowing he wouldn't respond, but still doing it. Still standing by his side, like she said she would, even when he was hurting her.

With trembling fingers, he opened the envelope and took out the letter.

Dear Noah,

I just told Cevilla about your illness. If you won't listen to me, maybe you'll listen to her. She says she's planning to visit you. I want to go with her, but she says she prefers to travel by herself. I don't think she's being completely truthful about that. I think she's trying to protect me. But this is what she and everyone else doesn't understand. I don't need protecting. I know what I want, and that's you.

I keep thinking about CJ's letters. How he was strong enough to pour out his heart and tell Cevilla how much he loved her. I'm doing that now, Noah. I love you. I want to tell that to you in person again. I think it's only fair that you hear those words from me instead of merely reading them on a page. If you won't come to Birch Creek, then I'll come to Iowa. I know you said you don't want to fight for us. That's okay. I'm strong enough to fight for us both.

I'm going to ask Cevilla to give you this letter. Hopefully I'll hear from you soon.

Love,
Ivy

Noah folded the paper, his eyes filling with tears. All the barriers he'd put around his heart came crashing down. Cevilla had broken through them, and Ivy had done the rest.

He couldn't live like this anymore. More importantly, he couldn't keep hurting Ivy.

Her life was at a standstill, and it was because of him. Because he didn't have the courage to do the right thing.

For the first time in weeks he got on his knees and fervently prayed. He begged God for forgiveness for doubting him, for blaming him for his illness. But he didn't pray for healing, which was what he'd been doing—when he'd bothered to pray at all. No, this time he was praying for something else. "Help me make the right choice," Noah said aloud. "Give me strength to follow *mei* heart."

Ivy sat in the kitchen, pen poised above paper, her head in her other hand. How long was she going to do this? How long was she going to keep sending Noah letters, and getting nothing in return? Hadn't his silence given her his answer?

Then she remembered the pain in his eyes when he told her how sick he was, the despair she saw in them. And even though he was pushing her away, she couldn't let go. Not yet.

When she sent her last letter with Cevilla, she gave him an ultimatum of sorts. That was over a week ago, and Cevilla had already returned from Iowa. But she hadn't even brought up Noah when Ivy saw her yesterday, and Ivy took that as bad news. Maybe she'd made a mistake pushing him that way. But she knew she needed to write the letter. She needed to either try to spur him into some kind of action or make good on her determination to go see him.

She would write him one more letter. Then if he didn't respond, she'd buy her bus ticket to Iowa.

She'd just written "Dear Noah" when she heard a knock on the front door. No one else was in the house, and when she opened the door, she gasped. Then her heart flipped into triple time. *Noah.*

"Hi," he said, looking at her intently.

"Hi." The word came out on a long breath as she stared at him. It hadn't been that long since she'd last seen him, but it felt like forever. He looked the same, but still thinner than normal.

There were also dark circles under his eyes. He was suffering, and it made the ache in her heart almost unbearable. "I was . . . I was just thinking about you." She swallowed, collecting herself. "I was writing you a letter, actually." She forced an unsure smile. "And now you're here."

His face remained impassive. Like stone. "Can I come in?"

Alarmed at his indifference, she nodded and opened the door wider. He came in, but he didn't walk any farther inside. Didn't come close to her. And that's when she knew she had lost him. She had pushed him for an answer, and he was here to give it to her.

"Cevilla's received another shipment of Glenda's belongings," Noah said, his hands in his pockets.

"I thought we went through all her stuff."

"Cevilla thought so, too, but apparently not. They sent a few more boxes. Cevilla asked me to *geh* through them for her."

Ivy nodded, unable to stop her chin from trembling. Cevilla hadn't said anything about the shipment yesterday. Even his aunt knew things were over between them. She tried to seem unfazed. "Maybe you'll find something valuable in them, like more jewelry."

Noah didn't say anything.

The only sound in the living room was the steady ticking of the cuckoo clock. Her father had mounted it on the wall after the auction. They stood there, not saying anything, as if they were complete strangers. All she wanted was to throw her arms around him and tell him she loved him. But the invisible wall around him was too high, too thick, for her to do that. "Is that the only reason you came back?" she said, unable to keep the bite out of her voice. "Because Cevilla asked you to?"

He shook his head and then reached into the pocket of his jacket. He took out an envelope and handed it to her. "I came to give you this."

She looked at his outstretched hand, her fingers curling into fists.

"Take it, Ivy."

When she finally did, he opened the door, gave her one last unreadable look, and then left.

She looked down at the letter. In it was his answer. She moved to the couch and sat down, staring at the envelope for a long time, tempted to throw it away since she already knew what it contained. But she couldn't bring herself to do that. She wasn't going to hide from the truth. Finally, she gathered the courage to open it and read.

Dear Ivy,

I don't know what words I can say, or even write, to tell you how much you mean to me. How I wouldn't have made it through these past two months without you, even though I pushed you away. I didn't write you back because although I couldn't face life without you, I didn't want you to be saddled with a deaf man with no prospects. You deserve better than that. You deserve better than me.

But as someone much wiser than me pointed out, this is your choice to make. I just told you how I felt while I was in Iowa. How hard it is for me to come to terms with what's happened. How uncertain I am about the future. The only thing I'm sure of is that I love you. I want to be with you more than anything. But the decision is yours. And I won't blame you if you decide you don't want me anymore. That life with me would be too tough for you. I'd never hold that against you. I want you to be happy. I want you to follow your heart, the way I'm following mine.

When you decide, let me know. I'll be at my aunt's house.

All my love,

Noah

Chapter 20

Ivy climbed up the attic stairs, her heart pounding so hard in her chest she thought it would burst. When she reached the top, she saw Noah arranging several boxes against one wall. This last shipment wasn't as big, and she knew he could make quick work of it himself.

It took everything she had not to run to him. She walked instead, still wearing her shoes because she couldn't make herself stop long enough to take them off, realizing he couldn't hear her footsteps on the solid wood floor, even though they echoed in her own ears. It brought his condition to stark reality. But she was prepared for that. She was prepared for anything, because this was the man she loved.

A few months ago, she'd thought she'd be alone for the rest of her life. At first she'd been resentful, then lonely, then accepting. And if she hadn't met Noah, she would have lived a good life as a single woman. She had learned that she could stand on her own.

But now she wanted something else. She wanted a future with this man in front of her, no matter how uncertain that future was.

When she touched his arm, he startled and turned around. His gaze was so intense she took a step back. "Ivy," he said. "You're here."

She saw the sheen of tears in his eyes. Gone was the impassive expression he'd given her when he was at her house, handing her the letter. Now she saw the old Noah—gentle, lively, a spark in his hazel-green eyes and a smile that lit up his face as he took in her own.

"I missed you so much," he said.

"I've missed you too," she whispered through her tears, sure he'd understand even if he couldn't hear her words.

He took her hand and led her to the bench in front of the window. But when she was about to sit down next to him, he swept her up in his arms and put her in his lap. "There," he said. "That's better."

She touched his face. "You can hear me better when we're closer?"

"*Ya*. But that's not the reason I want to hold you." He paused. "Ivy, I'm so sorry. I never wanted to hurt you." He averted his gaze, and then he looked back at her. "I remember when I said I wouldn't."

"And then I fell facedown in the snow."

"You were so cute with snow all over *yer* face." He drew his fingertip across her cheek. "I'm sorry I was so selfish."

"I understand. You're dealing with a lot—"

"That's *nee* excuse. I pushed you away because I was scared. I didn't want you to be stuck—"

She put her finger on his lips. "Don't you understand by now, Noah? I want to be stuck with you. Forever." She put her hand on his chest. "This is where *mei* heart lives."

He covered her hand with his. “I can feel that, Ivy. I just . . .” He swallowed. “I’m afraid.”

“Me too.” She gazed into his eyes. “But we’ll fight our fear together.”

He took her face in his hands and kissed her. Sweetly, longingly, lovingly. When they parted, she leaned her head against his shoulder. She felt his hand rubbing her back, and they sat there for a moment, silent in each other’s arms.

“I don’t know what the future holds,” he said, his voice a little hoarse. “I can’t promise I won’t lose *mei* hearing completely. Or that I won’t pass out. Or that any medication will help me.”

Ivy threaded her fingers through his. She looked at the size difference and snuggled closer to him. “We’ll deal with that together too.”

“I want to stay in Birch Creek,” he said.

She lifted her head. This was a surprise. She’d assumed he would want to go back to Iowa where his family and business were. She was prepared to go wherever he did. “You don’t have to.”

“I want to. I really like this place. It feels like home, and I realized when I was gone that I not only missed you, but I missed being here.” His face sobered. “I’m not sure what kind of work I’ll be able to do, but like you said, we’ll figure that out.”

“*Ya*. Together.”

He kissed her again, and when he whispered in her ear, she heard the words she’d been waiting to hear. “I love you, Ivy.”

“I love you too.” And she knew as long as they had their love, they could face anything.

Cevilla had smiled as she watched Ivy go up the attic stairs. Her nephew had done the right thing. Not that she doubted him. He just needed a nudge in the right direction.

Now she was sitting in her room, on her bed. She was tired. Matchmaking was an exhausting business. But a satisfying one. Noah had been able to gather his courage and face an uncertain future. Ivy had been brave enough to stand beside him. The two young people were inspiring.

Cevilla opened the drawer in her nightstand and took out an old envelope. She lifted the flap, its crease worn from use, and pulled out the letter inside. Her eyes were already filling with tears, but Noah had gathered the courage to face his pain. It was time she did too.

Dear Cevilla,

It's strange calling you by your first name. I'm so used to calling you Bunny. But since you asked me to not use that name anymore, I won't. It's been five years since I last wrote to you. Since the end of the war. Since you broke my heart into a thousand pieces. I know you didn't think you'd ever hear from me again.

I was so angry with you that day. I couldn't believe you would throw away what we had together. You told me you loved me, and I believed that love extended into happily ever after, two kids, a picket fence, and a car in the garage. The American dream. It was a dream I wanted to share with you, and I thought you wanted the same thing.

I also couldn't understand why you had to leave me when you joined the Amish, even though you explained your faith to me. For a short time I thought you would come to your senses.

Then I thought I might be able to make it work if I joined the Amish. But I realized I couldn't do that. I couldn't turn my back on my family and my way of life, not even for you.

That's when I knew you were right. That you had to follow your heart, like you said. I had always thought your heart was with me, but I should have known it was with God. And despite my anger, I admired you for that. It took a long time to acknowledge it, though. A long time to put those pieces back together and learn to trust someone again.

But I did, and I fell in love. I'm not telling you this to hurt you, or for some kind of revenge. Mabel is kind and sweet and the perfect woman for me. She knows I'm writing you this letter. She knows all about us. I thought it was only fair that she understood my past and knew about the woman who had once meant everything to me.

I hope you're as happy as I am, Cevilla. I hope you found what you were looking for when you rejoined the Amish. I hope you got married and had a passel of kids and that everything is perfect for you. Because it is for me now.

This is the last time you'll hear from me. Just know that I forgive you, Cevilla. Even though you hurt me, I now realize doing so hurt you too. You're that kind of woman. Big-hearted and strong-willed.

CJ

Cevilla wiped the tears from her eyes and folded the letter. When it arrived all those years ago, she'd been prepared for angry words. CJ had a temper, and she deserved anything he said to her. What she hadn't been prepared for was his forgiveness. His grace. His wish for her happiness after she had broken his heart. He was an amazing man—so amazing that she had never met a man who came close to him.

She rose from the bed and walked over to the wooden box sitting on her dresser. She never regretted not marrying. If she couldn't find a man she loved as much as CJ, it wouldn't be fair to marry someone just because marriage was expected. She'd known many nice men, and a couple of them had shown interest. But none of them compared to her first love. And even that love hadn't been strong enough to rival God's love, his bringing her back to her Amish roots and planting her firmly in its soil.

No, she didn't regret breaking off her relationship with CJ. But she had regretted hurting him, and when she learned he'd forgiven her, a burden had been lifted.

She opened the box, pulled out the stack of letters, and stared at them for a long time. She hadn't read them since she'd ended their relationship, and perhaps she never would. She untied the ribbon and added CJ's last letter to the bundle—where it belonged. She retied the ribbon and placed this part of her past back in the box.

Her secret was no longer a secret. Even though she had never meant for anyone else to read those letters, she was glad Ivy and Noah had. Maybe they learned something from her story.

Four years ago, she got word that CJ had passed away. She had mourned him, as well as the love and friendship they'd shared. She put her hand on the box. "Good-bye, CJ," she said, tears streaming down her cheeks. "I still love you."

Epilogue

MARCH (A YEAR LATER)

"I think it might be a little crooked," Ivy said as she looked up at the storefront and wrapped her sweater around her tighter.

"How should we move it?" Seth asked. Noah and her brother were holding up the Schlabach's Antiques sign they'd picked up from its maker last week. Both men were on ladders, each waiting for her answer on one side of the sign.

"I think it's fine, Ivy." Noelle moved to stand next to her.

"Are you sure?"

"Positive."

"Make up *yer* mind," Seth grumbled. "*Mei* arms are getting tired."

Ivy nodded. "It looks *gut*."

The men affixed the sign into place and then climbed down. Seth went inside to get a cup of coffee—his third of the morning—as Noah moved to stand next to Ivy. "*Ya*," he said. "It looks perfect."

"I'm so glad I finally have a neighbor." Noelle grinned. "I thought that store would remain empty forever."

"It was just waiting for the right business." Noah smiled, scratching his chin through his beard.

Ivy looked up at her husband. She hadn't seen him this happy since their wedding day last November. They'd gone to Iowa shortly after for a couple of months, where Noah wrapped up his business and visited several specialists for his Meniere's disease. He'd finally found a medicine that helped with the vertigo, along with an analgesic to combat the bouts of pain that still plagued him. Only Ivy knew about the two small hearing aids covered by his hair.

"I better get back inside. I'm opening up soon." Noelle squeezed Ivy's hand. "Good luck, neighbor."

Ivy smiled. "Thanks."

As Noelle left, Ivy looked up at the sign again. Their very own business. When the idea had come to her around Christmastime, Noah wasn't sure it was a good one. But she'd convinced him, especially since they'd found plenty of valuable antiques in the second shipment of Glenda's things. Noah was the one who remembered the empty store next to Noelle's, and he used his connections to build inventory. He also attended a couple of small auctions, which had been difficult at first because of his illness.

Her gaze dropped to the display she'd set up in the picture window. She'd put several of their best items there, and all were for sale, with the exception of one. In the center, on a small wooden stool, was a stack of old letters tied with a red ribbon, leaning against an old wooden box. Cevilla had given them to her, telling her she could sell them in the shop if she wanted. "It's time for me to let go of that part of *mei* past. Besides, I doubt they're worth anything," she'd said, an uncharacteristic touch of sadness in her eyes.

But they were priceless to Ivy.

"Tomorrow's the big day," Noah said, looking down at her. "Our grand opening."

"Do you think people will come?" Ivy said, suddenly a little worried.

"With Cevilla as our public relations person, do you even have to ask that question?"

Ivy laughed. *"Nee."*

"Here," Noah said. He handed her a folded piece of paper.

She put it in the pocket of her jacket before he squeezed her hand and went inside.

At their home that evening, while Noah was outside doing chores in the barn, Ivy pulled out the paper. On it were written three simple words. *I love you.* She smiled and went upstairs. She pulled out a keepsake box much like the one Cevilla used for CJ's letters. Noah had given it to her as a wedding gift. She opened the box and added the note to the dozens of others he'd given her since returning to Birch Creek—his words of love.

She would treasure them forever.

Acknowledgments

Thank you to my editors, Becky Monds and Jean Bloom, for their expertise, input, and grace. Thanks to Kelly Long and Eddie Columbia for always being there when I need to brainstorm. And as always, thank you, dear readers. I hope you enjoyed reading Noah and Ivy's story as much as I enjoyed writing it.

Discussion Questions

1. Cevilla's attic held lots of different heirlooms. Some were worth money, others were precious for another reason. Do you have a treasured heirloom? What is it, and how did you acquire it?
2. Before his illness, Noah was a workaholic. Do you have trouble "slowing down"? What are ways you take time to spend with God?
3. Ivy worries that she'll be lonely when Leanna and Karen start their families. What advice would you give to reassure her?
4. In his letter to Bunny, CJ says that suffering "hones our faith and belief." Was there a time when a trial you went through strengthened your faith?
5. Cevilla chose her faith over CJ. Have you ever had to make a similarly tough decision?
6. Noah, Ivy, and Cevilla all had to learn how to put their faith and trust completely in God. Is this something you struggle with? What helps you during those times of doubt?

About the Author

Kathleen Fuller is the author of several bestselling novels, including the Hearts of Middlefield novels, the Middlefield Family novels, the Amish of Birch Creek series, and the Amish Letters series as well as a middle-grade Amish series, the Mysteries of Middlefield.

Visit her online at www.kathleenfuller.com
Twitter: @TheKatJam
Facebook: Kathleen Fuller

READ MORE FROM KATHLEEN FULLER!

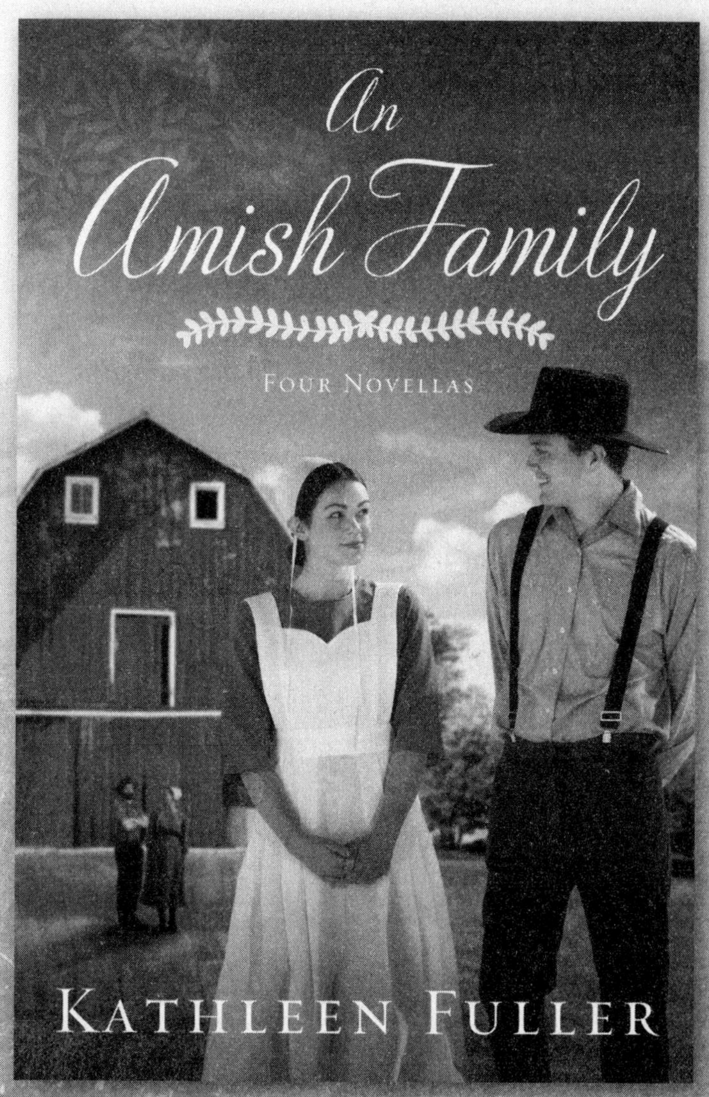

AVAILABLE JUNE 2018

The Middlefield Novels